FIRST AND BABY

KRISTA LAKES

ABOUT THIS BOOK

"Who the heck leaves a baby in a box on the doorstep of a professional football player?"

DYLAN CALLAHAN'S career needs a jump start. Between dropping passes and dropping sponsors, it's only a matter of time before he's traded away from his team. But what he really didn't expect was to get a baby dropped on his front porch, with a note saying it's his.

So he does what anyone would do. He buys a goat to feed the baby goat's milk.

Natalie's job in the ER keeps her busy, and she thought she was used to surprises, but that's before a goat appears outside her apartment door.

Natalie doesn't have time for football or flings, but she can't leave a baby in need. Agreeing to help Dylan while they wait for paternity results, she quickly learns there's more to him than his cocky grin and impressive stats. Between late-night feedings, hilarious mishaps, and one very opinionated goat, the line between teammates and something more starts to blur.

As the stakes rise on and off the field, can Dylan and Natalie make the play? Or will they lose the game of love?

<u>DON'T FORGET to join my mailing list as well for updates!</u> (clickable link)

For my sister: Thank you for walking around the pool with me for hours helping with this plot.

For Katy: Thank you for sharing your crazy stories over Indian food.

Thank you to all the people that keep us healthy and safe.

1

THAT IS NOT THE PACKAGE I WAS
EXPECTING

What's the difference between a quarterback and a baby?
One takes the snap, the other takes a nap.

Dylan Callahan

There was a baby in the box.

Herbert, the doorman for my very nice and very expensive apartment building, had called and said there was a package for me. I'd told him to leave it by my door and I'd get to it as soon as I got out of the shower.

Thank God I was expecting a food delivery so I hadn't left that box sitting out in the hallway for longer than it took to dry off and put on pants. When I saw that the top wasn't taped, just carefully closed, I was sure that someone had stolen or tampered with my groceries. I was ready to call someone and complain.

The box did not contain the organic meats and specialty protein pasta I was expecting.

No.

There was a baby. A sleeping baby.

I know nothing about babies, but I knew this one was young. It didn't look like it could sit up or play patty-cake. It looked like the pictures my mom kept on the mantle from when I was three months old. I wasn't sure if it was a boy or a girl since the blanket wrapped around it was yellow with green trim. It wore a matching green and yellow hat. Packers' colors. The thing was tiny, and luckily, fast asleep.

"Um, this is a baby," I said to no one in particular. The hallway was empty.

I stared at the box sitting out in the hallway of my apartment, not understanding what was going on. I half expected cameras to pop out with my teammates laughing that I'd just been punked. This had to be some sort of prank.

Who the hell leaves a baby in a box on the doorstep of an NFL player?

I looked around the empty hallway again and then back to the box with a baby in it. The baby sighed and wiggled slightly, but stayed asleep.

I couldn't just leave it sleeping out in the open, so I picked up the box and brought it inside. It was surprisingly light. Thankfully, the baby didn't wake up.

I set the box down on the kitchen table and stared at the box for a moment. It was just a plain brown box, so that didn't give me much information. I should probably call the police, but they would want more information. Also, I did not want to wake the baby up with a loud phone call. Cautiously, as if the baby were a dangerous cobra, I peered into the box.

Just a baby wrapped in a thin blanket. *Swaddled.* The word popped into my head and I felt like I might not be completely incompetent at child rearing. The baby was swaddled in a thin blanket, just like they did at the hospital.

And then I realized that I was a complete idiot. Knowing the word *swaddled* was not the makings of a good caretaker.

"Who are you?" I softly asked the baby, as if it could respond.

Yup, I was an idiot.

However, I did see a piece of carefully folded paper near its feet. Treating the baby as if it were still a cobra, I carefully reached in and pinched the note. A professional bomb squad technician would have been impressed at my careful and delicate movements.

The baby didn't move except for some gentle breathing. Success.

I read the note.

Dear Mr. Callahan,

This is your daughter. We slept together September 2nd at a party downtown. By the time I found out that I was pregnant, there was no way for me to reach you. I can't take care of her and she deserves to be with someone who can. She was born May 25th. The doctor said she was perfect. Tell her that her mother loved her, but

*there was no way for her to keep her. She will
have a chance at a better life with you.*

I STARED AT THE NOTE. The handwriting was neat and small, as if the writer had taken great care shaping every letter, as if she'd known it would be read thousands of times. There was no signature, no hint of who had actually written this note.

I was glad there was a chair at the kitchen table because I sat down hard. My knees went wobbly.

My daughter?

How the hell did I have a daughter? Sure, I liked the ladies. Neither my coach nor my agent liked the way I had a new woman on my arm every week, but I was living the high life. I was enjoying my freedom and sowing some oats while I was a hot item. I knew it wouldn't last forever and so I was taking what I could get while I had it.

September 2nd. I had no idea what I had been doing twelve months ago.

Other than this woman, apparently.

I guessed that meant the baby was three months old.

I fumbled for my phone, pulling up the calendar app and frantically scrolling back about twelve months. Yup. There was a party downtown. I remembered it. It had been a huge party thrown by a couple of rich fans. They'd rented an entire hotel downtown, hired a famous band, and then paid to have several of Omaha's most favorite football players attend.

I did not remember much from that night. Free food, good booze, and beautiful women everywhere. The cops had eventually had to shut the entire thing down because too many people were in the hotel. It had leaked there was a party, and everyone and their uncle tried to get in.

I tried to remember who I had been with that night. A blonde? I remembered a blonde. I remembered doing some things that could lead to a pregnancy, but her name? Nope. I couldn't make her face out in my memory.

Not a great look for me.

I peeked at the baby in the box again. Did she look like her mother?

No. She looked like a pink potato.

I distinctly remembered sleeping with a woman, not a pink (or any other color) potato.

I wasn't that much of a man-whore.

I wiped my hand across my face, trying to figure out what the hell I was supposed to do next. I was a father. Her father. Wasn't I supposed to have some sort of parental instinct?

The only instinct I had was that I should let sleeping babies sleep.

BRRRRRRRRNNNNNGGGG.

My phone started to buzz and ring, the volume set to as loud as humanly possible so I wouldn't miss it in the shower.

"SHIT!" I shouted, and then realized that wasn't a good idea. "Shit," I repeated, this time in a whisper as I frantically hit the answer button. "This is Dylan."

"Callahan. Turn on the news. Now." Coach's voice was low and serious. It was the kind of voice he used when I fucked up. I swallowed hard. At least the baby hadn't woken up.

For a panic-stricken moment, I wondered if this baby

was already on the news. My brain imagined the reporter standing outside my apartment building reporting that not only was I a deadbeat dad, I was a kidnapper. I wasn't sure how that worked, by my brain went with it anyway.

Carefully, I crossed the kitchen into the living room and turned on the big screen TV, making sure to lower the volume to just barely audible. I did not want to wake up the baby and have to explain that to Coach. It was already set to the sports news station.

"In other news, Dylan Callahan still can't catch a ball," an attractive female reporter announced into a micro-phone. The screen cut to footage of practice yesterday and I winced as they showed clip after clip of me dropping the ball at practice.

"After suffering an injury at the only postseason game the Quakes made, Callahan made some questionable off-field decisions," the reporter continued. "Sources say that Dylan Callahan's contract may not be renewed this season."

The screen cut to a picture of me drinking at a party. Three women hung on me like ornaments on a Christmas tree.

"The owners of the Omaha Twisters were willing to overlook the playboy behavior and partying when the man could make plays," the reporter continued. The screen shifted to the beginning of last year when I was made of speed and could catch anything. "But after a minor injury, he just can't seem to hold onto the ball."

Minor injury, I scoffed. I'd broken my wrist playing football. Those "questionable off-field decisions" were me trying to come to terms with the fact that I might never play again. If I had a little too much to drink and found some comfort in the arms of several women, was that really so bad?

My wrist would never be the same after the accident. I still had nightmares about that game. We'd lost. My Super Bowl dreams were crushed because of that "minor injury" and I wasn't sure I'd ever get them back.

"Sources say that if Callahan can't step up his game and start catching the football--" The screen cut to another montage of me fumbling the ball at practice and at yesterday's preseason game. My face heated. "Then he'll be cut."

"Well, it could have been worse," I said to Coach, muting the TV.

"Sure. They could have said you were already fired," Coach agreed. "Listen Callahan, I like you. You're a good ball player when you have your head in the game. But you haven't had your head in the game all summer. You were only in the team's good graces at the end of last year because you could run the ball. It's not looking good for you. We're cutting players tomorrow."

I grimaced and was glad he couldn't see me blushing. I rubbed at my now healed wrist. I didn't want to be cut from the team, but it wasn't looking good for me this season. My contract was due to be renegotiated, so I was in no place to make demands.

"Let me tell you this," Coach continued. "If you don't get your shit together, you're out. You're on medical for the week, but if you show up in the news at another out-of-control party, you're out. If you so much as get a speeding ticket, you're out. We can't afford to have players making fools of the team."

"A speeding ticket?" I asked. "Isn't that a bit much?"

"After the shit Williams pulled last week? Every news

article about the Twisters this week is negative. The owners want this team to be family friendly. Williams' harassment accusations are not good for the team. You are in no way to be the next player on the news."

"But I haven't done anything--"

"I don't care. Everyone is on notice," Coach cut me off. "The entire team better be choir boys the rest of preseason. You aren't playing well enough to get special treatment."

I wished I had a retort. I wished I could say that I could play better, but...

My confidence was not high. Ever since the accident, I felt like I needed to protect myself rather than going all out for the ball. I'd seen a therapist, a psychologist, a hypnotist, and even had a psychic cleanse my energy, but nothing seemed to be working.

I couldn't seem to hold onto the ball to save my life, let alone my career.

"Yes, Coach." I sighed, wishing I could sink into the floor. At least I was safe tomorrow. That wouldn't be true for a lot of guys on the team. "I'll be picture perfect. No scandal. No antics."

And that's when the baby started to cry.

2

ADVENTURES IN THE ER

"You know that feeling when you meet someone and your heart skips a beat? Yeah, that's arrhythmia. You can die from that."
-Unknown

NATALIE **Parker**

"YOU ARE NEVER GOING to believe this one," McKenna, my favorite EMT, said as she walked out of the ER room she'd just dropped a patient off at.

I didn't look up from the computer I was busy charting my latest nursing assessment on. "Let me guess... butt stuff?"

"Well, obviously," McKenna replied, leaning against the nurses' station counter. She swiped one of the pens and stuck it in her cargo pants pockets. "But you're never going to guess what."

I looked up to see her grinning devilishly at me.

"Um... a light-bulb?" I asked.

"That was last week," she replied, waving her hand. "This one is better."

"Gardening tool? Egg? Vegetable? Sausage?" I asked, getting a head shake no at each.

"Have you eaten yet?" McKenna asked. "Because it sounds like you're prepping an omelet."

I rolled my eyes at her. I hadn't eaten, but that's why nurses lived on coffee. Coffee counted as a food, right?

"Toothbrush? Phone? Wooden object?" I offered, going through a mental list of all the things I'd seen up someone's rectum in the ER before.

"Wooden object is far too generic to count as a guess, but it's not that," McKenna replied, stealing another pen like I wouldn't notice.

"Hamster?" I asked, hoping that I wouldn't have to call a veterinarian at midnight again. Working the night shift at the Omaha General Hospital made for some interesting late night specialty phone calls.

"Thank heaven, no." McKenna shook her head. "No live animals this time. I'm still traumatized by the guy with the boa constrictor."

We both shivered.

"I have no idea, but I'm sure he fell on it 'accidentally' and has no idea how this happened," I said, clicking save on my charting.

"Actually, this time he admits it," she replied, grinning at my surprise. "You're never going to guess what it is."

I thought for a moment.

"A dildo, but it doesn't have the flared base so it got lost up there," I offered.

"How'd you guess?" she asked, frowning and pulling back from the counter. "Did you cheat and look at the admitting info?"

"Nope. It's just hard to pretend you 'accidentally' fell on a dildo. A carrot? That's not believable but at least it's possible. A dildo only has one purpose," I explained. "No one accidentally falls on a dildo because no one keeps those out where people can fall on them."

McKenna nodded, stealing another pen. "We see weird stuff."

"Yup. Please put back three of the four pens you just stole," I said, rising from the computer to go greet my new patient. "You can keep one, but I need some pens tonight too."

"I only took three!" McKenna protested until I crossed my arms and waited for her to admit her guilt. "Fine, it *was* more. I just thought I was being sneakier."

She plopped three pens back into the cup on the counter.

"You going to miss all this when you're a fancy nurse practitioner?" she asked as I gathered my things.

"I'm staying in the ER," I reminded her. "I love the craziness here. I just want to be able to write my own orders and help more people."

"How much longer until school starts and you leave me to fend on my own?" McKenna asked with a dramatized pout.

"I will only be dropping one shift when school starts. It's a work study program sponsored by the hospital," I reminded her. "I just need more hours to qualify for the scholarship. Post graduate school isn't cheap."

I was so grateful my hospital offered this program. It

was for full-time nurses who wanted to become nurse practitioners. They would pay for my schooling as long as I had enough hours at the hospital.

I started school in just a few weeks and needed every shift I had to complete the work requirements for the scholarship. Once school started, my available work hours would drop, so it wasn't something I could make up later.

Becoming a nurse practitioner was a dream I'd had for a long time and I wasn't going to let anything derail me from it.

"Well, I've got another call," McKenna said, checking her work phone. "I'll bring you back something else fun."

"How kind of you," I deadpanned.

"Oh, and two more things," McKenna said, walking away from me and back to her ambulance. "I actually took five pens. And the dildo is the vibrating kind. Have fun!"

I shook my head as she waltzed out the ER doors with her pilfered pens.

The ER was a wild place.

* * *

"ARE YOU NURSE NATALIE PARKER?" A uniformed police officer stood on the other side of the nurses' station desk, looking annoyed.

"That's me," I replied, keeping my eyes on the screen. I had to finish my charting so I could get out of here and go home. My shift had technically ended ten minutes ago, but that meant nothing when the charting wasn't done. It had been a crazy night, but as a nurse, I had to document all of it even if that meant staying late. Once I had this chart done, I could go home. If I concentrated, I could have the charting done in seven minutes.

Yes, I was counting the minutes. Night shift in the ER in a big city is not an easy thing. I'd been running all night. I'd snarfed a granola bar as the only form of dinner I could smash down my throat in the two minutes I'd managed to get away from patient's emergencies. We'd had nonstop emergencies all night and I was hungry and tired. Coffee, as amazing a chemical as it was, could only go so far.

"I'm Officer Brown. Do you remember your patient, Hazel Smith, tonight?" Officer Brown asked.

I sighed. With him interrupting me, this charting was going to take even longer. At least ten minutes now.

"Was it the baby or the grandma?" I asked, trying to place the name. "Or the raccoon?"

"Definitely not the raccoon. You don't remember Hazel?" He sounded surprised.

"Sir, I have seen twenty-three patients tonight," I replied, looking at my very cluttered notes and doing a quick count. "Between CPR, an incident with a raccoon, a surprise baby, pneumonia, a bottle in a very strange and uncomfortable place, and an incident with an eyeball, I am lucky I remember my own name at this point."

The officer paled slightly. "An eyeball?"

"I don't think it was Hazel's eyeball," I replied. That patient had been a fifty-three-year-old male. McKenna had brought him to me after dildo guy.

Officer Brown shook himself as if trying to restart his mind. "No, Hazel is a three-week-old baby."

I paused for a moment, going through the night's patients.

"Right. Dehydrated. We sent her up to the Pediatric floor. Did something happen? Is she okay?"

That had been one of the more simple cases of the night. Baby Hazel's mom had brought her in. Mom hadn't wanted to go up to the unit, but due to Hazel's age, she needed more medical attention than a trip to the ER could give her.

"Hazel is fine. However, the woman that brought her in wasn't her mother," the officer replied. "Did you notice anything strange?"

"That wasn't her mother?" I stared at him. The woman had been incredibly attentive to the baby. Even McKenna had remarked about how concerned the mother had been for the child.

"No. The woman was a stranger. The real mother reported Hazel missing two days ago." He frowned. "Are you sure you didn't notice anything strange about her?"

"Well, strange is relative in the ER," I explained. "But it did seem odd that she didn't want to go upstairs to the Peds unit. She seemed very nervous and jumpy, but I just assumed it was because her baby was sick and a hospital stay is expensive."

"And you didn't notice that the child wasn't hers?"

"No, I mean it was a little weird that she didn't have a diaper bag with her. There wasn't a car seat with her either, but some parents leave it in the car." A sinking feeling started to grow in my stomach the more I talked. "She seemed unsure if Hazel was breast fed or took formula..."

"And how did the baby act around the mother?"

"The way a sick three-week-old baby acts around everyone?" I shrugged, knowing this night wasn't going to get better. "Although, thinking back, the mom held her like she might break. I just assumed she was a first-time mom. That also explained why she was so unsure about how to feed her child. Parents get so overwhelmed by their sick or injured child that they forget all kinds of things."

Now that I was thinking about it, I could see all sorts of red flags. No diapers, no diaper bag, no extra clothing, no socks, and just a soft fleece blanket that looked too big for a baby.

"I didn't see it. I just saw a sick baby. I didn't realize the baby was so dehydrated because she'd been kidnapped and the kidnapper didn't know how to feed her."

I felt like an idiot. Like I had failed this child.

This was the part of the job I hated the most. When I found out I didn't do my best. When I didn't help someone who could have used my help. I hadn't done everything I could to help this kid.

Officer Brown gave me a kind smile. "You aren't in trouble," he told me. "It's easy to miss child trafficking, especially with little kids that can't talk or show you they aren't with the right person."

I nodded, my stomach still plummeting through the floor.

"What should I look for next time?" I asked. I hated that I knew there would probably be a next time. The downside to working in the ER was that I saw the worst of what people did to one another.

"You said a lot of the warning signs- no bottles or baby supplies. Looking uncomfortable holding a child, not having things prepared, and of course acting anxious or like they don't know what they are doing."

I nodded.

"I'm sure you'll see it next time," Officer Brown assured me. "The baby is safe upstairs with her real mother. We're still looking for the woman that brought the baby in. There is a chance she could try and kidnap the child again."

"I'm not going to let it happen again," I promised him. "Now that I know what to look for, I'm going to make sure no one is stealing babies around me."

"That's all I can ask for," Brown replied. He handed me a card with his name on it. "If you think of anything else, let me know."

I pocketed his card, feeling the sudden heavy weight of it in my pocket. I was a good nurse. I loved my job in the ER. I loved helping people and the adrenaline of emergency care, but sometimes I hated how dark this place could be. Sometimes I hated seeing what humanity could do to one another. Who would steal a baby from their mother?

I sighed and looked back at the computer screen, trying to remember what it was I had been charting. I needed to get home and go to bed. Luckily, I had more done than I thought I did. I finished as quickly as I could, clocked out and hurried home.

The sun was bright and promising a beautiful day for me to sleep through. I felt like a vampire, creeping back into my lair before the sun could turn me to dust. I laughed. I handled a lot of blood at the hospital. I probably was part vampire and just didn't know it yet.

I paused for a moment at the entrance to my apartment building. I loved this place. The building was ten stories with the ground floor an open area for residents. We had a pool on the third floor, a state of the art gym, and a fantastic front desk staff.

Due to the prime location and the amazing view of downtown Omaha, several high profile people lived here. We had an NFL player, a famous author, and lots of high profile doctors and lawyers. I didn't see any of them, even though the NFL player lived on my floor. Working nights meant I didn't see much of anyone.

To be honest, the rent here should have been out of my price range, but my aunt owned the building. She gave me a very good deal on the smallest apartment in the building in return for watching her plants up on the rooftop garden once in a while.

I waved hello to the front desk as I came inside. The front lobby smelled like fresh coffee, but I didn't want to be up all morning, so I walked past it without stopping and to the main elevator. Everyone was on their way out, so I had the elevator to myself for the ride up. I was already imagining how comfortable my pillow was going to be after a nice bowl of oatmeal.

The elevator doors opened and I stepped out onto my hallway, ready for my day to be over.

But apparently it was just beginning, because as I stepped out of the elevator, a goat ran down the hall right at me.

3

THE GOAT

"Usually, the team that scores the most points wins the game."
-John Madden

DYLAN

"IS THAT A BABY CRYING?" Coach asked. "Why do you have a crying baby, Callahan?"

"Uh, just a commercial! Got to go!" I hung up on Coach. I'd probably be doing laps until he was tired for that, but there was no way I was going to be able to explain a baby.

Especially not right after he'd made me promise to be picture-perfect and scandal-free.

The baby wasn't as loud as I had expected. I had a little experience with toddlers, and they could scream. The baby wasn't so bad. Or at least that's what I told myself as I reached into the box and picked up the screaming bundle. In the process, I did figure out it was a girl.

She had minimal head control and her head lolled back as I picked her up. It didn't seem to hurt her, but it did make her cry more.

"You can't even hold your own head up?" I asked her, carefully tucking my hand under her delicate head. I had no idea how to hold a baby. I wanted to hold her at arms length, but she needed so much support I didn't dare hold her too far away.

So I tucked her in my arm like a football, keeping her close to my body. She stopped screaming, but she didn't go back to sleep. Instead she just stared up at me with big gray-blue eyes and a tiny rosebud mouth.

I had a feeling that this quiet wouldn't last long. I didn't know much about babies, but I did know that they needed food and diapers, both things a single twenty-seven-year-old man did not have in his house.

So, that meant I had to do what I always did when I needed something. I called my assistant.

"Hey, Alex, what do you know about babies?" I asked when he picked up.

"Do you have any idea how early it is?" Alex asked with an audible yawn. "I thought you were sleeping in today since it's your rest day."

I looked at the baby in my arms. Why did I get the sinking feeling I would never sleep again?

"Yeah, I woke up to work out," I replied. "But, babies. What do you know about babies?"

"Well, when a mommy and a daddy love each other very much--" Alex started.

"I mean how to take care of one," I cut him off.

"Not a clue."

"Well, I need you to get over here and help me figure out how to take care of a baby." I started to pace, keeping the baby pressed into my body. Her eyes did heavy sleepy blinks and I desperately hoped she would fall back asleep.

"Excuse me, what?" Alex sounded as confused as I felt.

"Just get over here," I told him. "I'll explain when you get here."

* * *

ALEX MADE it to my apartment in record time. He lived with his mom only a few miles away, but I was still impressed at the speed he got here.

"Why are you asking me about babies?" he asked, barging through the front door. We'd been friends since high school, so when I'd hit it big, I had hired him to handle all my day-to-day things. He liked it better than working at a regular job.

"Shhh!" I hissed at him, pointing to the baby in my arms.

Alex's eyes went wide. He looked at the baby, then up at me, then back at the baby, then up at me.

"How do you have a baby?" he asked. "*Why* do you have a baby?"

"She came in a box," I explained, pointing to the box still on the kitchen table.

"Babies aren't something you can order off Amazon," Alex replied. He moved to the box, looking at it like it might bite him if he got too close.

I sighed. "No, her mom left her on my front door in a box," I amended. "There's a note saying that I'm her dad."

"Shit, man." Alex stared at me.

"Yeah. I know." I sighed, but kept pacing. As long as I kept moving, the baby stayed asleep. As soon as I stopped walking, her little eyes would start to open and I figured she was probably getting hungry by now. Every time she woke up a little, she smacked her lips and looked like she was looking for something to suck on.

"I need something to feed her," I told Alex. "And diapers. Baby stuff."

"Okay." Alex nodded. "Where do you think they sell that stuff?"

I stared at him. "You're supposed to be *my* assistant. Where do you buy my food?"

"My mom helps," Alex admitted. "She knows all the organic shit you like."

"So you're telling me I should be paying your mom?" I narrowed my eyes at him.

"No, I do the work. I put it in your fridge. I am also the one who makes sure you have clean clothes. Mom refuses to do your laundry." Alex shrugged and I wasn't sure if he was kidding about his mom and the laundry. "Also, I'm the one who hooked you up with the recruiter and got you on the team. And bailed you out of jail that one time."

"Yeah, and you never let me forget it," I mumbled. I took a deep breath. "I need you to get me baby stuff."

"Sure." Alex shrugged. "I'll text my cousin. She has tons of kids and will know everything."

"Hold up." I crossed the room as fast as I could and stopped Alex before he could call his cousin. "This cannot get out. Coach has me on probation, not just for the dropping balls at practice but for all the bad press too. No one can know about this. I will lose my spot on the team if it gets out."

Alex looked at the baby in my arms. She was starting to wiggle since I wasn't moving.

"I don't know how long that's gonna last," Alex informed me. "Babies are hard. And noisy. I swear my cousin Sheila broke windows with her crying. You don't think anyone is going to notice you suddenly have a tiny infant?"

Panic clawed at my chest, but I forced it down.

"I just need some time. I need a lawyer. I need my agent on this," I told him. "But those will both take time. Right now, I really need something to feed this kid. I think she's hungry."

"You know, I remember reading that goat's milk is the closest thing to human milk," Alex informed me.

"Sure. Goat's milk is really good for muscle repair," I replied with a nod. "My trainer is always talking about how good it is. Also, if we're feeding her, we'll probably need some diapers."

"We?" Alex raised an eyebrow at me. "Are we co-parenting here? I didn't exactly get to participate in the creation process."

"You'll help me unless you want to be out of a job," I reminded him. "If I get kicked off the team, your salary goes along with my career."

"Right. Cool. How many do you think you'll need?" Alex asked. "Like, ten?"

I shrugged. "She's tiny. We probably don't even need

that many right away. How many diapers could a baby possibly need? I only go through one pair of underwear a day."

"Okay. Milk and diapers. I'll ask my mom about baby stuff, but I'll make sure she doesn't suspect anything," Alex promised. "I'll be back in ten minutes. They have to have something at that new convenience store down the street."

"Go fast Alex." I looked down at the sleeping baby in my arms and knew that I didn't have long.

* * *

I NEVER PROPERLY LEARNED THE words to the Itsy Bitsy Spider. Luckily, the baby didn't seem to know or care. But that's probably because she hated my singing more than the wrong lyrics.

Alex had been gone for seven minutes and thirty-six seconds when the baby woke up. I tried to get her to go back to sleep with the walking, but she was done. She kept turning her head and opening her mouth like a little fish trying to catch a hook. When there wasn't anything there to catch, she started to cry.

I tried rocking her. I tried singing.

She did not appreciate either.

My girl was hungry, and now it was becoming apparent, she was also hangry.

If I wasn't sure of her parentage, that certainly helped convince me. I got angry when hungry as well.

"Come on, kiddo," I whispered. "Please, just be quiet. Uncle Alex will be here any minute with something super tasty for you. Promise."

She looked at me with huge blue eyes, then screwed up her face, opened her mouth, and started to scream.

"Come on, it's not that bad," I tried to convince her. I turned on the TV, but she didn't care. She didn't want football or the kids' show with blue dogs that every parent seemed to be in love with.

"Well, your apartment has good soundproofing," Alex announced coming in the front door. "I didn't hear her out in the hallway."

"That's good," I said, turning to greet him with a desperate hope.

So you can imagine my surprise when, instead of much needed supplies, he brought in a goat.

A real-life, hairy, white goat.

"Why do you have a goat?" I asked, the baby still crying. She didn't care there was a barnyard animal in my house.

"For goat's milk, obviously," Alex replied. He tugged on the rope tied around the goat's neck and pulled it into my apartment. "And I got some diapers."

"How did you get a goat? We're in the middle of a city." Sure, Omaha wasn't exactly New York City big, but it wasn't the middle of farm country Nebraska either. I stared at the creature. It was a dirty gray color and about the size of a very large dog. The goat stared at me with devil eyes. "Also, are you sure it's a girl goat? It has horns."

"All goats have horns," Alex replied loftily. He tied the rope around one of the kitchen table legs. "I'm surprised you didn't know that. This is a milking goat. An Alpine goat, which is a breed known for their milking abilities."

"The person you bought that from told you that, didn't they?"

Alex deflated a little bit. "Yeah, but still, how lucky are we? What are the odds that I would find someone selling a goat right outside the gas station?"

"I should probably buy a lottery ticket," I agreed. "But did this person show you how to milk the goat?"

The baby was still crying. I had no idea how to milk a cow, let alone how to milk a goat.

Alex's face fell a little bit. "No. And I just realized I didn't get any bottles. Do you think the baby would just nurse off the goat directly?"

We both stared at the goat, tilting our heads to look at her udder.

"It's too big," I said after a moment. "Besides, she can barely hold her head steady. There's no way she could sit and eat off of it."

"I'm sorry, man." Alex sighed. "Not quite as amazing as I had hoped."

"It's okay," I assured him. "We just need to practice. I'm sure all new parents go through this."

"Yeah..." Alex agreed. He frowned, looking thoughtful. "I don't remember Auntie June having a goat, though."

"You got diapers?" I asked, changing the subject.

Alex held up a small plastic wrapped cube. "They didn't have much, but they did have these swim diapers. That should work, right?"

"It'll be fine. At least until I can figure out what to do," I replied. I hesitated. "Have you ever changed a diaper before?"

"Do I look like I've changed a diaper before?" Alex asked me.

"You at least have siblings," I countered. "I'm an only child."

"Yeah. *Older* siblings," he replied. He shrugged. "I could call my mom?"

"Do *not* call your mother." I wished this baby would stop crying so I could think. "We're smart men. It can't be that hard. Human beings have done this for centuries. We can do it too."

Alex nodded weakly, giving the baby an unsure look.

I took her to the rug in the living room by the couch and lay her down. She screamed even harder, her little fists balling up and her face going red.

"It'll be okay," I promised. There were little button snaps on the bottom of her shirt, so I unsnapped them and pulled up the cloth. The diaper she had on looked completely different than the one Alex was handing me.

But I was a smart guy. I undid the little Velcro straps and opened her very full diaper. Luckily, it looked like it was just pee and I made sure to tell Alex to add wipes to his shopping list. I wrapped the icky diaper up.

"I'll go throw this away," Alex said. He picked it up like it was a live bomb about to explode as he took it to the trash chute in the hallway.

The swim diaper did not have little Velcro straps. It was more like underwear. It took me a couple of tries to get her wiggly little legs into the correct holes, but I had her in a clean diaper in less time than I thought.

I could do this.

I picked her up. She was still screaming mad, but at least she wasn't wet anymore.

"Okay, let's figure out how to get you something to eat," I told her, patting her back. She seemed a little calmer now that she wasn't wearing a sopping wet diaper.

I looked at the kitchen, the open apartment door, and sighed. I did not want to be quoting Jurassic Park, yet I had to say it.

"Where's the goat?"

4
———

MY NEIGHBOR IS A KIDNAPPER

Nurse: the first person you see after saying, 'Hold my beer and
watch this!'
—Unknown

Natalie

There was a goat in the hallway.

I blinked twice, sure that I was hallucinating. I really did need to get to sleep. What had been in that last cup of coffee?

I lived in a high-end apartment building with a doorman and security. This was supposed to be a pet-free floor, although I knew that Mr. Salvador down the hallway often babysat his niece's puppy for long weekends. No one ever minded because the puppy was adorable.

But a goat was something all together different. Especially because it was trying to eat the carpet at the end of the hallway. For a moment, I considered just walking into my apartment and pretending I never saw the goat.

But my stupid morality wouldn't let me. Or my curiosity. I needed to know why there was a goat in the hallway and if this was going to become a regular occurrence.

"What in the world are you doing here?" I softly cooed, coming up to the goat. It seemed friendly enough. It didn't try to run away as I came closer. A collar looped its neck and a leash hung on the floor. I picked it up and the goat didn't object.

She was cute, in a creepy demonic way. I kind of liked the strange shape of her pupils and the fact that she instantly leaned into me for butt scratches.

"You're just a big goofy puppy, aren't you?" I asked her. She wagged her little floofy tail and bleated, very clearly asking me to continue giving her scratches. "Well, let's figure out where you belong because I don't want you out here getting in trouble."

I glanced up and down the open hallway. Only one door was open. The football player. I rolled my eyes.

Of course *he* would have a goat. It was probably for some fresh goat's milk for muscle building or something ridiculous like that. We weren't supposed to have pets, let alone farm animals here, but of course the famous football player wouldn't follow the rules.

Why would he? He was famous. He had enough money to do anything. Why follow the rules?

The goat nibbled gently on my scrub pant leg and looked up at me. She bleated softly again, as if she was saying, *"Hey, you don't know the guy. He's not that bad."*

I sighed. "Well, he left you out here. I don't know why you're defending him."

She looked at me, and I swear she sighed.

Great. Now I was having complete nonsensical conversations with a goat. Did that mean I needed more coffee or less?

I needed sleep, I decided. I tugged on her leash, and the goat obediently started following me back to the open door. At least she seemed to be well-trained.

Be nice, I told myself as I approached the open door. *You've seen weirder stuff. Just give the man his goat and go to bed. It will absolutely count as a good deed for the day and you can enjoy that karma later.*

I didn't know much about the guy other than he played for the NFL. I'd ridden up on the elevator with him a few times, but I tried to avoid him. Most of the time he seemed happy to keep to himself, but then I'd hear about him on the news for being at some crazy party and having a new girlfriend every other weekend.

Definitely not the type of guy I wanted to be around.

Not that I had any other prospects at the moment, but there was more than enough drama in my life working in the ER and prepping for school. Dating a high-profile player did not sound like something I wanted to entangle myself in.

Two men stood inside the apartment. One was tall, muscled, and looked like a football player. The other was around the same age, but without the "I'm in the NFL and bowl people over for a living" look. Their backs were to me, both of them bent over a phone. I could hear a woman's voice instructing the watcher to be gentle with the teats, but use a strong firm pressure.

Still not the weirdest part of my night at least.

I knocked on the open door and cleared my throat. Both men looked up and turned around in surprise.

The football player had a baby in his arms. A little baby- probably only a few months old.

That seemed like something that should have come up on that sports show my patient was watching this morning. I knew he wasn't married. Maybe he was just babysitting. Or maybe it was the other man's baby?

"Uh, are you missing a goat?" I asked, holding up the leash with the goat.

"How did she get out again?" The football guy looked at his friend in surprise. "I thought it was too quiet in here. We are going to have to watch that door better."

"Be sure to praise your mama as you milk her and tell her that she is doing a good job. Even if she doesn't speak English, your little mama will know that she is doing a good job," the phone blared. "Mamas give good milk."

Luckily, I could now see a video of a goat being milked on the screen or that video would have been very strange. The smaller man quickly shut off the phone, but not before his cheeks darkened.

I walked into the apartment, leading my new goat friend through the door and into the apartment foyer.

His apartment was much bigger and nicer than mine. My entrance area only had enough space to store two pairs of shoes. His could fit an entire shoe store. The open concept kitchen to the left was full of stainless steel appliances, while mine had an old fridge that didn't have an ice-maker. A huge leather couch with matching recliner sat in front of a TV big enough to charge movie theater prices and several doors leading off to other rooms.

But what I really noticed was the lack of baby things. I knew several people with babies. Their houses were always full of toys, diaper boxes, high chairs, and baby accessories. Even when they cleaned up for guests, there was always evidence that a small human lived in the space. There wasn't anything for the baby in this apartment.

No bottles on the counter. Just shaker bottles and protein drink mixes. No diaper boxes stacked by the door, just regular grocery boxes. The only diapers I could see were a package of swim diapers for a six-month-old. No diaper bag.

Nothing indicating that this baby was supposed to be here or belonged to either of these men.

"I'm sure you'll see it next time." The cop's voice echoed in my mind.

Was it just my imagination, or did the football player look uncomfortable holding the baby?

Fuck.

"So, why do you have a goat?" I asked, hoping I sounded nonchalant. The goat was currently leaning against my leg as she grazed on an empty cardboard box in the recycling bin.

"For the milk," the smaller guy replied. "It's the closest thing to human milk there is."

It took a second for my brain to register what he said. Despite working in the ER and hearing lots of random facts, this one took me by surprise.

"You mean other than formula, right?" I asked, hoping that maybe they were just a really unique gay couple that was using alternative medicine and diet to make sure that their precious baby had the most expensive options to thrive.

The smaller man paled. "Formula?"

"I mean, yeah, in the 1700's, goats' milk was a great substitute," I continued. "These days though, most people just use formula."

"Formula would definitely be easier than trying to figure out how to milk a goat," Football Guy replied, giving Smaller Guy an annoyed glare. Smaller Guy gave him a *"well, you aren't doing any better"* face right back.

The alarm bells going off in my head started to get louder. Did these two knuckleheads really think they could just milk a goat and feed it to a baby?

Considering there was a goat trying to nibble on my shoes and no sign of formula in the house, I was more than just a little suspicious.

"I'm sure you'll see it next time."

"You don't have any formula for the baby?" I asked, making sure that I wasn't reading the situation wrong.

"Yet. We don't have any formula yet," Football Guy clarified.

"On it, Boss. Formula." Smaller Guy stuffed his phone in his pocket and took two steps toward the door before pausing and looking at me. "Do you have a recommended brand?"

"For this baby?" I pointed to the bundle in Football Guy's arms. "How old is it?"

"Um, newish?" Smaller Guy shrugged.

The alarm bells were clanging in my mind now. He hadn't bothered to correct the gender. He didn't know the age.

"Infant formula. It should say 0-12 months on the container," I advised, trying to remember what I'd seen at my friend's house with a new baby. "You should probably look to see if there's a pre-mixed kind."

Lord knew what these two idiots would do if they had to mix it themselves. I took a breath. Hopefully, I just didn't know the entire situation. Hopefully, this was an emergency situation and they weren't really in charge of taking care of an infant. Maybe the mom was a friend and had just gotten out of a bad situation so that's why there wasn't any baby stuff.

"I'm sure you'll see it next time."

"You should probably get some more diapers, too," I added, pointing at the package of swim diapers on the table. "Real ones. Not swim diapers. I'd guess a size one or two. And some wipes to go with them."

"Size one diapers. Wipes. Formula," Smaller Guy mumbled, clearly making a list in his head. He gave me a polite nod and rushed out the door, leaving me with Football Guy holding a baby, and a goat now trying to eat my pant leg.

"So, where do you want the goat"" I asked, lifting the dog leash. It didn't look like they had anything in place for the goat either.

"Um... the office?" Football Guy offered, looking around the room. "She'll be fine in there."

He led me to one of the closed doors, pushing it open. It was a very nice office with an expensive looking desk, chair, and computer.

"Are you sure?" I asked, glancing at the goat. "She is going to eat everything in here."

"She doesn't look hungry," the man said with a shrug.

"She was eating the carpet in the hallway. She is a goat. She'll eat your computer," I warned.

"Goats can eat computers?" His eyes widened and he moved to block the goat from the office.

"I know they eat tin cans," I replied. "Did you buy a goat without knowing what they eat?"

Football Guy shifted his feet uncomfortably.

"I didn't buy the goat," he informed me, lifting his chin. "Alex did."

Alex must be Smaller Guy who had run off to buy diapers and formula.

"So, is this your baby or his?" I asked, keeping my voice as neutral as possible.

"You can put the goat in the guest bathroom." Football Guy closed the door to the office and opened one a little further down. It was a nice size room with a tub. The shower curtain was the Omaha Twister's emblem. "If she eats all the TP, I have extra."

I pulled the leash, putting the goat into the bathroom. She ignored the toilet paper and went straight for one of the fluffy white towels hanging on the wall.

"I didn't like those towels anyway," Football Guy said, closing the door and trapping the goat in the bathroom. "Thanks so much for your help. You can head back home and don't worry about us."

"I'm sure you'll see it next time."

There was no way I was leaving this baby alone now.

The baby started to cry. It was the classic "neh" sound made to break a mother's heart.

"Oh, she's hungry," I said, stepping closer to him.

"You can tell that from her cry?" He looked down at the baby in his arms, his dark eyebrows creasing his attractive features.

"I worked in the NICU before I switched to the ER," I

explained. "The hungry cry has a 'Neh' sound at the beginning. Also, see her mouth? She's looking for the nipple to suck on."

I wanted to take the baby from him and run all the way to the ER to get her someplace safe. Every bone in my body told me that this baby was not supposed to be here. But this man was much bigger than me. *Much* bigger. He was huge. I had to be careful. I had to do this right or the baby and I could end up in serious trouble.

"Well, Alex should be back in a few minutes with the formula." He looked down at the baby and gave her a reassuring smile. "We'll get you something to eat, promise."

"Is she yours?" I asked again. "How old is she?"

"She's mine," he replied, not taking his eyes off the baby. "And she's only a few months old."

Despite the sweet look on his face, all I wanted to do was grab that baby and run. But I wasn't sure how far I would get. He wasn't set up to be a parent. Was this an illegal adoption? A custody battle gone bad? A kidnapping?

There was a crash from the bathroom.

"Oh boy," he groaned. "Well, at least I know what the goat is doing."

"I can hold her while you go check on the goat," I offered. It was only partially because I was a good person. It was also my chance to check out the baby and make sure she was healthy. It was my chance to make sure that the horrible twisting feeling in my gut wasn't real.

But my gut was usually right.

He paused, holding the little girl close to his chest. "You said you're a nurse?"

I nodded. "And I worked for six months in the NICU. I know how to take care of babies. I promise."

He chewed his lip, considering if he could trust me. There was another crash from the bathroom, this time with a loud thud and the sound of liquid. He winced.

"Just... don't leave the living room." He looked down at the infant in his arms, as if unsure that he wanted to hand her off to me. My heart warmed a little at his protectiveness.

"I won't go anywhere," I promised, holding out my arms to take her.

He sighed, glancing back toward the strange noises coming from the bathroom before moving in close to me. With absolute gentleness, he carefully handed her over to me, making sure that she was securely in my arms before letting go of her. He looked me over once I had her cradled into me, obviously judging if I was going to suddenly drop her and he would need to dive in and rescue her. The sound of hooves on tile echoed out of the bathroom, making me think the goat had jumped up onto the sink.

"I'll be right back," he promised before dashing into the bathroom and closing the door behind him so the goat couldn't escape. I drifted back to the living room, looking around at his very nice apartment. The guy was loaded. Everything was top of line and nice.

But I wasn't here to see his swanky apartment. I snuggled the little girl into me and she cooed with delight. Her delicate dark hair smelled like baby shampoo and warm milk. I inhaled deeply, soaking up the sweet baby smell. I'd read somewhere that it was coded into our DNA to think babies smelled good and I wasn't about to disagree with that science. She had the good baby smell that I could sniff all day. It was definitely encoded into my DNA to enjoy them.

I did a quick assessment on the baby. Overall, the baby looked good and healthy. She was well-fed with bright eyes and good movement. I guessed she was somewhere around three months given that she responded to my silly faces with smiles, although she was definitely very hungry. She kept trying to snuggle into my shirt, hoping to find the good stuff.

"Sorry little one," I whispered. "There isn't anything there. Hopefully your uncle will be back with some food for you in a minute."

My stomach twisted again. That man wasn't her uncle. Uncles knew to feed babies formula. The little girl's mouth opened and shut as she rooted for something to eat. Maybe there was a pacifier around here somewhere? I didn't see any on the very clean kitchen counters. Luckily, she found her hand and sucked hard at it. I hoped that the other guy returned soon with some food for her. The fact that there wasn't any was worrying me.

"He's just clueless," I told myself, although I wasn't sure who I was trying to convince. There was something very off about what was going on here.

Suddenly, my arm was warm and wet. I looked down to see the baby leaking pee straight out of the diaper. The entire front half of her onesie was soaked and leaking onto my arm.

I sighed. At least at work I got paid when someone peed on me.

I looked around the room for a stack of diapers. I had changed many an infant in my nursing days and figured it was the least I could do for this very confused little family.

I could hear her dad yelling at the goat and crashes as things fell in the bathroom. I heard what sounded like a shampoo bottle, the water running, and the rip of what I could only assume was the shower curtain. That goat was giving him a run for his money.

"No, you can't eat the shower curtain! Or the shower rod? How about some water instead? No, not soap!"

I shook my head and continued looking. I finally saw a plastic package, but it was full of swim diapers. The apartment was spotless, and there wasn't a single diaper bag to be seen. There was no clear spot for me to change a diaper either. There was only a box on the table with a blanket in it and a tiny pack of swim diapers. There was nothing else that even looked like it could be for a baby.

"Oh... no..." I groaned, that twisting feeling getting worse. I peeked at the little girl's diaper, hoping that it wasn't going to be a swim diaper. But no. The cute little blue and green diaper that wasn't meant to hold liquid was the reason my arm was now wet. There was no food for this baby. There were no diapers. There were no supplies.

This wasn't his baby.

Maybe there was a reasonable explanation. Maybe there was a good reason that this man was completely and utterly unprepared to even babysit a baby.

The police officer's words echoed in my mind. That I would do better next time.

My hand went to my pocket and immediately found the policeman's business card. I didn't even have to look for it. It was just in my hand. It was like fate was telling me that I could help this little girl. The universe was making it easy for me to do the right thing. I knew what I needed to do. This little girl needed my help. She needed me to be the voice she didn't have yet.

Maybe this guy was just a clueless dad. Maybe he'd just gotten custody and didn't have a clue. Maybe he was just babysitting.

But this baby was old enough that she should have supplies, even if he was just babysitting. This baby was hungry and had no food. There were no diapers. There were no wipes. There was nothing to indicate that a baby lived in this apartment at all. The things needed to care for an infant just weren't here. This was not a safe place for her to be in.

Better safe than sorry. If I didn't call, I would worry and feel awful about potentially leaving a defenseless child in a terrible situation. If he was just a babysitter, it would easily be cleared up. No harm, no foul, right?

My phone was out and I was dialing before I had time to stop. I didn't have much time before the fake-dad came back from dealing with the goat. I had to get this sweet little baby help before something bad happened to her.

The detective answered on the first ring.

"Hi, Officer Brown. It's Natalie Parker, the nurse from the ER today. I think I may have another baby in trouble situation."

5

—————

AVOID GETTING ARRESTED

How do football players deal with their problems?
They tackle them head on.

DYLAN

I DIDN'T KNOW that toilet brushes were edible. Nor did I know that goats found them irresistible.

Along with toilet paper. And shampoo. And the expensive towels my home decorator had absolutely insisted upon. The goat also seemed to think that the shower curtain was some sort of delicacy.

My house cleaner was going to freak when she saw the mess the goat had made in here, but I found myself rather liking the devil-eyed creature. She was sweet in an eat-everything kind of way. She kept rubbing her head against me, obviously asking for pets, in between eating my various bathroom components.

I had no idea what I was going to do with her. I didn't have a place to keep a goat. I lived in an apartment in the middle of the city. But that was something to worry about in twenty minutes. Right now, I had to figure out the baby situation and what I was going to do with my brand new child.

After making sure that only non-toxic items were left in the bathroom (was a shower curtain considered toxic? It was a bamboo mix, so I guessed that meant it had some sort of plant in it) I closed the goat in the bathroom and returned to the living room.

My neighbor was smiling and talking at the baby in her arms. She hadn't seen me yet, but she looked so natural with my daughter that it made me pause for a moment. Her oval face was framed by messy dirty-blonde hair, but it was her smile that drew me in. When she smiled, the whole world lit up. I had no idea how I had never noticed her walking the building before. Maybe I'd overlooked her because of the scrub pants. Maybe I'd just never seen her smile at me before. I'd known there was a nurse on my floor, but I'd never paid attention before.

I was paying attention now.

"So, how come I haven't seen you around here?" I asked, coming over to join them. She looked up, surprise flashing in her eyes.

"I work nights," she explained, shifting the baby to her other hip. "I'm usually asleep during the day, so I don't get out much. Vampire hours are not great for a social life."

"Do you like being a vampire?" I asked her. She

frowned at me for a second before figuring out what I meant.

So much for my charming social skills.

"I like the people I work with, and I like the job that I do," she said slowly. "But the hours? I would very much like to come back to the daylight."

She flashed me a grin that made my knees go a little weak. Damn. She had a smile that could light up a room. No wonder the baby had been watching her with rapt attention. She said she worked in the ER and I was now thinking that all those concussions football was famous for weren't so bad. They were the perfect excuse to see her again.

"I'll take her," I said, reaching for my daughter. The woman hesitated for a moment, but handed her to me.

"So, I don't mean to be rude, but..." Her smile faded and worry replaced it. "Why do you have this baby?"

"It's mine," I replied defensively, without even pausing to think. It surprised me with how quickly the words came. I'd only been a father for thirty minutes, but I already was prepared to fight for my child.

She raised an eyebrow and lifted her hands in surrender. I sighed.

"She's mine," I said, trying to keep my voice calm. The baby squirmed in my arms, sensing my feelings. This woman was a nurse and lived down the hallway. She was a great resource, one that I couldn't afford not to utilize. Plus, the baby seemed to like her. "She was left on my doorstep."

Her eyes went wide.

"She came in that box with a note saying she's mine," I continued, motioning toward the box on the table. I reached over and handed her the note that had come with the baby. "I only found out about her thirty minutes ago."

Her eyes somehow became bigger as she read the note. They were a really pretty pale blue. "Oh... oh... that's why there isn't any baby stuff here."

I nodded. "I sent my assistant to go get all the things we'd need, but he doesn't have kids. I plan on setting everything up and making sure she has the best of everything, but to say I was not expecting to be a parent today is an understatement."

"Shouldn't you call the police?" she asked, handing me back the note. "Or a social worker or something?"

"I can't. I'll lose my job," I explained. "I'm in hot water with my coach and the team owners, and something like this would be candy for the press. Can you imagine the field day they would have with this?"

I looked down at my daughter. She was sucking furiously on her hand.

"I saw you on the news. They were saying your position on the team is in jeopardy," she said, her voice quiet.

"I want to do right by her and I want to take care of her," I told her, cradling my daughter in closer to me. "I just need to make sure I can keep my job in the process."

"Oh." Her face went pale and slightly greenish like she was about to be sick. "Oh boy."

"Are you okay?" I asked, taking a step toward her. "You said you work nights. Do you need to sit down? I have some electrolyte drinks in the fridge. You probably need some hydration. Or if you need to eat, I have tons of protein options."

She shook her head. "No, that's not it. I just...." She took a deep breath, reaching up and smoothing her blonde hair back. Her eyes met mine, guilt shining bright in her gaze. "I think I made a big mistake."

"Mistakes are fixable," I said automatically. I flashed her a small grin. "At least that's what my mom always used to say."

She fidgeted with the hem of her shirt, avoiding my gaze for a moment before taking another deep breath. She still looked like she was about to puke.

"I called the cops on you."

The words echoed around the room like tiny gunshots.

"You what?"

"I called the cops on you." Her shoulders crumpled inward, making her small. "I thought you kidnapped the baby. You don't have anything for her."

Anger started to rise up hot from the pit of my stomach, mixed with a little bit of dread and no small amount of fear.

"And you went straight to calling the cops?" I tried not to shout, but she still shrank back from me like I'd thrown the words.

Her eyes went to mine and she took a deep breath, lifting her chin and throwing her shoulders back like the linemen do when they know a hit is coming and they just have to take it.

"I had a kidnapped little girl in my ER last night." Her words were quiet but strong. She wasn't apologizing, but explaining. "It could have been bad. Luckily, it wasn't. She's fine, but, it means that I'm looking for the signs of a kidnapped child. There's no diapers. There's no food. There's nothing to indicate this little girl belongs here. I was making sure she was safe."

I want to be angry, but she's right. There was nothing

in my house for a child because until thirty minutes ago, I didn't have one. She was wrong about the why and I wished she would have asked instead of jumping right to calling the cops, but a part of me was glad that she wanted to protect my little girl.

"She's mine," I repeated, looking down at my daughter in my arms. I knew it in my core and that I would do anything for her, even if I'd only had her for a few minutes. "She's mine."

"I get that now," she said, raising her hands in surrender once more. I hadn't realized that I'd said the second one out loud. "But, there is a police officer on the way. He should be here any minute."

I frowned. "You didn't call 911? You called an actual police officer?"

She nodded, looking guilty. "He gave me his card at the hospital. I figured he was the best person to call."

I just stared at her for a moment, trying to come up with a battle plan. My brain went blank. This is why I didn't want to be quarter back. I liked being the running back because I got to react to what the boss wanted. I didn't have to come up with the plan, I just had to figure out the best way to accomplish it.

"What do we do?" I asked, more to myself than to the nurse. "I don't exactly have anything showing that she's mine and that note isn't exactly great for staying under the radar with my coach."

She chewed on her lower lip. "I tell him that I made a mistake. That I was wrong."

"But he's going to see all the same red flags you saw," I countered. "The lack of diapers, no milk, and the fact there is a goat in my bathroom."

Luckily, the goat had been quiet the last few minutes. I hope that meant she was napping in the bathtub, her tummy full of shower curtain.

She looked thoughtful, tugging her lower lip between her teeth for a moment before brightening.

"We tell him this is your assistant's baby. You're babysitting, that's why nothing is here. He's in a bind and you're being a great friend and helping him out."

There was no way that was going to work, but I didn't have any other ideas. I looked around the apartment, desperately wishing that magical baby items would just appear and solve all my problems. Shockingly, no baby bottles or diapers whisked out of the ether and filled my home. It was up to the two of us.

"Maybe you could call him--" I started to say just as the doorbell rang. Her eyes went wide with terror. "You gave him my address?"

She nodded guiltily. "I am so sorry."

But there was nothing to be done now. I took a deep breath. I'd been in stickier spots before. I let my eyes close for two steadying heartbeats, the way I did before every play of a game. You can't think if you aren't calm. Brains and brawn win the game, but brains hurt a lot less. I could get through this if I just used my head.

I nodded to her to open the door since she was closer to it. She winced as she put her hand on the door handle, but straightened her spine and lifted her chin.

"I am so sorry Officer. I made a terrible mistake." The door wasn't even all the way open before she started speaking. "I was absolutely wrong about the situation. There isn't a child in trouble and--"

"Dylan Callahan?" The police officer stared at me the

way so many surprised fans stared at me when they met me on the street. As if all their hopes and dreams had suddenly come true. As if just being in the room with me was everything they could have ever hoped for in life.

Sometimes, that look was welcomed. Sometimes, I hated that look. Sometimes, I just wished they would let me buy my damn toilet paper in peace. Today, it was a gift from heaven that I wasn't about to let go to waste. I put on my camera worthy smile and walked over to the man as if I had known him my entire life and he was my best friend.

"Hi Officer, I am Dylan Callahan." I flashed my smile just a little wider. "Are you a fan?"

"Um, yes. I mean, I'm a huge fan. My son and I watch your games. He's eight and thinks that you can do anything in the world." The man bounced on his toes like he'd just won the lottery. "He's going to flip when I told him I met you today!"

"Oh, I'm always so excited to meet my fans," I said, pushing the door open a little wider. A team banner hung on the wall specifically so that everyone walking in would know who I worked for. "Please come in. Can I get you a water?"

The man gaped like I'd just offered him pure gold. Nurse, however was glaring daggers at me.

"What are you doing?" she hissed as I closed the door behind the cop. "You don't want him in here."

I ignored her. The meet-and-greet of fans was something that I was actually pretty good at. It came naturally, almost as easily as running a ball down the field did. I reasoned that the thought patterns were actually pretty similar- guess what the other person was going to do, what they wanted you to do, and then react accordingly. It was all just reading people's body language, and right now, this cop wanted to hand me the key to the city. If I kicked him out, he would be suspicious, which would actually be worse. I needed him to feel like his time had been well spent and for him to go home feeling like a hero.

He would never look around for the baby stuff if he was too interested in getting football fame for his son.

"You said your son is a fan?" I asked, leaning against the counter. "I have an extra hat from preseason training. They're pretty exclusive, so I'd really like to give it to someone who will appreciate it."

The cop's mouth dropped open and he stared at me for a moment. "Seriously?"

I nodded. "Of course."

"That would be amazing," he stammered, excitement tripping his words up in his mouth. The smile on his face should have made me feel like a king, but I felt like a fraud.

I went over to my gym bag and rummaged around for the extra hats I always keep stashed there. The team gave us each a dozen or so to hand out, so I always tried and keep one or two on me to hand out to fans. I loved giving them out to kids best because they were genuinely excited about it, and they probably weren't going to turn around and try and sell it for a profit. Although, if a ten-year-old kid made a hundred bucks selling his hat, he deserved it. Kids deserved everything that brought them joy.

I pulled out the hat and a marker, bringing it over to the counter so I could balance the baby on my hip while I signed the brim of the hat.

"Who should I make it out to?" I asked, smiling at the police officer. He beamed as he told me his son's name and

I could almost believe we were home free. "So, is there anything else I can do for you, officer?"

"Uh no." His smiled dropped as why he was here crashed back into him. Damn. We were so close. "There was a concerned citizen that needed me to check on a baby."

"That was me," my neighbor interjected, raising her hand and stepping into the conversation. "I was wrong. I mean, obviously, our beloved Dylan Callahan, star player of the Omaha Twisters, wouldn't steal a baby. That would be ridiculous."

The police officer looked at her and then back at me and then at the baby in my arms.

I could feel my stomach sinking into the floor. This was it. This would be how my career ended. I could already imagine it on the nightly news. "Star running back Dylan Callahan of the Omaha Twisters was arrested today on charges of kidnapping." Yup. That would make my coach thrilled. My agent would love me. All the fans would clamor for my autograph.

"You thought the best tight end in the league kidnapped a baby?" the police officer repeated, looking once again at my daughter.

"Oh, I'm not the best. It's nice of you to say though," I said, trying to keep the mood light.

"I should arrest you just for saying that," the police officer informed me. "You're amazing. Your stats last year won me the fantasy league."

I wanted to say that those were last year's stats. That this year I was not doing nearly as well. That this year, I wasn't going to win him any fantasy football leagues, but he just continued.

"That injury at the last game just has you rattled. You'll bounce back. I'm counting on you to win me the championship again."

It was always weird getting psychoanalyzed by complete strangers. Everyone seemed to think they knew what was going on in my head, like they knew me just because they had watched me run around on their TV screen once a week. The worst part was when they were actually right.

I was about to thank him when a loud thud came from the closed bathroom door. The goat. Behind the cop, I saw the nurse's eyes close and her shoulders sag.

"What was that?" the police officer asked, his posture suddenly upright and on guard.

"They're working on some pipes in the building today," the nurse quickly lied. "There was an email about it. Weird noises from the bathrooms are totally expected today."

I thanked my lucky stars that she could lie so quickly and convincingly. As long as the goat didn't decide to eat the door or bleat too loud, we still might make it out of this.

"I'm back!" Alex announced, throwing the front door open and nearly smashing the cop in the process.

"Oh good, the baby's uncle is back!" Nurse cried out, once again saving the situation with quick thinking.

"I am?" Alex asked, freezing in the doorway as he registered the cop standing in the middle of my living room. Every line on his body went rigid as his panic filled eyes met mine.

"What the hell man?" he asked, using his eyes.

"Just go with it," I answered psychically. *"It'll be fine."*

His gaze cut back to the cop and then to me. *"If you get me arrested, you owe me a million dollars."*

"Done."

"And if there is jail time, you have to explain it to my mom."

"I'd rather give you another million," I silently replied. He just glared. I sighed. *"Fine. I explain it to your mom."*

"So you're the baby's uncle?"

We both turned, realizing that the police officer was speaking to us and not part of our silent conversation. Once again, his body language had shifted back into wary investigation.

"Yeah, yeah." Alex nodded. "My sister just had a baby and she dumped it on me for the day. I have no idea what I'm doing, so Dylan said he'd help me out."

The nurse's eyes flicked back and forth between the cop, Alex, me, and the baby like we were the most interesting TV show on the planet.

"He's a great mentor," Alex continued, not even sounding a little sarcastic. "He's really great with kids. Even babies. Especially babies."

The cop narrowed his eyes, looking Alex up and down and then back at the baby in my arms. I really hoped he didn't notice how much different Alex's skin tone was or that he'd just think it was just weird genetics. They both had dark hair, but that was where the similarities between Alex and the baby ended. My breath hitched in my chest, but I kept the confident smile plastered to my face. Fake it 'til you make it. Never let 'em see you sweat.

Something thudded in the bathroom again and I groaned internally.

"Like I said, Officer, it was my mistake," Nurse broke

the silence of the room. "I am so sorry for wasting your time."

This was it. I willed my pulse to stay steady, to keep my breathing even and muscles loose. Fourth down and inches. We were so close.

"I can see that the incident at the hospital rattled you," the officer finally said. "But you really need to use your brain. Dylan Callahan stealing a baby? That's ridiculous."

Another thud from the bathroom. I needed to get the cop out of the house before the goat started screaming. Goats did that right? I seemed to remember a screaming goat meme at some point.

"We really should get her down for a nap," I said, moving to the door. "And you have your hat, right?"

The cop clutched the signed hat to his chest like a little kid with a treasure. "I do. I really appreciate this, Mr. Callahan."

"Oh, it's my pleasure, and please, call me Dylan," I said, making sure to flash him another photo worthy smile. "I do have a request of you though. Could you keep this quiet? I mean, I have a reputation to uphold. If the other guys hear I babysit, I won't have a minute of free time after practice. This place would become a daycare."

"Oh, absolutely. I won't say a word about the baby," he assured me, taking slow steps to the door.

"Thanks, I really appreciate it."

"Anything for the man about to win me this year's fantasy league title." He was going to say more, but the baby started to cry. I couldn't blame her. There was milk in those grocery bags and she was hungry.

The cop chastised the nurse one more time before thanking me yet again and then finally exiting the door.

"Good luck with the season!" is all I heard as Alex closed the door behind him.

"So, I'm an uncle now?" Alex asked me with a glare. He turned back to the baby. "I'm absolutely buying you a drum-set for her first birthday."

6

APPARENTLY I NEEDED ANOTHER JOB

"This will only be a little pinch."
-Lies nurses tell

NATALIE

"WHAT IS GOING ON?" Assistant Alex asked, looking at his boss. "How did I become an uncle? Why is she still here? Why was there a cop in your place? Where is the goat?"

The questions came fast and hard, each one punctuated with a step further into the house.

"In order, one: because we needed you to be. Two: she was helping with the baby but called the cops, leading to three: The cop was here to check on why there was a baby here. And four: The goat is in the bathroom," Dylan explained, ticking off his fingers with each answer. Alex just stared at him open mouthed.

Another crash from the bathroom echoed through the room, followed by a sad bleating. I was so glad the cop had left. There would be absolutely no explaining the goat in the bathroom. Unfortunately, the sound of water gurgled from the bathroom this time as well.

I was really, really glad this was Football Player's apartment and not mine.

It felt like things were falling apart. The paper strings that we'd had tied around this scenario were now melting under the water currently creeping under the bathroom door.

And that's when the baby started to cry in earnest.

Her tiny hand was red and wet from her sucking on and not getting anything out of it and she was not happy. Poor little girl was at the absolute end of her rope. Both men winced as they looked at her, unsure of what they were supposed to do next.

"I'm better with plumbing than babies, so I'll go rescue the goat," Alex said, dropping the groceries on the floor and rushing toward the bathroom. I couldn't blame him. The baby was screaming full force now, and she was using every available muscle in her little body to be as loud as possible.

Football Player just stared at the baby in his arms like he didn't have a clue.

Probably because he didn't.

So I fumbled around in the grocery bags until I found a formula bottle. Thank heaven he had listened to me and purchased the premixed bottles of formula. Three separate brands of formulas, six different bottles, and what looked like four different kinds of wipes rolled out of the bag I went through first.

Well, at least he was thorough.

I chose one of the pre-mixed formula bottles with a nipple attached to the packaging.

"Come here," I said, motioning to Dylan. "You're going to have to learn how to do this."

I ripped open the packaging and screwed the lid onto the bottle.

"You should wash your hands before doing this," I said, handing him the bottle. "But she's at the furious hunger stage."

"Doesn't it need to be warmed up?" He held the bottle like it might bite him.

"I think she's hungry enough she'd take it ice cold," I replied.

He didn't move. The baby continued to scream. She looked so tiny in his arms, but he held her delicately and gently.

"Here." I moved his arms, putting the baby in the standard cradle position. "Run the nipple under her lower lip and she'll find it."

He swallowed hard, like he was nervous about feeding a baby, but did what I said. The baby fussed for a moment and then attacked the bottle with gusto. She sucked hard, her breathing coming hard and fast as she swallowed loudly.

"There, that's better," I cooed at her. I looked up at Dylan and caught him looking at the baby with absolute pride. It was a soft smile. A loving smile. A father's smile. If I hadn't known that he'd only had her for an hour, I would have believed that he saw this baby being born and loved her from that moment on.

"Position the bottle so it's a little more upright," I

coached, moving his arm into a better placement. "That way she'll suck in less air."

The baby reached up, grabbing his hand as if she was afraid he might take the bottle away from her. Her hand was so tiny against his, and he smiled down at her again with that smile that had my ovaries singing. Really, any woman who even remotely liked the human race at all would have their ovaries exploding at the endearing way this man looked at the baby. It was irresistible on an evolutionary level, so I told myself I didn't have to feel guilty about it at all.

"You're a natural," I told him, my voice low and soft. He lifted his eyes to meet mine and I realized how close we were. I was still touching his arm. He smelled really good. I felt my face go hot and took a step back. I hurried into the kitchen and found a towel hanging on the stove. It was just a dark blue towel, no football emblem on it, which surprised me. Wasn't a football player supposed to have team gear everywhere in his house?

"Should we give her another?" he asked, lifting up the now empty bottle. It was only a few ounces so I wasn't surprised she downed it so quickly.

"Let's burp her first. If she wants more in a few minutes, we can give her more, but I'd rather not overwhelm her stomach," I explained. I draped the towel over his very broad shoulder and he gave me a quizzical look. Being this close to him again had my heart speeding up. His clean soap scent was rather distracting. "Put her stomach on your shoulder and then gently pat her back. We're going to burp her."

He followed my instruction, moving carefully yet confidently. He checked in with me to make sure that the baby was in the right position on his shoulder before delicately tapping her.

"A little harder," I coached, ignoring the dirty line of thought my brain and screaming ovaries wanted to go down. "We want to get the bubbles out of her."

"She can't do that on her own?" he asked, just as the baby burped. A little milk dribbled out onto the towel. He looked surprised. "I wondered what the towel was for."

"Babies kind of suck at staying alive," I replied, going over and using the towel to wipe her face. Her eyes were glazing, the milk hitting her stomach and soothing her. "We have to help them with everything. Eating, pooping, burping... they are a lot of work."

He grunted, moving the baby off his shoulder. She immediately snuggled into him, her eyes slow blinking as she started to fall asleep. He smiled at her as her breathing became slow and even.

And then his smile disappeared.

"Why am I wet?" he asked.

"Because you got swim diapers," I replied, doing everything in my power not to snicker or laugh. "Swim diapers are only good for keeping the solid stuff in. The liquid stuff goes right through them."

"But they're diapers!" he protested.

"That's why you don't swim in the baby pool," I informed him.

He looked absolutely horrified and I couldn't help but laugh at his expression.

After a moment, he relaxed, shaking his head. "Why would they do something so gross?"

I rooted around in the bags again until I found a package of diapers. Real ones with pictures of baby animals in yellow and green on the edges. "Here, I'll help you change her. Have you ever done a diaper change before?"

"Oh, loads," he replied with a nonchalant shrug. "It's part of what the team trains us on during the off-season."

I frowned, wondering what the heck kind of training program these elite athletes had. Maybe it was some kind of weird hazing?"

"I'm just messing with you. I've never changed a baby before," he told me with a chuckle.

With a grin, I showed him how to take off the onesie and wet blanket (which we tossed into the kitchen sink to deal with later) and to properly wipe her from front to back.

Despite his large hands and muscular frame, he was surprisingly gentle and delicate in his motions. He moved deliberately, watching my movements carefully before copying them as best he could. The diaper change was quick and easy, but now we had a naked baby. Despite it being summer, his apartment was just cool enough that I knew the baby wouldn't be comfortable for long without something on.

Alex didn't pick up any clothes on his shopping spree, so that would have to wait until tomorrow. Luckily, babies were pretty happy to be naked.

"We'll need a blanket," I replied, looking around the room. "One you don't mind getting dirty."

"Use the one on the couch." He quickly walked over to the very fancy white leather couch and pulled off a gorgeous teal cashmere blanket. I assumed it was real cashmere because I didn't have the money to own anything quite that nice.

"She's going to ruin it," I said, looking at the blanket and imagining all the stains the beautiful fabric would hold being wrapped around an infant.

"My interior decorator picked it," he said with a shrug. "I don't ever actually use it."

"Okay..." Then I remembered that he played for the NFL and was rich enough that using a gorgeous cashmere blanket as a baby blanket wouldn't dent his pocket book in the slightest. He could dress her in nothing but cashmere and wouldn't ever worry about the bill.

So I wrapped her up in the blanket. She sighed, her eyelids fluttering for just a moment before she fell into a deeper sleep. It had been a busy day for her.

"That is not what we do!" A shout came from the bathroom. "Not cool, Goat! Not cool!"

"Should we go check on him?" I asked, afraid of what might be going on in that bathroom with the goat.

Dylan nodded, his face grave. "He will probably need medical attention."

But we found him sitting on the edge of the bathtub, the goat's head in his lap with her eyes closed and looking like it was the absolute best day of her life.

"Are you a goat whisperer?" Dylan asked, looking around the room. "She was a demon when I put her in here!"

"You just need to show her who is the boss," Alex replied, crossing his arms and looking smug.

Three Skittles fell out of his pocket, and onto the floor. The goat quickly slurped them up and then put her head back on his lap.

"Or bribe her with Skittles." Dylan shook his head at his assistant.

"Skittles work on everyone," I agreed with a grin that faded quickly. "Except babies. Don't give Skittles to babies. They can't chew. It's a choking hazard. She can't have them until she's eating real food and has actual teeth."

Both men stared at me like I was a crazy person, but I couldn't get the image of the two of them feeding the baby Skittles to keep her quiet from filling my mind.

"We know better than to give a baby candy," Alex informed me. The two men's eyes met and they both shook their head like I'd told them that the sky was blue. "We're not complete idiots."

I decided not to reply to that.

Instead, I let out a jaw-cracking yawn that shook my entire body. I'd forgotten for a few minutes that I had been up all night working my shift. It was way past my bedtime and all this excitement suddenly had me very tired.

"Okay, so feed her when she gets hungry. Change her diaper, wiping front to back. Put her in the box to sleep, not the bed, and not with any blankets other than the one swaddled around her," I listed off. "I will be right down the hall if you need anything, but I have to go to bed before I fall over."

Alex gave me a strange look. "Bed? It's like nine in the morning."

"She works nights," Dylan answered for me, and I was slightly impressed he'd remembered.

"What if she gets cold?" he asked, keeping her tucked to him.

"Since she can't move the blankets off her face, she can't have them. We'd rather her be cold than not able to breathe," I explained. "And that's why the box as well. If she rolls over on the bed, she may not be able to get her face out of the pillow."

"Oh. That's why my aunt insisted nothing in the crib..." Alex remembered. "Makes sense."

"You'll also need a car seat if you want to take her anywhere."

"Even I know that one," Alex informed me.

"It's a rest day," Dylan added. "I was just going to watch film at home today, so I can hold her while I do that."

I smiled softly. I had a feeling he wasn't going to put that little girl down today.

Reaching into my pocket, I pulled out a scrap of paper with three different sets of vitals scrawled across it along with a pen I'd stolen from the hospital. On it, I wrote my phone number and handed it to him.

"Here," I said, trying very hard not to blush. I wished I had business cards as he inspected the scrap paper with a raised eyebrow. "Call me if you have any problems. I'll keep the volume on high so it will wake me up."

He grinned at me, sliding the paper into his pocket. "I guess that's one way for me to get your number."

I rolled my eyes, laughing. "Ah yes, the old 'get a baby and a goat' trick. Gets me every time."

7

PARENTING IS EASY. JK

*"Nobody in football should be called a genius. A genius is a guy
like Norman Einstein."*
-Joe Theismann

DYLAN

"So, how many diapers do you think we need?" Alex asked, frowning at the screen of his phone as he scrolled through a grocery delivery app.

I shrugged. "She's little. How many could she actually go through in a day?" I asked him, repeating my thoughts from earlier. "I mean, I only wear one pair of underwear a day."

"Unless it's game day," Alex corrected me, not bothering to look up from the screen. "Also, you don't routinely poop your pants."

"Good point," I conceded. "So, what? Three a day? I think that feels pretty average bathroom usage."

Alex nodded thoughtfully. "That sounds good. Oh, here's a huge box. It says it's a size five. That probably means five hours, right?"

"Get that one," I agreed, peering over his shoulder. "It has 120 in the box. That'll last us for weeks and it's the same brand as the ones she's wearing now. I think she likes them. She hasn't complained."

Alex lifted an eyebrow at me. "I'm glad she's not speaking to management about the service," he said dryly.

I ignored him. "What else do we need?"

Alex scrolled on his phone. "We got everything on the list."

I went through the list we'd found on a "How to be a new parent" website we'd found. I couldn't believe babies needed so much, but I'd had Alex help me pick out one of everything they said we needed:

- a crib

- bibs

- burp cloths

- a mobile for the crib (we'd spent a long time finding a cool football themed one.)

- some clothes (bodysuits and a team jersey of course.)

- more formula (she kept drinking it and wanting more.)

- diapers (they only seemed to last an hour, which must have been why they were labeled "1". Hopefully the fives would last a little bit longer.)

- a wipe warmer

- a white noise machine

- nipple cream (not sure why, but all the websites said to get it.)

- lube (I was a little afraid of this one, but I purchased it.)

- cabbage leaves (why a baby would need cabbage was beyond me, but I was obviously not trained in being a parent.)

- a changing pad

- baby monitor

- baby shampoo

- swaddle blankets

- the worlds best car seat

- and a partridge in a pear tree.

Looking at the total at the bottom of the screen made me a little nauseous. It was a lot and we hadn't even bought any toys. No wonder people were always complaining about the price of kids. I was just glad I had a good money manager and several TV commercials making me crib-buying money.

"Okay, this should all be delivered in a couple of hours," Alex said, hitting the buy button without pausing. Why should he? It wasn't his money. "You good? I need to go pick up some stuff for *mi abuela* before her big doctor's appointment, but I can stay if you need me."

I'd nearly forgotten that today was the doctor's appointment day. I hoped that it was just a normal run of the mill "you're seventy-years-old" results and not a big scary one. Alex lived with his mom and his grandma, not because he couldn't afford it, but because his grandma's health wasn't the best. He stayed with her to make sure she stayed healthy. His grandma was the strongest woman I'd ever met. She was the one that kept Alex's family going. Without her as head matriarch, I wasn't sure the Castorena family would survive.

"No, man, I've got this," I assured him. I re-positioned the baby in my arms. She'd had another bottle and gone right back to sleep in my arms like she thought I was the safest place in the whole world. That thought made me warm and fuzzy all the way to my toes. "Hey, your mom raised three kids. Could you ask her for tips?"

Alex hesitated. "You want parenting tips from my mom?"

"Well, she raised you," I replied. "You seem to have turned out okay."

He smiled at me. "That is because I am simply amazing. I'm sure she'll say something like, 'kids need to respect their elders' and 'don't let them watch too much TV' or some shit like that."

"Right, because those are terrible things for people to do," I said, walking over to the couch and settling down. I thought about putting the baby in her box, but I didn't want to let her go. I loved her sleepy weight in my arms, and I knew if I put her in the box, I'd just stand there and watch her sleep. At least on the couch, I could put on some film and pretend to get work done.

"I'll ask her," Alex said, sliding his phone into his back pocket. "I won't tell her it's you. It might be a good distraction if we need something to talk about." He swallowed hard, his face going dark and worried at the same time. "I gotta go."

"Good luck today," I said as he headed to the door. "Let me know how it goes. If she needs anything..." I let the words trail off. I would always make sure that Alex's family got what they needed. Alex was not only my employee, but also my best friend. What good was my million-dollar contract if I couldn't help the people I cared about?

Alex gave me a quick nod before escaping the apartment to take his grandmother to the doctor. I settled in with the remote control, the baby sleeping peacefully in my arms.

This parenting thing was easy.

* * *

THIS PARENTING THING was stupid hard.

All the stuff had come, but the doorbell had woken up

the baby. Since I didn't have a good place to put her while all the delivery people piled baby gear into my entryway, I just stood there, holding a crying baby like an idiot. They gawked and the baby screamed. It was fun.

Nothing I did soothed her. She didn't want to eat. I ruined three diapers trying to figure out how to change her. Natalie had made it look so easy, or maybe the baby just liked her better and didn't try to squirm as much. As it was, I got pee all over the floor. Twice.

Then, when I did finally figure out where the little fastening straps went and how tight they needed to be... she pooped. And I had to do it all over again, except this time, it was the most disgusting thing I'd ever seen, smelt, or touched. Because it got on my hand. I nearly threw up. I used up nearly an entire container of the baby wipes getting her, the floor, and my hand clean.

I was going to need more wipes sooner than I thought. That and an industrial strength steam cleaner.

And she still didn't stop fussing. Sure, she'd stopped wailing once I'd fed her and gotten her in dry pants, but if I set her down or stopped moving around the apartment, she started to whine. If I didn't start walking, her little eyes would well up with huge fat tears, her lower lip turning upside down as she looked at me like I'd betrayed her entire family and then kicked her puppy. She also had to be held a specific way. She wanted to be upright against my chest and would not accept anything else. My arms were getting tired, but I tried to tell myself it was just a new kind of weight training.

So I'd looped the couch three hundred and eleven times the past hour while telling my arms to just suck it up and hold her.

It also meant that I hadn't been able to set any of her stuff up. I had everything I could possibly need to take care of her; a crib, changing table, bottles, and clothing. But I couldn't use any of it because I couldn't stop walking or set her down. The supplies to make my life easier sat there, mocking me, so close and yet so far. I felt more inadequate and dumb than I had in years. This was worse than high school math class.

Plus, now I had to pee.

I couldn't do this any longer. I was going to break.

I pulled out the little slip of paper, squinting at it to figure out which numbers were her phone number, and which were some poor guy's blood pressure. The slip of paper was somehow heavy in my fingers. I didn't want to bother her. She was supposed to be sleeping. She'd worked a long shift and had looked like a zombie when she'd left. It had only been a few hours and I knew that I would hate to be woken up early by some dude who just couldn't seem to figure out how to take care of a baby.

I imagined her waking up, her hair messy and sleep still in her eyes. She would be gorgeous in the morning, I decided. She would be gorgeous any time. Those scrubs didn't hide her figure of curves and softness.

But I couldn't afford to think about her like that right now. Having sexy thoughts about women and acting on them was what had gotten me into this situation. I needed to do something else.

I thought about calling Alex, not that he would be much help. He'd be just as confused as I was by all the baby stuff, but at least he knew how to use a hex wrench and could make the crib while I kept making the endless laps around the couch to keep the baby happy. I didn't put his number on the screen. He was at the hospital with his grandma. I didn't want to bother him. That route was blocked. Pick a different run pattern.

"It's just a baby," I told myself as she fussed and whimpered until I got her position just perfect again. "People do this all the time. Teenagers do this. Cavemen survived saber-tooth tigers chasing them while caring for a baby. I can do this."

I didn't believe myself.

The baby fussed again and I checked her diaper. I'd discovered that wet diapers felt squishy while the dry ones had a crackly feel to them. It wasn't an exact science, but little girl had a squishy diaper. It was time to change it.

"I can do this," I told myself. I felt like I should do my pregame hype routine. We were out of the pack of diapers Alex had brought home with the second purchase, so I opened the giant box of number 5 diapers.

And it was huge. There was no way it was going to fit on my little girl.

The "five" was a size, not a time frame. I was an idiot. For a moment, I was incredibly glad that Natalie wasn't here to see me fail at this parenting thing yet again. I wanted to impress her and buying the wrong diapers for the second time today was just too much.

"Nothing but to do our best with what we've got," I told my daughter, wrapping the giant diaper around her as tightly as I could make it go. The darn thing was nearly up to her armpits. She looked like a baby doing a terrible impression of Steve Urkel.

She fussed until I had her upright again and she reached out a tiny hand toward the TV. I turned to see what had caught her attention and it was an advertisement. Lots of flashy colors and fast movement. And then me. I wore my jersey as Marcus threw water balloons at me. I wasn't sure how that was supposed to sell houses, but the company said it was giving record sales and they kept paying me.

The rest of the team flashed up on the screen. Something squeezed in my chest. Those were my friends. My family. Sure, some of them were complete assholes, but they had my back. When I was injured last season, they were there for me. They checked in on me. Even now, when I kept dropping passes like they burned my hands, they still showed up for me.

Would they show up for me with something like this?

I didn't want to risk it. Coach told me to keep my nose clean and having a surprise baby was the exact opposite of that. It would leak. The press would find out and paint me in a bad light because that was the better angle to sell papers. *"Deadbeat NFL Dad"* was always in season.

I needed a different team to help me because I knew I couldn't do this on my own. Tomorrow, I would have preseason practice and I didn't think I could wear the baby to the pads practice.

I looked down at the scrap of paper again. I hadn't set it down. Her handwriting was messy yet readable.

"You win games with the team you have, not the team you want," I told myself. But I did want her. She was cute and smart and had a great laugh. I liked her, which was dangerous if I was going to ask her what I wanted to ask her.

But I didn't have a choice.

So I picked up the phone and called her.

"This better be an emergency," she answered the

phone. I winced and tried not to think of how little sleep she'd had today.

I held the baby up to the phone. Her little screams echoed hard enough to cause feedback.

"Sleep is overrated anyway," Natalie groaned. "I'll be right there."

8

———

BABY LESSONS

Does binge watching Grey's Anatomy count toward my
Continuing Nursing Education hours?

NATALIE

I KNOCKED on the door of the NFL player's apartment.

There was a statement I never thought I'd see myself say. I didn't usually hang out with the jocks. I tended to gravitate toward the nerds or those with slightly dark senses of humor. But, he seemed like a decent enough guy.

At least he was trying his best to be a dad.

The door swung open and I was hit with the sound of a baby wailing bloody murder. He looked like he hadn't slept in days despite the fact that it had only been a few hours.

"Well, sounds like you're jumping into this parenting

thing with both feet," I told him, stepping inside and closing the door behind me so that the neighbors wouldn't hear a crying baby and come investigating.

I held out my hands, surprised that he hadn't foisted the baby onto me the moment he had the chance. Despite the fact that she was screaming her little lungs out directly into his ears, he didn't want to let her go. I felt my cold heart melt just a little bit.

"She won't stop crying," he told me, finally handing her over. He made sure I absolutely had her before letting go.

"What's the matter, baby?" I asked her, not really expecting an answer, but it seemed the polite thing to do. I walked her over to the table, noticing several empty formula bottles on the counter. She wasn't making the hungry cry, but rather the "I'm uncomfortable!" one. Time to figure it out.

First, I did the easy things. I burped her, getting an adorable little burp out of her that was worthy of a viral video, but it didn't make her happy. I ran my hands over her fingers and toes, making sure that nothing was pinching her. Nothing seemed to be poking or irritating her skin, so I ruled that out.

I laid her down on the table and she erupted in screams. I felt terrible, but I didn't pick her up, instead checking her diaper.

"Did you get a new size?" I asked, undoing the little Velcro straps and making sure that she was dry, and also checked for diaper rash. Her skin looked good and the diaper was clean, but far too big. I was rather impressed that he'd managed to get it to stay up on her.

"Blame Alex," he mumbled, anxiously watching me over my shoulder.

I felt her stomach, making sure that things were working correctly. It made her cry harder until I picked her up and had her upright again.

"Has she pooped today?" I asked, rubbing her back. She stopped crying, instead making sad little whimpers that somehow broke my heart more than the sobs.

Dylan turned a pale shade of green. "Yes."

I raised an eyebrow. "And?"

"There was so much..." He stared past me in a hundred yard stare that had me concerned for his mental health.

"What did it look like?" I asked, patting her back in small circles. She was the perfect size to snuggle and love on. And she smelled so good.

"Why in the world would you want to know that?" he asked, looking at me like I had three heads. "It was the most disgusting thing I have ever seen in my life. And I had to touch it."

I smothered a smile. "What color was it? Consistency?"

"You're sick, you know?" he said, shaking his head. "It was yellow. And frothy. I didn't know poop could come out in that color and texture until today..."

He trailed off again, turning a slightly darker shade of green.

"And how much was there? Did the diaper overflow?" I continued, already guessing what was making our little girl so upset.

"It can do that?" His expression changed to a new variety of horrified. I waited until he shook himself. "Um, no. It didn't overflow. It was the size of a pudding cup? Oh boy. I don't know if I can ever eat pudding again after thinking of that."

I kept the small smile to myself. "I think I have a theory." I went to the carpeted area of the floor and laid the baby down, making her unhappy again. With gentle fingers, I began to massage small circles on her belly. She stopped fussing, her face pinched and unhappy, but no longer crying. I cooed to her as I moved her legs like she was riding an invisible bicycle. It only took a few moments of massaging her stomach and moving her legs before she let out the biggest fart I'd ever heard.

The fart echoed through the room.

"How did that come out of such a small package?" Dylan asked, obviously impressed. "I thought little girls were supposed to be delicate and petite. No wonder she was unhappy!"

I kept massaging and moving her legs. "It's the new food," I explained as she let another man-sized fart rip out, this one a little wetter than the first. "She must have been on a different brand of formula, and the change is upsetting her stomach a little bit."

"What do we do to help her?" Dylan asked. The worry in his voice made me smile.

"This," I replied, showing him the motions I was doing. She let out a wet fart and giggled. "And you can hand me some wipes."

"They won't be warm," he warned, handing me a brand new pack. "I haven't set up the warmer. I haven't set up anything yet."

"I actually recommend not using the warmer," I replied, waiting as he gathered the supplies together to change her into a clean diaper.

"But she'll be cold!" He stared at me like I was advocating a form of child abuse.

"Yes, but if she doesn't start with warm wipes, she will never know what she's missing. You will be happy about that when you're out of the house and have to use cold ones. They'll just feel normal for her," I explained. "I promise, the room temperature wipes are not that bad."

He narrowed his eyes, but didn't comment as I began to change her. I could feel him watching my every move, taking notes and learning. Out of habit, I began to narrate what I was doing like I was in a nursing clinical or teaching a student in the ER.

"Always wipe front to back. This will keep the bacteria from her poop getting up to her urethra and causing a urinary tract infection," I reminded him. "She needs to be changed as soon as she becomes wet, and especially if she has pooped, as both of those things are really hard on skin."

"I'm guessing that the bigger the diaper isn't better," he remarked, watching me try to tighten the straps to keep the diaper on her.

"No. See the leg holes?" I motioned to the diaper. "The bigger sizes are made for bigger legs. You're going to have a lot of leakage with these ones."

He sighed. "So what do I do with them? The box is open, so I don't know if they'll take it back."

"Keep them for later. She'll grow into them," I advised.

His entire body stilled for a moment, as if realizing for a moment that she was going to be with him for a long time. He swallowed hard. I let him be, instead wrapping the cashmere blanket back around her.

"Wait, do that again," he commanded, halting me mid-swaddle.

"Sure." I unwrapped the baby, letting her limbs flail for a moment. "Take the edge, either side, and tuck it in here. Then tuck the tail of the blanket up so that she can't wiggle her legs too much, and then the other side tucks in just like this."

"Why do we wrap her up like a little present?" he asked, his eyes still taking in the swaddle as if he were dissecting it so he could know exactly how to do it next time. "I don't like being tangled up in blankets myself."

Not unless I'm with the right person, I thought to myself. I didn't need to say *that* out loud to a handsome man.

"Babies are in the womb for a long time. They are used to being warm and confined. When they are born, the world is suddenly so big. If you watch, she'll throw her arms out and startle because she doesn't hit anything," I explained. "The swaddle makes her feel like she's back safe in the womb and it will help her sleep."

I undid the blanket and moved to the side, motioning him to take my spot.

He swallowed hard, and then with a confident gentleness I didn't expect, managed a half-decent swaddle. His motions were slow and calculated, as if had already practiced this in his mind when he watched me. I gave him an appraising look. This man was more than just a sports guy with no brain. He was quick on the uptake and more observant than I first thought.

"Not bad," I told him. I didn't want to tell him that it looked better than a lot of students I worked with. The man already had a big enough ego that I didn't need to add to it.

"At least she's not crying anymore." He flashed me a quick self-satisfied grin before glancing toward the bathroom. "And the goat hasn't eaten down the door yet."

"Have you fed her anything?" I asked, curious about what he was going to do with the goat.

"I gave her some cabbage. I have no idea why the parenting website recommend purchasing it, but the goat liked it a lot. Last I checked on her, she was napping in the bathtub."

"The parenting website recommended cabbage leaves? And you bought them?" I echoed, unable to keep the giggle out of my words. "Do you know what the cabbage leaves are for?"

He shook his head, picking up his daughter. She was fast asleep in his arms, her breathing coming slow and even. She knew she was safe with him.

"It's for nursing mothers looking to stop their milk supply," I explained. "Cabbage leaves on the breast help with engorgement."

His cheeks flushed. "Oh. Well, I guess it's good it went to the goat then."

I shook my head, chuckling softly. I had a feeling this parenting thing was going to be a wild ride for him.

"What else did you get that sounded strange?" I asked. I started picking up the kitchen, just to help out.

"Nipple cream," he replied.

I tried not to laugh. "That is also for nursing mothers. Unless you were planning on milking yourself?"

"Not this pregnancy, no," he replied, his cheeks pink. "I'm guessing the lube was also not needed for the baby."

"Lube? No. Not unless you also got a rectal thermometer," I informed him. He shook his head. "Then it's probably because nursing mothers can have dryness issues. Hormones do crazy things to women's bodies."

He sighed, looking at the counter of supplies. "I'm now wondering if I found a parenting supply list for nursing mothers. I guess I'll find a use for it all eventually."

"Have you eaten?" I asked, realizing that there were no food wrappers mixed up with the baby bottles. "You need to keep up your strength. And stay hydrated."

I couldn't help it. It was the nurse in me. I had to make sure that everyone was being taken care of.

"Um... no." He paused as if thinking about it and going over his memories trying to remember if he did eat something.

"Put her in the box since she's sleeping, and we'll get you something to eat and drink." I moved toward the kitchen wondering what kind of protein shakes this guy probably had in his pantry.

I looked back to see him hesitate at the box. He very obviously did not want to set her down. It was rather sweet. She had only been in his life for a few hours and she already had her fingers wrapped firmly around his heart. With a deep breath, he gently laid her down, making sure to move slowly so that he wouldn't wake her. She sighed softly as he backed away slowly.

Once she was safe in her box, he strode confidently into the kitchen and straight to the fridge. There he downed a Gatorade in two sips, sagging against the kitchen counter like he'd just finished running a marathon. His shirt rode up on his stomach as he chugged, showing a sliver of defined ab muscles. It didn't help that the arm position showed off his gorgeous biceps. I turned away so that I wouldn't be caught staring.

"What does a nurse make in a month?"

I was glad I wasn't drinking my own Gatorade or I would have sprayed it all over the spotless chrome kitchen.

"Are you thinking of applying for a job?" I asked, trying not to sound offended. "I would imagine it's not as good as the NFL and you you probably have better benefits."

His cheeks flushed slightly, accenting the strong line of his jaw. "I'm sorry, that didn't come out right. I'd actually like to offer you a job."

"A what?" My mind started to race.

"A job," he continued. "I don't know what I'm doing and you're really good with her. You also haven't gone to the media to tell them all about this top story."

"No, I just called the cops on you," I replied, still feeling guilty.

He smiled at me, making my heart do a little flutter. Good lord, that man was attractive. Maybe it was just the fact that a baby looked so good on him, but he was growing on me.

"I can't really ask anyone to help me out here," he continued. "My lawyer wants a DNA test to make sure she's mine before we do anything public. I can't ask my coach or anyone on the team. Alex is great, but he's got a lot on his plate with his grandma right now. I don't really have any options on people I can trust to keep this quiet and keep her safe."

I stared at him. This was not where I thought my day was going to go.

"So, I'm asking you. I'll pay you double whatever your hourly wage at the hospital is to help me watch my daughter. It won't be for long. Just a few weeks. Once the DNA test comes back and my lawyer has things ironed out, I can hire a nanny." He stepped close to me, peering into my eyes. They were a warm brown that seemed to swirl with intensity. "But, right now, I need you."

The *"I need you"* made my stomach do bubbly things and I suddenly felt hot and flushed.

"It wouldn't be all the time either. She's my daughter, and I plan on being a good parent, but I do need to work. I have to go to practice. I have to go to games. I have responsibilities to my team. It's mostly during the days, but there are a few games that will go into the night." His words came fast, as if he was afraid he wouldn't get them out once he started.

I was tempted. SO tempted. That much money? And only for a couple of weeks?

But I loved my job and I couldn't cut my hours. I had to get my full hours in order to be eligible for the hospital scholarship. I needed that scholarship to pay for my grad school, and even as generous as Dylan's offer was, it wouldn't be enough to cover my tuition. I couldn't cut my hours, but I could see he was desperate. I understood his desperation. He couldn't ask anyone for help without risking his position on the team. I'd seen another news article on how tenuous his position on the team was. I didn't know that they were cutting team members as part of the summer training program.

I was going to regret this. I could feel it in my bones, but that didn't stop the words from coming out.

"I can't help you on nights I work," I told him. "But, luckily for you, I already requested all the game nights off."

"But you'll do it?" He looked like a hopeful puppy. There was no way I was backing out of this now.

"Yes. I'll do it."

His entire body relaxed, his shoulders lowering from his ears and his expression softening.

"Thank you," he said. "I didn't know she even existed until a few hours ago, but I want to make sure she has everything this world can offer her. Is that sappy or what?"

He laughed, running a hand through his hair. His shirt rode up with the motion, once again showing his ab muscles and flexing his biceps. He didn't even realize he was doing it, but the motion was incredibly masculine and sexy.

Oh boy. He was growing on me. He obviously adored his new daughter. He was hot.

And he was also a single dad and my new employer. I needed to get any temptation thoughts out of my brain now.

"So, you're a fan?" he asked, smiling hopefully at me.

"A what?" It took me a moment before I realized what he was referencing his football team. "No. Not a fan."

His expression fell a little bit. "Oh. But then why do you have all the games off?"

"Because I hate working on game nights. It's all anyone talks about the entire time, and we get so many stupid alcohol-induced injuries," I explained.

His eyes lost the hint of smile they'd had and I realized that I'd just kind of insulted him and his job. It was a good thing I hadn't said more or gone off on one of my usual diatribes about the dangers of concussions and the lack of safety around football as well as the increased alcohol injuries of those watching. He was probably not the best person to share those opinions with on the first day of meeting him.

"I mean, nothing against you. I just am not a football person." The words felt lame coming out.

"It's okay," he said with a shrug. "It's not for everybody. But, if it means you can watch my daughter, I'm very much okay with you not liking the games."

I smiled, turning away so that he wouldn't see that it was a fake smile.

"Since I'm here, can I help you set up some of this stuff?" I asked, pointing to the mountain of boxes on his floor. "In addition to being amazing with children, I am actually pretty good at following poorly written instructions."

"Really?" He smirked at my boast. "And how does one get good at following poorly written instructions?"

I shrugged one shoulder as I picked up a box. "Haven't you ever read a doctor's handwriting?"

9
___

THIS IS A SET UP

"Well, we've determined that we can't win at home and we can't win on the road. What we need is a neutral site."
-John McKay, a former Buccaneers Head Coach

Dylan

"And viola! You now have a crib!"

Natalie beamed at me as she brushed a strand of hair out of her eyes and proudly motioned to the crib she had just finished putting together for me.

"And it only took a few tears," I added. "Mostly from the baby."

She laughed and stuck her tongue out at me. I loved her laugh. It wasn't like a bell or musical, but it came straight from her soul and went directly into mine. When she laughed, it made my heart rate surge and I couldn't help but laugh with her.

"Have you come up with a name for her?" Natalie asked. "I know you've named the goat Penelope, but what about the human?"

I shifted the baby in my arms. She was fast asleep, her little mouth a rosebud and her eyes fluttering softly as she dreamed.

"Eleanor." My voice cracked slightly with emotion as I said her name. I'd been thinking about it and it fit, but I hadn't said it out loud until now. "That was my mom's name. But, I want to call her Ellie for short."

"It's a beautiful name," Natalie replied. "I like it a lot."

"Thank you." I looked up from my daughter to smile at Natalie. She grinned back at me. "And thanks for helping me get all this baby equipment set up. I know I didn't do much, so I really appreciate it."

"You did the important part of keeping the baby safe." Natalie waved a hand through the air. "I'm happy to help get little Ellie settled."

When Natalie said her name, I knew it was the right choice. My daughter, my Ellie. It sounded right in both my ears and my heart.

"So, where's your bedroom?" she asked, looking down the hallway at the three closed doors. One led to the guest room, the middle to the bathroom with the goat, and then the master bedroom.

"Isn't that a little forward?" I teased her. "I mean, we just met and you're already taking me to my bed?"

I loved the way her cheeks flushed. She ducked her head, not meeting my eyes and my heart fluttered again.

"The crib should be in the bed, I mean your room. I

mean..." She let out a flustered sigh and narrowed her eyes at me. "For safety reasons, the crib should be in the room you sleep in."

I grinned at her as I stood up from the couch with the baby in my arms. Beside me in the recliner chair, Penelope the goat bleated her dislike of me standing and blocking the TV. We had let her out of the bathroom about an hour ago when she kept bleating at the door and Natalie had taken pity on the poor creature. We had put up a baby gate around the recliner and put on the TV. I had never seen a happier camper than that goat sprawled on the recliner watching *Supernatural* reruns.

"We'll be right back," I assured Penelope. She looked at me with sad eyes, but rolled onto her back, letting her legs splay out as she sat in the recliner. I shook my head and sighed. We'd put one of the large diapers on her to keep the mess down. She didn't seem to mind it, and it made buying the wrong size diapers feel a little less wasteful.

At least she was eating all the expired food in my fridge. I also made sure to order more cabbage, since she seemed to like that more than anything else. Alex was going to stop at a farming supply store tomorrow to pick up some better goat food and other supplies. I had a feeling that mushy lettuce and week-old chow mein noodles were not good for a goat's long-term diet.

My daughter was in a heavy sleep as I walked to the table with the box. I was getting used to her soft weight and the way she snuggled her little face into my chest. My heart grew three sizes each time the little girl nestled into me and held onto me like she already knew that I would jump in front of a train to protect her.

Carefully, I laid my daughter in the box, hopefully for

the last time. She fussed slightly, but the swaddle held and she stayed asleep. I knew it wouldn't last for long. She hated any time I set her down. To be fair, I hated it as well. I much preferred to have her in my arms.

"Bedroom is this way," I told her, pointing to the third door. "Although, I did think we'd at least have a dinner date before I brought you there."

She stuck out her tongue at me as she picked up her side of the crib and helped me carry it into the bedroom.

"Dang..." she whispered, as she stepped into the room.

I would be lying if I said that didn't do something for my ego, even though I knew the bedroom was impressive. It had originally been two rooms, but it was now one large room with a giant bed in the center. There were masculine nightstands on either side in dark wood colors. I'd told the room designer that I wanted something masculine yet warm and comforting. She'd delivered. Heavy wood, a dark blue bedspread, and sturdy furniture filled the room, but the paint and artwork were light and warm. I loved how the room turned out, and so did most women I brought in here.

And that was just the room. Women usually ended up with more reasons to be impressed.

Also, thank God the maid came yesterday. All the dirty undies were off the floor and the bed was made. At least I didn't look like a total slob, and I made a mental note to tip my house cleaner extra in the coming weeks.

Together, Natalie and I tucked the crib against the wall near the head of the bed where I could easily access it during the night. I tried to keep the thoughts of how little sleep I was about to get out of my head, which was easy when I looked over at Natalie.

She sat on my bed, evaluating the crib placement. I knew she didn't mean anything by it, but seeing her on my bed did something to me. I couldn't help but notice the shape of her body. Her clothes were loose and comfortable looking, but I could see the line of her leg, the curve of her hips, the soft swell of her chest.

Explicit thoughts started to race through my mind. The way she would flush when I laid her down. Would she be quiet or loud? What would her moans sound like...

Get a grip, I told myself. *Stay in the game.*

"It looks good," she said, standing from the bed and flashing me a smile. She had no idea that I was imagining her naked and very much liking the idea.

In the other room, the baby started to fuss. And the goat began to bleat.

I wondered if the goat was attentive to the baby like a good nanny goat or if she just didn't like the sound of the baby crying. We'd also discovered that she liked to nibble on the diapers if left alone- both the clean and the dirty ones.

My feet were out in the kitchen faster than I thought possible to pick up my daughter. I didn't want her to ever think I didn't want her, even for a moment. I'd already missed out on the first part of her life and I wasn't about to waste a second if I could help it.

Penelope flopped her head back on the chair and continued watching Sam and Dean slay demons once she saw that someone was being responsible for the baby.

"I think she's hungry," I said to Natalie, heading toward the kitchen to get her a bottle. "She's doing the mouth sucking thing."

I looked behind me to see her smile. "You're picking

this up quickly. You're a natural." The praise went straight to my head.

"Nah," I informed her. "I'm just good at having people yell at me. Marcus and Coach Frank especially."

"Marcus?" She raised an eyebrow. "That name sounds familiar..."

"Marcus Johnson." I popped the formula pod into the bottle maker thing. It was basically a Keurig for formula. Just insert pod, push a button, and boom- a perfect bottle without worrying about boiling water or thinking. The machine whirred and hummed for a moment before presenting me with a perfect batch of baby juice.

"I still have no idea who that is." She shrugged and looked at me like I was the crazy person for talking about someone she didn't know.

It was so strange to meet someone that didn't have any idea about football. In a strange way, it was rather refreshing to not have her already know Marcus' stats or that the two of us weren't communicating like we used to. Three guys at the bar last week had told me that I needed to suck it up, swallow my pride, and do whatever Marcus wanted so that we could get back to winning.

"He's the quarterback of the team," I said. She still had a slightly confused look on her face, so I continued. "He's the one that throws me the ball. He's also the one yelling what we're going to do most of the time." I looked down at my daughter greedily sucking away at the bottle. "A lot like her."

"I get it now." Natalie nodded and then grinned at me. "Hopefully he poops his pants less."

"Usually."

She laughed, the sound making my knees do the

wobbly thing that was usually reserved for the five seconds before the game whistle sounded. It was my favorite feeling in the world- exhilarating and like lightning was about to strike.

"So, scheduling?" I needed to get back to business and not think about her laugh. Or the way she smiled. Or the fact that she had looked so good on my bed. I needed to keep this professional.

"Right. I work until 7:30 in the morning. I usually get home around eight," she informed me.

"I need to leave right around eight," I replied, letting out a small sigh of relief. "That will work."

"I will be napping with her, just so you know," she reminded me. "Downside of working nights is that I still need to sleep."

"As long as Ellie is safe, I am okay with it," I said, holding up my hands. "This is only temporary. Once my lawyers have gotten everything settled, I'll hire someone to watch her full time. For now, I'm not worried about her learning her ABCs or colors during the morning hours."

Natalie chuckled. "Okay. On the nights I work, I leave at seven. I'll give you my schedule since it changes every other week. Luckily, I won't have to work any of the games for the next three weeks. You think you'll have someone by then?"

"We have bigger problems if my lawyers haven't figured things out by then," I informed her. "And your schedule looks good. This week is a bye week and the next two games are home games."

The football gods must have known my life was going to be complicated and had decided not to make this harder with travel games.

"Okay." She focused on her phone, making sure that our calendars synced. I found myself admiring the little scrunchy space between her eyebrows. "That was easier than I thought it would be."

"Anything else I need to know about you?" I asked.

"I'm a serial killer," she replied gazing up at me and widening her eyes. She snickered, ruining the creepy look. "Um, what do you want to know?"

I wanted to know if she was single, but I didn't want to be obvious about it.

"I only want you to watch Ellie," I said. "So no boyfriends or girlfriends or family members over while you're here."

"That's fine," she said with a shrug. "I'm not seeing anyone and I don't have any family other than my aunt that live nearby. I've been so busy with work that I haven't had time to do anything else."

Was it my imagination, or did she answer that really fast? I wondered. *Had she wanted to tell me she was single? Don't read too much into it,* I told myself.

I was a single parent now. I needed to keep my thoughts on my daughter and my job. Not the hot nanny I'd just hired.

"What about you?" she asked, nonchalantly playing with her hair. "Do I have to worry about a girlfriend coming by and getting mad that there's a woman and a baby in your house?"

I swallowed hard, suddenly feeling my heart beating in my throat. That was definitely obvious interest.

"Nope. No girlfriends," I replied, keeping my voice calm. "I'm focused on football right now."

"Okay."

We stared at one another for a moment and I was sure she could see right through me. I was sure she could see just how much of an idiot I was and how much I hoped she couldn't see that.

All I saw was a gorgeous woman that was smart enough to be out of my league.

"Do you want me to stay for a little while longer?" she asked after a moment. "I mean, I know we got most of the baby stuff set up, but I'm happy to keep helping you until I have to go work tonight. Or I could run to the store and get you some new diapers."

"Stay. I'll have the diapers delivered." The smile on my face was genuine. "I can use all the parenting lessons I can get."

"Yeah, you do." But she smiled as she said it, giving me a hope I didn't deserve to have.

10

DREAM OF PAIN

"Football is easy if you're crazy as hell."
-Bo Jackson

DYLAN

I WAS DREAMING. It was like being there again. I couldn't stop it anymore than I could change the past. I knew I would wake up, covered in sweat with my wrist aching. I just had to survive the dream.

* * *

SNOW MAKES EVERYTHING SLIPPERY.

Frost coats the edges of the field. It's wet and slippery under the lights, but it's the playoffs.

We made it. I made it.

My legacy will go down in the history books. I can feel it. All I have to do is catch the ball.

That's easy. Easy as breathing.

We line up. I take the left side. Marcus nods twice. That's our signal. It's not in the playbook. Coach doesn't know about it. It's just for the two of us. A secret code that he's going to get me the ball if I can get open.

He calls out the play. "Twenty-three, thirteen, twenty-two... hike, hike." He stomps his foot like a bull about to charge.

I take off running. My muscles clench and spring forward as I put everything I have into this drive. If I score, then we're going all the way. I can already taste the victory champagne. I can already hear the cheers.

My legs pump down the field. None of their defenders can keep up with me, and the ones that think they can I juke and run around. I can fly out on the field.

I was made for this.

I glance back, relying on my peripheral vision. There's three guys coming up on my left. Three! I grin that they think I'm that big of a threat that they need to send three guys after me.

They really should send four because those three aren't going to catch me until I'm in the end zone.

I can see the white lines. The hash marks are long behind me.

I don't have to look. Marcus and I have a psychic link. I know he's aiming the ball right for the space between my hands. I don't have to look. I can feel it.

The crowd gasps and I know he's thrown it all forty yards. They hold their breath, waiting to see if I catch it.

But I always catch it.

Even in my dreams. That part is never the problem.

The ball hits my outstretched right arm. It nearly wobbles out of my reach, but time slows. My left arm moves up to catch the ball. I feel the ball in my grip. I have it.

But there's a problem.

One of those three guys is suddenly in my space. It's slippery. He can't control his body or his speed. I see his eyes widen as he realizes he's out of control. He's not going to tackle me. He's going to crash into me.

I have to choose. Do I hold onto the ball or do I stop my fall?

I choose the ball. I should choose the ball. I panic. I choose my body. I throw a hand out to protect myself.

Today it is the wrong choice.

Bodies collide. I should have held onto the ball, but instinct made me put my arm out to stop the fall. I try to hold onto the slippery pigskin, but is slides out of my grasp like it's oiled.

I don't feel the snapping of bones, but I hear them. I hear the crowd gasp. I hear someone scream on the sidelines.

The ball is loose. My hand doesn't work anymore. I don't have control and the ball skitters away from me and directly into someone else's hands. I scream, but no sound comes out. I reach for the ball, desperately trying to bring it back to me, to rewind those last ten seconds. It feels like they were never real anyway. Those seconds were never mine. I just watched them like the viewers on TV. They didn't actually happen to me.

This is all wrong. This is not how this was supposed to happen. This is not supposed to be my legacy.

The ball is gone and I'm on the grass. My hand is bent the wrong way. There is bone showing. The crowd is screaming. Coach is screaming. Marcus is screaming.

I should be screaming, but I'm just staring at my arm.

It's broken. I can't move my fingers. I know on an instinctual level that this is bad.

It should hurt. I should be writhing on the ground in agony, but I'm more angry that I fumbled the ball. My legacy is running down the field to the wrong end zone.

The game will not end in a W.

And it's my fault.

Marcus threw me the ball. We'd used our secret signal. No one had known.

Yet I lost the ball. If I'd held onto it, protected it, rolled with it, I wouldn't be staring at a shattered wrist.

But I'd valued my arm more than the ball.

I didn't protect it with my life.

And now my life might be over.

I hear the air horns blast a touchdown. That should have been mine, but now it's my fault.

The pain is coming now. I welcome it.

I lost the ball.

I lost the game.

11

PARENTING HURTS

I was wondering why the football was getting bigger. Then it hit me.
-Unknown

DYLAN

I ACTUALLY WAS ENJOYING the ice bath today.

Not because my muscles ached. Not because of practice or the lack there of. And definitely not because I liked ice baths.

No. It was because I could actually rest. I was tired and the ice bath was the first place all day that no one had bothered me.

I had no idea just how little babies slept. How the hell did anyone get anything done with a baby? How did they function without coffee? I'd never felt so tired in all my life and it had only been one night so far. Thank God it was a bye week so we didn't have a heavy practice today. I'd been able to get by with a light workout and some extra time in the medical area with the trainers, and now the ice bath was quiet and more relaxing than I'd ever experienced.

I might even fall asleep.

The idea that this might be all the sleep I would have for the day was rather daunting. Raising Ellie wasn't going to be easy.

But at least I would have Natalie.

She'd popped into my thoughts all day, even more than Ellie. I kept wondering what she and Ellie were up to. I wondered if she would stay for dinner tonight- and then that led me to all sorts of other thoughts that did not help my football playing skills. It was a good thing that I didn't have my phone on me during practice or I would have messaged her multiple times.

"Time to get out, Callahan," one of the physical trainers, Sara, called out. "You don't have to go home, but you can't stay here."

With a groan, I pulled myself from the cold water, suddenly feeling the ice creaking through my bones. Perhaps I wasn't as comfortable as I had thought I was. The towel around my waist was scratchy, which, considering how much money was spent on medical stuff for the team, surprised me, I wandered back into the locker room and nearly turned around and walked back to the ice bath.

I could hear the voices of two men talking in the locker room. Marcus Johnson, the quarterback, and Cameron Right, the center. I would have said they were my best friends last season, but since the accident, it seemed liked they both were avoiding me. Given how I was dragging down the team, I couldn't blame them.

Marcus and Cameron were the only ones left in the locker room. The two of them were having a quiet conversation, but I could hear enough of the conversation to know what it was about. I hung back behind the door, hating that I wanted to hear what they were saying about me.

"He's not off the team," Marcus said. "But he's only safe from being cut because Coach put him on medical leave. Once he's off medical, they're going to have to whittle the team numbers down and he's not looking like he's worth the price. We're better off with a rookie like Franklin. At least he seems to want to show up to practice."

"Yeah, he couldn't catch a cold today," Cameron agreed. The big man sighed. "I don't know what happened to him. He used to catch everything."

"The hit last season did something to him," Marcus replied, stuffing clothes in a gym bag. "He snapped his wrist and it snapped his confidence. And he won't do anything about it except tell me that I'm throwing it wrong. It's not my fault he can't catch a damn thing."

I winced. He was right. I'd been blaming him for bad throws, but everyone else seemed able to catch them. I was the problem and I knew it. I just didn't know how to fix it. I didn't understand why I couldn't keep the ball in my hands.

I also knew I couldn't afford to get hit like I did last year. I couldn't afford to be injured like that again.

Panic started to swirl in the pit of my stomach. I had to get off the medical list and back on the team roster. Football was the only thing I had ever been good at. Not math or music or writing. I wasn't even that great of a runner, but put a ball in my hands, and I suddenly could figure out patterns, read plays, and sprint like I had wings on my feet. Football was the only thing that made my life make sense.

The idea of not having football was terrifying. There was nothing left in my life without it.

I stepped back into the hallway and coughed just loud enough to make it echo before heading into the locker room. Marcus and Cameron both greeted me like they hadn't just been discussing my future, or rather the lack thereof.

"You okay, man?" Cameron asked as I went to my locker and pulled out dry clothes. "You were with the medics all day."

"My wrist," I replied. It wasn't a total lie. It ached most of the time. The doctors said that with the severity of the break, I would probably always have a little bit of pain, but it was the memory of the pain that kept me awake at night.

Well, that and a three-month-old baby that insisted on being fed at two A.M. And three A.M. And four A.M.

"I've been feeling it in my knees," Cameron agreed. "Pressure change is coming."

"Yeah, we're probably going to get rain or something," I mumbled, pulling a t-shirt over my head. "How was practice for you guys?"

"Somber," Cameron replied. Apparently he was going to be doing all the talking. "Cut day always sucks. I hate seeing guys have to leave."

I nodded. We'd had enough preseason games now for

the coaches and the higher ups to make decisions on who was going to be on the official team this fall. Today was the day when NFL dreams were cut short. The team could only hold so many players. Only the best could stay.

I *should have* been cut from the team. I *deserved* to be cut from the team with the way I had been playing the last few weeks, but I still had enough good will and fan support that Coach had saved me for a few more weeks. But I was in danger. I either had to clear medical and play, or I was off the team. I'd be traded or become a free agent. Neither sounded like something I wanted.

"I'm out. See you tomorrow," Marcus said. I wasn't sure if he was speaking to Cameron and me or just Cameron. Still, I said a goodbye. Cameron was right behind him, leaving me alone in the quiet locker room to finish dressing. I finished getting dressed and sat down to lace my shoes.

"Hey, you in here?" Alex stuck his head in the locker room. "I saw Marcus on the way out. He said you were the last one in here."

"At least he's talking to you," I murmured.

Alex shrugged. "You alone in here?"

I looked around the gray square room lined with metal lockers. It smelled like gym socks and sweat, but it felt like home. "Yup. I'm the last one out today."

"Good." Alex hurried over to me and sat on the cement bench under the locker. "I think I have it narrowed down to three women that could be Ellie's mom."

I sat up a little straighter. I didn't want to give Ellie back, but I did want to know more about her. "And?"

"Here's what I got. Three possibilities. I went through all the photos on your phone from the nights in the right range," he said, handing me his phone. "And man, you have got to get some better photography skills. I mean, the phone does most of the work for you these days. It's like you were trying to take awful pictures."

I scanned the three photos. They were all blonde and thin, with big fake boobs and tight dresses. One didn't have a face because somehow I'd put my thumb on the lens. I felt my optimism that I might remember Ellie's mom fade.

"All I remember from that night was that the girl I was with had amazing breasts. Real ones," I told him, handing him back is phone. "At least I think they were."

"You think?" Alex scoffed.

"It was dark." When his nonplussed expression didn't change I added, "And fast and dirty."

"Obviously." He rolled his eyes. "I hate that I'm even asking this, but would you recognize her if you felt her boobs?"

"Are you seriously suggesting that we go around feeling women up Cinderella style to see if they are my child's mother?" I asked.

"Well, when you say it like that..."

"What about the front desk?" I asked, changing tactics. "Did she remember anything about the delivery person?"

Alex shook his head. "I asked. Unfortunately, she was wearing a hoodie and sunglasses, so there's no way to ID her. The front desk girl just remembers that a woman came up and said there was a package for the 'damn player'." Alex shrugged before continuing. "Considering that you are public enemy number one to everyone with a fantasy league right now, she didn't think it was weird at all."

I sighed. Of course, my inability to play would come back to bite me in more ways than one.

"You also said you were expecting a package and to have it sent right up," Alex continued. "So she did."

"I didn't even get my protein powder delivered," I grumbled.

"Yeah, I got a refund coming to you," Alex said, leaning his thin back against the locker. For someone who never played football, he was surprisingly comfortable in the locker room.

"I think we struck out with the front desk for now." I closed my eyes, trying to find another way around the problem. "Any news on the DNA test?"

"I'll be by your house this evening with some cotton swabs and test tubes," Alex replied. "Richard has a service that's discreet, but it's going to take a week."

Richard, my lawyer, had not been happy about the phone call we'd had this morning. He was insistent that we make sure Ellie was actually mine before we legally did anything that could come back and bite me harder than things already were.

"And there's no way to expedite it?" I asked, imagining those old TV shows where they determined if someone was the father between commercial breaks.

"Not if you want it to stay quiet," Alex answered. I imagined myself with the host saying *"You ARE the father"* on live TV and shuddered. "The lawyer says to do it this way. I'll have a bunch of forms for you to sign tonight. It's why you pay us the big bucks."

"Thanks," I said, feeling the gratitude for my friend all the way down to my toes. This would be impossible without having Alex to do the legwork and keep everything quiet. "I appreciate it."

"I got you, man," was all Alex needed to say.

"How's your grandma?" I asked, needing to change the subject. "She had those tests."

"They came back as good as they can," he replied with a shrug. "She's a fighter. She doesn't quit."

We sat in silence for a moment as I laced up my shoes, my brain going a million miles an hour.

"Hey, I hate even saying this out loud, but it's something that I can't stop thinking about." I swallowed hard. "Do you know anyone that wants to adopt?"

"You don't want the baby?" Alex asked, turning to face me.

"I do, I just...." I sighed, running a hand through my sweaty hair. "It's just a lot of responsibility. I'm not really ready. I need to focus on this season if I want to keep my spot, and a baby is not helping me concentrate."

My stomach lurched with every word, but I wasn't sure if it was because I didn't want it to be true or because it was. I loved that little girl, but I wasn't sure if I was the best person to raise her. I wasn't sure that I would do a good job.

"I get it." Alex nodded, his eyes looking past me but without judgment. "I have a cousin- the one out in the sticks on that hobby farm. They have two boys and I know they were talking about trying for a girl sometime soon. Do you want me to ask?"

"Maybe?" My stomach twisted again and I felt nauseous at the enormity of even the possibility of the decision. "I don't know. I'm just trying to keep my options open."

Alex held up his hands, showing me that he wasn't attacking. "It's not a problem. Nellie is awesome and I know she's chill."

"Don't do it for now." The words came out faster than I expected. "But it's good to know that there's a good family for her. Just in case."

"Just in case," Alex agreed. "Baby poop makes us all need options."

12

DAYCARE FOR GOATS

We didn't tackle well today, but we made up for it by not blocking.
-John McKay

DYLAN

N**ATALIE AND** E**LLIE** were napping together when I got home.

Natalie was curled up in a tight little ball, her head on the arm of the couch and her arm hanging off and down into the pack-and-play where Ellie was sleeping. Natalie's hand rested on the baby's back, rising and falling with every breath. Neither of them stirred when I opened the door.

I stared for a moment, just taking in the scene. Natalie had her dirty blonde hair pulled back in a ponytail, but strands had gotten loose while she'd slept and now haloed around her face, giving her an angelic look. Not that she needed help looking like an angel, she was beautiful. Her mouth opened slightly and she sighed in her sleep. I held my breath, not wanting to wake her or the baby.

A fierce protective pride washed over me. It was primal and deep, a masculine urge to fight a hungry lion to keep these two women safe. They were *mine*.

Which made me scoff at myself. I didn't own either of these two women. Definitely not Natalie, and I had just told Alex that I was thinking of giving Ellie up for adoption. Since the DNA test wasn't done yet, I wasn't even sure if Ellie truly even was mine.

Still, the feeling remained. Not possessive, but protective. I wanted them both safe and happy and I knew deep in the core of my being that I would do just about anything to make sure that happened.

"You're back." Natalie smiled at me, her voice still rough and full of sleep. She sat up, rubbing her eyes and attempting to smooth her hair back into the ponytail. "Looks like we were having a good nap."

"I didn't mean to wake you," I said, dropping my gym bag at the front door and heading to the kitchen to make something with protein for a snack.

She looked at her watch and shrugged. "We actually just had a very good two hour nap. It was time for me to wake up anyway."

From the pack and play, Ellie gurgled, letting us know that she was also awake. I stopped making my snack and went to pick her up. She smiled at me and my heart melted as I snuggled her into me, her little hands fisting into my shirt. Suddenly, I wasn't nearly as cranky about all the missed sleep last night. How could I be when Ellie so obviously wanted me to hold her?

"Aw, I think she missed you." Natalie swung her legs off the couch and stood, stretching her hands over her head. I had to turn away so I wouldn't get caught staring at her lithe body and the little strip of skin between her shirt and shorts.

"I'll make her a bottle," Natalie said, heading toward the kitchen. "You sit and rest."

"I can do it," I said, but the couch did seem to be calling my name.

Natalie smiled at me. "You worked today. I got to nap with a baby. I can make the bottle."

I wasn't about to complain or fight her on it. I was tired and sitting on the couch sounded amazing. The whir of the bottle maker hummed as I smiled at my daughter and enjoyed the quiet of the house.

Which suddenly made me very nervous. The house should not be this quiet.

"Where's Penelope?" I asked, hoping my voice sounded calmer than I suddenly felt. I had images of the goat roaming the apartment hallways or perhaps she was sleeping in my bed. She was a nice goat, but I did not want her in my bed and my sheets smelling like barn.

"On the roof." Natalie handed me the bottle.

"What?" The roof was not a place for a goat either.

Natalie laughed. "She's with Marnie."

"Who?" I needed better one word questions because I was just getting more confused. Ellie fussed and I realized I was just holding the bottle, not giving it to her. I quickly stuck it in her mouth and she made a happy sigh.

"My Aunt Marnie," Natalie finally clarified. "She owns

half the building and has a very nice garden up on the roof attached to the penthouse suite. She said she'd love to have the goat up there to eat all her dead plants."

I just stared at her.

"Marnie is obsessed with that garden," Natalie continued. "She has been talking about renting a goat for months to get the 'all natural' weeding experience, although I don't know how a goat is going to be better at pulling weeds from planters it than just doing it yourself. Maybe in a real farm setting, but in planters?"

"So you gave her mine?" I managed to break into the monologue.

"I told her I had access to a goat through someone at work," Natalie explained. "You were not mentioned in any way. She will keep the goat for one week from sunrise to sunset. She's sent me pictures, and I think that Penelope is having the time of her life."

She handed me her phone and I scrolled through over a dozen pictures of an older women with the same shape nose as Natalie posing with Penelope. Her garden looked like something the local botanic gardens would grow. It was a lot more than just a couple of planter boxes filled with petunias.

"It's only for the next week and a half though," Natalie explained. "She's planting her mums and late autumn plants, so the garden will be off limits. But we've got goat daycare for the week!"

"Definitely better than hiding her in my bathtub," I agreed.

Goat day care. There was something I never thought I would have to deal with in my life, yet here we were.

I held out the phone for Natalie to take back. She

slipped it into her back pocket before joining me on the couch. Even though she sat a respectable distance apart from me, it still had my heart speeding up. I wondered if it was just my imagination or if I really could feel the heat of her from this far away. Was that her perfume? She smelled amazing.

"So, any luck on finding Ellie's mom?" Natalie asked, oblivious to the sudden tightness in my chest and the fact that I was sure my voice was going to squeak coming out like I was twelve years old and talking to my crush again.

"No." Thank God my voice didn't crack. I also decided not to mention the Cinderella boob option. I wanted her to like me. "All I know is that she said something about a 'damn player' to the front desk person. That's our only clue."

"I knew that you weren't the city's favorite player right now, but that seems harsh," she replied, crossing her legs. I noticed that they crossed in my direction and I prayed that the "body language expert" from the day time talk shows was right and that meant she was into me.

"I get the feeling that you aren't really a football fan," I said, remembering how she'd reacted to the sport when I'd met her.

She winced, then covered it with a nervous smile. "It's not you. It's..."

"It's a spectacle for the masses. Bread and circuses of the millennial man. A modern day gladiator fight in which tribal alliances can have a safe outlet for violence," I offered, using my snootiest voice.

She gaped at me.

"I get it," I said with a shrug. "It looks violent and brain dead."

"I wouldn't say it quite like that…" But her blush said otherwise. "You don't seem brain dead."

"Given the entire goat and diaper debacle of yesterday, I would beg to differ," I replied with a self-deprecating chuckle. "But there is a mental part to the game that I do love."

"There's a mental part? You sure?" She raised her eyebrows, obviously making fun of me. "Sorry. That's mean."

I laughed, liking her teasing. "It's a simple game, but the simple things are usually the most difficult to get right," I replied. "There's a fair amount of strategy that goes into every play, and a lot of that depends on the team and utilizing one another's strengths."

She raised her eyebrows again. "Utilizing one another's strengths?" she repeated. "That sounds like jargon."

I grinned. "Have you ever worked with a group of people that just get it? That absolutely understand what the goal is and are all working toward it in a way that helps the group?" I asked.

She nodded solemnly. "It's the best days of the job."

"It's a rush," I agreed. "Between figuring out the best path and working with people that also see that path, it's the best game in the world."

"You're making it sound a little less awful," she admitted, bumping me gently with her shoulder. I caught a scent of her shampoo when she did it, something light and coconut. It was fabulous.

"What about you?" I asked, trying to keep my head on straight. "Why do you work at a hospital?"

"Well, your whole spiel about working with people to accomplish something? That's a good day in the ER," she replied. "Also, it's an adrenaline rush. There's always crazy stuff going on. It is never boring, and I really like getting to help people."

She lit up as she spoke, her entire body becoming animated. Her eyes sparkled and she gained energy as she smiled and explained herself.

"You love it," I said, watching her sparkle. "Which is why you don't want to quit to be a full-time Ellie-sitter."

She laughed at the new word. "I wouldn't mind being a full-time Ellie-sitter, but I have a scholarship and dreams. I have to have a certain number of hours to qualify for the scholarship, but once I do, the hospital will pay for school."

"And you'll become a more professional nurse?" I asked.

"Kind of. I'll be a nurse practitioner which will mean I can do a lot more to help my patients," she explained.

"And I'm guessing that kind of schooling is expensive?"

"Very. Especially the school that I was accepted into," she agreed. "But the hospital has ties with them, so I can get the entire thing covered. I can't afford it without their help, even with the very generous salary you've offered."

I nodded. "That's why you don't want to call in sick."

"Yup. I'm registered to start school in a few weeks, but if I don't have the hours, the hospital won't pay. That's why I can't call in sick. I can't even call in dead."

I laughed and realized that our legs were touching. Not much, just our knees bumping together without either of us noticing it.

I felt like I was twelve and sitting next to Jennifer Lynston at lunch. How did Natalie have that effect on me?

It wasn't everyday that a woman made me feel like I could go back in time.

"I should get going," she said, clearing her throat and standing up. I wondered if she'd noticed our knees touching like I had.

"Thanks for this morning," I replied. "I'm glad this is working out."

She grinned at me, and it was Jennifer Lynston all over again. Suddenly I could smell cafeteria food and craved chocolate milk.

Hopefully it didn't end with her breaking up with me via passed note during fifth period. I don't know if I could live with that kind of heartbreak a second time.

13

YOU CALL THAT WORK?

*A new nurse listened while the doctor was yelling, "Typhoid!
Tetanus! Measles!"*
The new nurse asked another nurse, "Why is he doing that?"
*The other nurse replied, "Oh, he just likes to call the shots
around here."*

Natalie

"I'm really sorry, but there are no monkeys allowed in
the ER," I stated, pointing to a clearly marked sign on the
ER door. *No Monkeys Allowed.*

The gorilla did not care. It banged on its chest and went
to the blanket warmer to wrap itself up in blankets.

I wasn't even mad. The blanket warmer was the best
thing in the ER.

My phone started to chirp. I tried to answer it, but it wasn't my work phone. It was my personal phone.

I frowned, because I knew I wasn't supposed to have my personal phone on me at work. Gorillas were fine, but not phones.

And then I realized that I wasn't at work. I was in my bed dreaming about work.

I groaned. I needed to get a new life. One where I didn't think gorillas at my job place was weird.

"This is Natalie," I said, hitting the answer button on the phone and trying to convince myself that five hours of sleep was a respectable amount.

"Oh good, I didn't wake you," Dylan replied. I glared at the imaginary Dylan on the other end of the line. It was a good thing he and his daughter were cute.

"Oh, you did. I just have a really good phone voice," I replied, laying my head back down on the pillow and closing my eyes. If I tried, I hoped I might be able to fall back asleep for a little while longer.

"Sorry about that," he mumbled, and I only felt the tiniest twinge of guilt at his chastised voice.

"Wait, is Ellie okay?" I sat bolt upright suddenly very awake.

"She's fine," he quickly assured me, but my heart rate wouldn't slow down for a few minutes. That little jolt of adrenaline was better than a cup of coffee to get me up and moving. "But, I do need your help."

I flopped back onto the bed. "What's the problem?"

"I need to work today," he explained. "I have to go to the practice center for a couple of hours and then I have some things I can do at home, but I'm struggling to concentrate with Ellie around. Babies are very needy."

Kind of like NFL players, I thought to myself.

"I thought it was a bye week. I thought you didn't have any games this week." I covered my head with my pillow, but I knew it was too late now. I was awake. There was no going back to sleep.

"It is a bye week, but just because we don't have games doesn't mean we don't have work," he explained, sounding incredibly patient, which just made me want to thwack him with my pillow that much harder. "Please, Natalie? I really need you to watch her for just a couple of hours."

I did the mental math. "You owe me double time for this. I was supposed to have the day off from everything."

"Done."

I was surprised at how quickly he agreed, but I wasn't actually that angry. A day hanging out with Ellie was not a bad way to spend my day off of work. I liked the little baby, even if it meant I would miss my yoga class this morning. I would just change my plans to binge-watch something on Netflix. Maybe Bridgerton? Ellie was still too young to know that TV was interesting and we could watch what I liked for a few more months yet. I wasn't stuck watching sing-song shows focusing on being nice to our friends.

"I'll bring her over now," he said and hung up the phone.

I glanced at the clock and saw it was only ten in the morning. Ugh. That was not nearly enough sleep, even though it was my night off. I rolled out of bed and threw on a hoodie over my tank top. I did not have the energy to put on a real bra and T-shirt, so hiding under an old college sweatshirt was the way I was answering the door. I managed to get the pot of coffee started before my doorbell rang.

"Hi, thank you again for doing this," Dylan said as the door swung open. He stuttered when he saw me, his eyes doing the up and down thing before he caught himself.

"Yes, these are my pajamas," I replied. "I was sleeping."

"And I will pay you double," he assured me, keeping his eyes firmly planted on my face. He held out Ellie and the diaper bag. "Thank you again. I just can't concentrate with her around."

I brushed a strand of hair out of my eyes before taking the little girl into my arms. "I get it."

I wished I felt annoyed, but I didn't. How could I when Ellie immediately snuggled into me and sighed with contentment?

"Penelope is upstairs with your aunt, Ellie just finished a bottle, I changed her, and there are three spare outfits, three bottles, and a partridge in a pear tree in the diaper bag," Dylan explained. A soft smile crossed his face as he looked at the two of us. "Again, thanks."

"Get out of here," I said, smiling as I closed the door on him. "Go do work."

* * *

AT FOUR IN THE AFTERNOON, Ellie and I had both had an excellent nap and had discussed the finer points of 19th-century flirting techniques. I felt that she was ready for more episodes, but I was TV'd out for the day. I was ready for a walk, even if it was still late summer and warmer out than I preferred. I just didn't want to sit on a couch with a wiggly baby anymore. I headed over to Dylan's apartment to see if he had purchased a stroller yet. Given his thoroughness on all the other purchases, it seemed likely. The man had purchased nipple cream. He had to have some sort of stroller.

"Come in," came the yell through the door when I knocked.

I opened the door and nearly chucked the diaper bag at his head.

Because Dylan wasn't working. Oh no. He was watching a football game. It wasn't his team but there was no way this counted as doing his job. He was watching a live game and was just sitting on the couch, absolutely absorbed by the little men throwing a ball around on the screen.

"Oh, so this is what you call work?" Sarcasm so strong it hurt dripped out of my mouth. "This is what you can't do with a baby? I didn't know that watching TV required so much concentration."

"Natalie..." He turned, confusion painting his face. "I still need another hour. The game isn't over yet."

"But it's work?" I wished I could cross my arms, but Ellie was in them so the best I could do was an angry hip cock.

"It is." He frowned, looking at me and then back at the TV. Then his eyes widened. "And I can totally see why you wouldn't think that it wasn't."

I kept the angry hip jut. I wished I could have lasers coming out of my eyes. That would have made me feel better if I could have lasered the TV. I'd spent the entire day taking care of Ellie. I'd skipped my yoga class, I'd skipped my fancy coffee, and I didn't get any of my household chores done for the day because I'd been snuggling a baby. Sure, I probably could have gotten the chores done, but now I was angry and I wasn't going to take the blame for anything.

"We're playing the Broncos next week," Dylan explained, standing up and hitting the pause button. All the men froze in strange half running positions. "Their defensive line is intense. I need to know their strategies and what I'm up against."

"And that makes your time more valuable than mine?" I wanted to spit.

"No, no, not at all," he assured me, hurrying around the couch and to where I stood. Ellie held out her arms for him, the little traitor. "But it is my job. Here, come sit with me and I'll explain."

I thought about just throwing the baby at him and tossing the diaper bag at his head. It would feel good, but I didn't want to do that to Ellie. Besides, he was giving me wholesome puppy dog eyes and a hopeful smile that was very hard to say no to. So I just glared.

"I will make snacks," he offered. "I have popcorn... and it's the good stuff."

I raised an eyebrow. "How good?"

"Like the kettle corn they sell outside the stadium on game day," he replied. He leaned over the couch and picked up a bowl, letting the delicious scent of fresh kettle corn popcorn waft through the room. "I only get it when I watch film."

"Is that so that when you smell the kettle corn on game day you remember all the film better and have a better performance?" The popcorn smelled amazing. Sweet and salty filled the air and I could practically taste the chewy kernels of deliciousness.

"Sure. That sounds a lot better than the real reason, that it's a bribe to myself," he said with a shrug. He shook the bowl again. "But come sit with me so I can share this delicious food with you."

I narrowed my eyes. "Food is absolutely the way to my heart," I said with a voice that let him know I was still mad.

He grinned, his entire face lighting up as he jumped over the back of the couch, somehow keeping the popcorn bowl steady in the process. Not a single kernel fell out of the bowl. It was a rather impressive physical feat, but there was no way I was going to tell him that.

I did not hop over the back of the couch. I pretended that it was because I still held the baby, but it was also that I knew I would fall flat on my face if I tried to flip my legs over the back of the couch the way he did. He was an athlete. I was not. I took a seat, baby on my lap and popcorn bowl nestled between us.

He turned the TV back on.

"So, the goal," he said, pointing at the TV, "is for the offense to move the ball down the field and score in the end zone. They have four downs—or chances—to move the ball at least ten yards. If they succeed, they get another four downs. If not, the other team takes over." His hands gestured as he spoke, like he was sketching the game plan in the air. I nodded along, but while the words were English, they were going over my head.

He must have noticed my puzzled expression because he shifted to strategy.

"Okay, look at the quarterback," he said, motioning toward the player standing behind the line. "That's the guy in charge of reading the defense. His job is to decide whether to pass, hand the ball off to a running back, or sometimes run it himself. See how he keeps looking around? He's scanning for gaps or weaknesses in the defense."

"That would be Marcus on your team, right?" I asked, remembering the name.

"Yes!" He grinned and turned to watch a play unfolded, a receiver sprinting down the field to catch a long pass. "That's what a good quarterback does—he finds opportunities, like that guy who just got open. But it's all about timing. If he holds the ball too long, the defense will sack him."

"And that's what you do, run the ball or try and catch it?"

"Exactly!" He looked so happy that I was understanding the game.

"And why do you have to watch it on TV?" I asked, motioning to the big screen. "And not have a baby in the room?"

He held up a notepad I hadn't noticed.

"I'm learning their defense. I'm learning which players have which strengths, or, more importantly, their weaknesses. See that safety?" he asked, pointing to one of the guys on the screen.

"Is he unsafe? Running with scissors or something?"

He looked at me with an "are you serious" look. When I cracked a smile to show I was joking, he rolled his eyes.

"That's Nick Latts," he said. "He's the best in the league right now. I need to know what he's going to do to cover me. He's fast and has great coverage, so I need to figure out a way to get around him. So far, I've noticed that he likes to stick to the inside. I can use that."

He let the game run. I did not see how that one random guy mattered, but Dylan was busy scrawling in his notebook. He stopped, rewound the game, and replayed a pass pointing out exactly what Nick had done to stop the tight-end on the video from getting the ball.

"It's like a chess game," he added, his excitement contagious now. "The coach calls plays, but the players have to adjust in real-time depending on what the defense does. Watch this next play; they'll probably run it since they only need a few yards for the first down." Sure enough, the running back plowed forward, breaking through defenders for just enough yardage. I glanced at him, realizing he'd pulled me into the game without me even noticing.

I stared at him. Maybe this wasn't a game for the brain-dead after all.

"This actually sounds more complicated than smashing bodies together and fighting for the ball," I told him. I stuffed some popcorn in my face, trying not to moan with how good it was.

"You should come to one of my games," he said. I would have said he sounded nonchalant, but every muscle in his body tensed like he thought I was going to tackle him.

"I can't afford one of your games," I replied. "They're sold out unless I want to pay scalper prices, and remember? I'm a broke college kid now."

He laughed. "I always wanted a college-aged nanny," he teased. He winked at me. "Although it played out differently in my head."

It was my turn to laugh. "You better be good, or I'll put you to bed without dessert."

Dylan's pupils dilated and he looked away. Blood rushed to inappropriate areas of my body as I realized how sexual what I just said could have been taken.

He's your boss. He's a single dad. He's a player. He's not available.

I tried to keep that ringing through my mind instead of the *he's hot. He wants me. His bedroom is right there. The baby wouldn't even notice!* that kept trying to sneak in my thoughts instead.

I cleared my throat. "Ellie's asleep," I said, standing from the couch and carefully setting her down in the pack and play Dylan now kept in the living room for her naps. I focused on not looking toward the bedroom. Nope. I was not thinking about his giant bed or how warm he had felt on the couch next to me. Nope. Nope. Nope.

"Would you like some dinner?" he asked. "It's roasted chicken and portobello deli sandwiches with honey-glazed carrots and whole grain pasta."

"You cook?" I asked, glancing at the kitchen. He did have a lot of fancy equipment in there.

"Sometimes, but not this," he admitted. "They make us meals to take home during training camp. Nutrition is important, so they tend to send us home with extra. It's actually really good. Our chef is amazing. If you like salmon, I will have to bring you some."

"You have a personal chef?"

"Lauren and Chad are not *my* personal chefs," he corrected. "They work for the team. But I did help Chad out last year, so he always sneaks me extra food. They don't work for the team all year, just during training and for game stuff."

I nodded like that was a normal statement. "Sometimes we get pizza in the ER if a vendor is trying to sell equipment." I realized that sounded terrible, so I quickly added. "I would love some dinner. Thanks."

He stood up and went to the kitchen, humming softly. The game was finishing up the last few clips on the TV. I didn't mind it for once. I tried to see the teamwork and skill rather than just the brute force and potential injuries. For the first time, I could see the appeal of the sport. I wasn't going to start recommending it to anyone, but at least I didn't feel the visceral hate I usually did when football was on the TV.

While our food warmed in the microwave, the doorbell rang. I answered, and Penelope was standing in the hall with my aunt.

"She was an excellent goat today," Aunt Marnie informed me, giving Penelope scratches on her head. "I can't believe how much progress we're making."

"I'm so glad. Thank you again for watching her," I said.

"It's my pleasure." She patted the goat, said goodnight and headed back to the elevator.

The goat walked in the door like she owned the place, went over to the pack-n-play, checked to make sure the baby was doing well, circled the couch, hopped the baby gate around the arm chair, and curled up to watch some TV. She bleated at the TV, clearly not enjoying the football. She didn't stop yelling until Dylan changed the channel to *Supernatural*. She happily laid down and watched Sam and Dean fight monsters.

"She seems to be finding her new lifestyle agreeable," I

remarked as Dylan handed me a box of food. It was one of the nice expensive-feeling boxes and the food inside smelled amazing. A girl could get used to a private chef. I snuck a bite of the sandwich, and sighed with pleasure. It was delicious. Way better than the frozen chicken pot pie I had planned for dinner tonight.

"We can eat on the couch," he said, sitting down and motioning me to do the same. "It's not fancy, but neither am I."

I settled down next to him. It felt right to be here like this. Natural. Like this was how life was supposed to be. We ate in comfortable silence, making small talk occasionally about how the spice of the sandwich or what we thought was in the sauce. I said it was paprika and he thought there was a hint of anise as well. It was one of the better meals I had eaten in a long time.

Suddenly, the baby began to cry.

"Hello, gorgeous," Dylan said, picking up his daughter and snuggling her into him as she protested that we were eating without her. "Were we terrible parents?"

I pretended not to notice that he had included me as a parent. I pretended not to notice how happy it made me, all the way down into the pit of my stomach. I pretended not to notice how much I wanted it to be true.

"How about I change our princess and then we can watch a movie?" Dylan offered. "That is, if our resident goat will allow us."

Penelope bleated once, blinking her eyes at him with a slow, loving blink.

"I think you have a fan," I said with a laugh.

"Good, I need at least one," he replied.

14

FOOTBALL ISN'T EASY

What do you call a person who walks back and forth screaming
one minute, then sits down weeping uncontrollably the next?
A coach.

D YLAN

"CALLAHAN, get your ass off my field! You're done for
the day!"

Sweat dripped down my forehead and back. Every
inch of me was hot and sweaty, and not in the good way. I
could already smell myself in the summer heat. I really
needed to stop eating onions at lunch. My wrist surprisingly, didn't ache though, so that was a bonus.

"Get off the field, Callahan," Marcus snapped at me
when I didn't immediately move. I did a double take,
surprised at the anger in his voice, but decided that

punching him was not the best play for the day. I'd already dropped the last three passes. I'd misread the last two plays and only managed to get into a halfway decent position by the skin of my teeth.

It was not my best day. In fact, it might have been my worst day.

"Switch out Callahan!" Coach yelled from the sidelines. Reluctantly, I left the field, but I felt like I made it look like it was my choice and not Marcus's.

"Hey man, don't sweat it," Cameron said between slurps of water at the coolers. He dumped a paper cup filled with water over his head, and ran his fingers through his hair, spraying droplets of water everywhere in the summer sun. "Marcus is in a bad mood. He got dumped last night."

"Sandra left him?" I asked, sipping on the water. It wasn't cold anymore. It hadn't been since lunch. I didn't want it cold anyway, it went down easier if it was lukewarm.

"Sandra?" Cameron barked a laugh. "She left his ass weeks ago. You're behind, man."

I shrugged. It had been weeks since Marcus had said a full sentence to me. I still didn't know what had him so pissed off, but since he was pretending to be five years old and giving me the silent treatment, I wasn't going to find out. Besides, I had problems of my own. I didn't dare tell Marcus or Cameron about Ellie.

Even though I really wanted to tell them. These men were my teammates. My family. We'd shared blood, sweat, and tears.

But I didn't dare share with them about Ellie. I couldn't risk it.

All it would take was one stray word to one reporter up on that hill watching us practice and my life would devolve into legal fees and media circus. Given that I was barely holding onto my position on the team, that was the last thing I could afford to do. If even a hint of this reached the team owners, they'd boot me faster than I could run a touchdown.

"Hey man." Cameron caught my eye. "You doing okay? You look beat."

I wished I could tell the tight end that I hadn't slept more than two hours in row because of my daughter. The words hung in my mouth, but I couldn't get them out.

"My wrist," I mumbled.

"That sucks." Cameron tossed his paper cup into the trashcan. "That was a shitty break."

He had no idea how true that statement was.

He gave me a nod, bumping his chin in Coach's direction. I sighed but headed to where Coach stood watching the scrimmage with a scowl.

"You gonna figure out how to catch a ball again?"

I wished my shoulders didn't slump when he said it. I wished that I had a better answer than "my wrist hurts" or worse, the quiet fear that I was going to get tackled and feel that snap again.

"Callahan, you have talent." Coach uncrossed his arms and put one hand on my shoulder. "I don't want you to waste it on whatever nonsense is happening right now. I don't know why you and Marcus aren't talking, but it isn't good for the team."

"He started it," I snapped before I realized I sounded like a four-year-old. Man, I was tired.

Coach's eyebrows raised. "And I'll make sure to tell his

mommy. Fix it. Fix it before the next game or I won't be able to save you with medical."

I nodded. "Yes, Coach."

"Now get that wrist iced. I want you here early tomorrow going over the routes." He clapped my shoulder and left me to yell at the team that practice was over.

I barely listened to the closing remarks and skipped going to medical. I knew what to do better than they did. Ice, wrap, pain meds. Besides, I wanted to get home to Natalie and Ellie.

"Who's your daddy!"

I didn't know that it was possible for that phrase to not have a sexual connotation and still make me so damn happy.

I walked in through the front door and was greeted by two lovely ladies. Natalie wore comfortable looking sweat-pants with a t-shirt proclaiming that she donated blood around Halloween last year. Ellie was of course wearing something completely different than what I had left her in. My laundry bill this month was going to be outrageous. How the hell did someone so small make so much mess? She didn't even eat food, yet somehow she stained multiple outfits a day with it.

Natalie handed Ellie over to me with a giggle and a grin. I asked her to stay for dinner, which she accepted. We had a routine now. I would come home, we would have small talk about the baby, we would eat dinner, and then she would leave me with the baby for the evening. In the morning, she would take the baby and I would head off to practice. So far, it had worked wonderfully.

Not bad for three days. I was killing this parenting thing.

"Would you mind if I finished the episode?" Natalie asked, pointing to the TV after we finished dinner. "It's only supposed to be another ten minutes."

"Not at all."

In fact, I liked it when Natalie was over. It wasn't just that I felt more comfortable with her around because of the baby, but I liked her. She had a quick sense of humor and nothing seemed to phase her. She took everything in stride, staying calm and collected even when the baby was puking everywhere and the goat was eating my shoes. She just would take a breath and fix things.

Natalie flashed me a grin as she settled into the couch with Ellie in her lap to finish her show. I did the dishes in the kitchen, smiling as I worked. It felt domestic and just right for us to be like this.

I was definitely growing fond of her. The future didn't feel so frightening when I thought of her in it. Which was dumb, because once I established paternity, I would be hiring a nanny. Probably. The adoption idea was still in the back of my mind. I'd been killing this parenting thing for three days, but that didn't mean I was good at it. If I lost my position on the team, I wasn't sure I deserved to be a father.

Suddenly, a very naked woman dominated the TV screen, her lovely breasts on full display.

"Cover her eyes!" I shrieked, leaping over the couch and covering Ellie's eyes.

Natalie just laughed. "You realize that she's supposed to be drinking from a boob, right?"

I kept my hands over Ellie's face. "It's inappropriate."

Natalie raised an eyebrow. "You know she doesn't have any distance vision yet, right? She can barely see past our faces when we hold her."

"Seriously?" I let my hands drop. "Does that mean she needs glasses?"

Natalie shook her head. "No, it's normal. She's perfect." She smiled at the baby and Ellie cooed with delight at the attention.

"Well, I still think you should monitor her TV habits better," I chastised as the scene came to an end and the credits began to roll. Ellie didn't give two shits what was going on but I felt a little overprotective. The looming feeling that someday this would be important and these big decisions were coming down the pipeline lay heavy on my shoulders. How the hell was I supposed to make sure that she grew into a functioning adult? I wasn't even a functioning adult at heart.

No one should trust me with a baby.

But Natalie did. She set Ellie down in the pack-and-play where she could still see me.

"You're doing great," she told me, moving over on the couch to give me room to sit. "So, how was work? You watch more TV?"

"It was fine. No TV today, just lots of running," I replied, accepting the gentle teasing as I slid into the couch. My body was tired from training and it felt good to get off my feet.

She got up and went to the kitchen, bringing me back a Gatorade.

"It was hot out," she said with a shrug. "You probably need this."

Something deep in my chest loosened. A knot that had been tied so tight it tangled my ribs and made it hard to breathe suddenly went slack.

She was taking care of me.

It had been a long time since someone had taken care of me that wasn't actively getting paid. Sure, Alex was my assistant and my friend, but it wasn't the same as someone genuinely caring about my well being without being asked.

"Thanks." I took a sip.

"I also made dinner, if that's okay." She chewed on her lip. "It's not as amazing as those sandwiches, but it's pretty good."

I raised an eyebrow. "I'm not going to complain about free food."

She smiled, still looking a little nervous. "I'll get you a plate."

That's when I realized that the house smelled delicious.

"It's not pretty, but it tastes really good," she assured me, handing me the plate. She was right. The food was not pretty. It was a chicken breast covered in a creamy sauce with sun-dried tomato bits. A scoop of mashed potatoes finished out the plate with a small helping of peas.

I handed Ellie to Natalie so that I could focus on the food.

And I moaned as I tried the chicken.

"This is better than the portobello sandwiches," I informed her, stuffing another bite into my mouth. Chicken, herbs, bacon, sun-dried tomatoes all in a creamy sauce that I would have licked the plate for filled my mouth. The sauce made the perfect addition to the mashed potatoes and peas.

"What is this called? I need a recipe," I said, forcing myself to chew and not inhale the food. This woman was a goddess. She was good with kids, goats, and could cook.

She blushed. "Marry Me Chicken."

"Yes." I nodded, scraping my fork on the plate to get every drop of it. "I will marry you."

"You can marry the chicken," she replied. "That's how it got its name. Chicken so good you want to marry it."

"Do you think it would want a civil ceremony or one in a church?" I was considering licking the plate.

"Elopement," she replied, grinning as she watched me eat. "I don't think they'd want to wear a dress or a suit."

"Is there more?" I asked, holding up my empty plate.

Natalie beamed. "Of course. I'm so glad you like it."

She took my plate and made me a second helping. Once again, it felt good to have someone taking care of me.

"Have you eaten?" I asked, realizing that I was not being a good host.

"Making a plate for myself too," she replied from the kitchen. "I wanted to make sure you liked it."

"You can cook for me any time," I told her.

"Well, you say that..." She shook her head as she handed me my plate and sat on the couch next to me. "But this and spaghetti are about all I can reliably cook." Apparently, we were couch eaters, and I couldn't have been more okay with that. I liked eating on the couch. It felt familiar and less forced than the dinner table.

"I like spaghetti," I told her. "The only thing I don't like to eat is lima beans. Everything else is fine."

"Lima beans?" She took a bite of her dinner. "Any

reason why?"

"I had to eat them as a kid and I thought they looked like toes. Never got over it."

"Got it." She nodded. "No lima beans in the spaghetti."

I made a face thinking about lima beans in spaghetti and it made her laugh.

"Thank you." I didn't say it just for the food or not putting lima beans in our spaghetti. I meant it for her kindness and watching my daughter and the smile she was currently giving me.

It was for being there for me when no one else in my life could be.

"You're welcome," she said, her voice soft and warm. She smiled at me, like she understood what I was trying to say.

Ellie started to fuss, unhappy at being left out of dinner. I didn't know when babies started to eat food, but I had a feeling she was going to love eating when she figured it out.

"Tell me more about the team you're playing next week," she said, crossing her legs underneath her and watching me hold my daughter. "What are you going to do to get around that one guy?"

"That one guy?" I asked, raising an eyebrow.

"The danger guy? The guard guy?" She shrugged. "The guy who is supposed to stop you."

"The safety." I shook my head. She was never going to be good at this game, but I appreciated the effort. "Well, we have some plans."

And she nodded and let me talk about work.

I changed my mind. It wasn't the worst day ever after all.

15
———

AN ACCIDENTAL KISS

Why did the nurse need a red crayon? To draw blood.

NATALIE

THE HOT WATER of my shower felt insanely good.

It was still late summer and scorching outside, but the hot shower was exactly what I needed after a long shift. My muscles ached from running around the ER for the last twelve hours. I'd lifted patients, pushed carts, and hauled linens all night. I was exhausted, but my day was not done yet.

It was time for me to go to my second job.

I crawled out of the shower, sipping on the coffee I'd left by the sink. It was a good thing caffeine still worked on me. If it ever stopped, I'd probably die. I put on comfortable shorts and a t-shirt and headed across the hallway.

I knocked and opened the door, stepping inside to see three faces light up at seeing me. That was better than coffee any day of the week.

"Bahhhh," said Penelope. She didn't bother leaving her recliner. She wouldn't move until my aunt came to get her, then she would gleefully hop off and follow my aunt upstairs to her garden heaven.

"Arghlsyehs," cooed Ellie. I wasn't sure she could actually see me, but I appreciated the greeting anyway.

"Good morning." It was the deep voice that had my heart fluttering and my smile brightening, though. Dylan grinned at me, his brown eyes warm and looking at only me.

"Hi." I didn't mean for it to come out as a squeak, but it did. I was definitely good at this flirting thing. I cleared my throat. "How'd your night go?"

"We slept for a grand total of six hours," he replied. "Unfortunately, not sequentially. She should take a nice nap for you since I haven't fed her yet. How about you?"

I reached out and took the baby from him, settling her into my arms as she gurgled and cooed. "Just a night in the ER."

"I just made fresh coffee in the pot, and there's whiskey above the sink," he told me with a wink. "I won't even tell your boss."

I chuckled, watching as he gathered his things to head to practice. It was hard not to admire him as he moved. He was a professional athlete, after all, and he had the smooth movement and muscle to prove it. Plus, it didn't help that he was wearing a pair of dress slacks that accentuated his very muscular ass and a dress shirt that did not hide his broad shoulders or well-muscled arms.

The man was definitely nice to look at.

"What kind of practice do you have today?" I asked, trying to keep my mind from going into the gutter. Admiring was one thing, fantasizing was something I firmly needed to stay away from.

"It's light pads today," he replied, slinging a gym bag over his shoulder. "I'm still on medical leave, but I'll be expected to play. You want me to bring home dinner tonight?"

I grinned. If he kept feeding me dinners, he was going to absolutely win my heart. "Yes, please. Spaghetti can wait."

His eyes crinkled with an answering smile as he crossed the room to where I still stood by the door. He kissed my cheek and headed out the front door to go to work.

I didn't even register it until the door closed.

He'd kissed my cheek.

My skin went hot and my heart hammered in my chest. I could feel the spot on my cheek where his lips had touched me.

"It didn't mean anything," I told Ellie, looking down at the baby in my arms. She had no idea what had just happened. "Your dad and I...."

I wasn't sure how to complete that sentence. Her dad and I were not a thing. We were not dating. We had no plans to date. I didn't date men like him and I was sure that he didn't date nobodies like me.

Yet, I really liked the way his kiss felt on my cheek. I really liked the way his eyes lit up when he smiled at me. I really liked that he made sure there was always fresh coffee and clean blankets on the couch. He'd bought two different kinds of creamer because I'd casually mentioned I liked the vanilla and the caramel kinds at work. Fresh strawberries had randomly appeared in the fridge yesterday with a note to enjoy them.

A girl could get used to a life like this.

But was this what I wanted?

I wasn't ready to be a mother yet. I wasn't ready to parent or raise a child. I watched Ellie because she was a baby and it was easy, plus she was absolutely adorable.

And Dylan? That man was made to play the field. He was swoon-worthy and had dated models and cheerleaders. Besides, I hated football, right? How could I date someone in a sport that I didn't like.

"Blgrh," Ellie informed me.

I sighed. "You're right, kiddo. Blergh. I don't know what to do with that. So how about some breakfast instead? We can eat our feelings."

"Blfgh adjd," Ellie intelligently replied. She was right.

I went to the kitchen, my cheek still warm with the memory of his kiss. I was sure he hadn't meant anything by it. He'd probably been meaning to kiss the baby and had been busy thinking about practice and all the fancy run plays he needed to do today. Yup, that was it. He'd meant that kiss for Ellie. He probably didn't even realize that he'd done it.

"What would we even look like together?" I said out loud, not really talking to Ellie, but needing to talk to someone. "He's a famous football player. I'm just a random nurse. I've seen those reality TV shows where they have the wives of famous athletes." I shuddered just thinking about some of the women on those shows. "I'm just not sure it's even possible."

Ellie did not have anything to say in her father's defense.

"But he's super sweet," I continued, making a bottle with the machine. "And he's really good with you."

Ellie gurgled her approval.

"But..." I sighed, heading over to the couch to feed Ellie. We sat with a soft thump. "Maybe I'm just tired. Maybe I'm not ready for a relationship. Maybe I'm not ready to be in a parental role."

Ellie squeaked indigently.

"Oh, right." I gave her the bottle. "See? Not great parenting skills. Also, me complaining to a three-month-old about my grownup problems? Also not appropriate."

I sighed.

My cheek still felt warm. Just thinking about him made my chest flutter and my stomach tighten in the most delicious way.

I wanted him to kiss me again. I closed my eyes, imagining if he came home right now. The way he would walk through the room like he owned it (because he did) and lean over the couch, his strong arms framing me in on either side before he slid one hand behind my head to pull me into a kiss. My breath came fast just thinking about it.

The front door opened and I stood up so quickly that Ellie nearly lost her bottle.

"Dylan...." I gasped, hoping, praying that he was back because of that kiss. That I had somehow summoned him with my fantasy.

"Nope, just your aunt," Aunt Marnie announced. "I'm

here to get my goat. Dylan gave me keys to make it easier this week."

"Oh. Right." I cleared my throat, hoping that my cheeks weren't bright red. I felt like I had a neon sign over my head pointing down and proclaiming that I had dirty thoughts going on about Dylan. It did not help that his daughter was still in my arms.

I was not proud of myself.

Penelope jumped from her recliner, cleared the baby gate effortlessly, and happily bleated as she hurried to Aunt Marnie.

"There's my good girl," Aunt Marnie cooed, hooking a leash to the goat's collar. I realized now that it was bright pink and had her name on it. I'd seen him ordering it online a few days ago. Yet another reason to like Dylan. He took care of his things.

"How is the garden going?" I asked, ensuring Ellie was still enjoying her bottle in my arms. She didn't seem to mind that I had jumped up from the couch like I'd been on fire. She just chugged happily away at her bottle.

"Fabulous," Aunt Marnie replied with a beaming smile. She had my mother's eyes but a different smile. The same hair, but my mother never would have worn it as short as Aunt Marnie did. She reminded me of my mom, but not at the same time. "Penelope and I are fast friends."

"I know you said you only needed her for a couple of weeks, but if you're interested in adopting her..." I trailed off. Penelope wasn't really mine to give away, yet I didn't think Dylan had plans to keep her. Technically, she still wasn't allowed in the building. It wouldn't be long before the front desk noticed and Dylan got in trouble for her. Besides, this was not the best place for a goat.

"I love her, but once I plant the mums, she can't be up there. She'll eat them all. Plus, I will be leaving for Paris in three weeks." Aunt Marnie patted the goat fondly on her head. "I'm afraid I can't take her forever, even if I wanted to."

"Of course." I forced a smile. "Thank you for taking her now."

"Of course, dear." Aunt Marnie turned her fond smile to me. "Oh, I meant to tell you that the lake house is available this weekend."

I stared blankly at her.

"Did I not tell you?" She laughed, shaking her head. "The updates are all done. I had them put in that new outdoor shower I saw at Beth's place. The dock is fixed, but the kayaks are still leaky from last year. I won't get to use it for the next month or so, but you are always welcome to it. You know where everything is and you always take such good care of it."

"Thank you," I replied. "I don't know if I have any time off soon, but you know I love it out there. Thanks."

"You are my favorite niece," she informed me. "You might as well enjoy the perks."

"I'm also your only niece," I gave her my standard reply.

"Which makes you the best," she agreed. Penelope pulled on the rope and I had to reach over and pull an unused diaper out of her mouth. Ellie giggled when it went by her head, reaching out a chubby fist that made Aunt Marnie smile again. "I'll leave you to the little one."

She clucked at Penelope who happily left the stack of diapers and pranced alongside my aunt as they headed out the door and up to her garden.

I settled back on the couch. The room was quiet except for the gentle sucking noise of the bottle, but Ellie's eyes were glazing over. She was almost done with the bottle and would be asleep soon. Just like me. Weariness tugged on my body, weighing me down and making it hard to untangle my thoughts about Dylan, Penelope, and Ellie.

Just sleep for a little bit, I told myself. *Maybe it will all make sense when you wake up.*

I thought of Dylan's accidental kiss again.

Or maybe I'd have a really nice dream to make it even more confusing.

16

FOOTBALL STILL ISN'T EASY

"When I played pro football, I never set out to hurt anyone deliberately - unless it was, you know, important, like a league game or something."
-Dick Butkus

DYLAN

I KISSED HER.

I couldn't believe I had done it, but it had felt so damn natural. I'd picked up my stuff, said goodbye to my daughter, and I'd kissed Natalie on my way out the door. It was very "Leave It to Beaver" if Mr. Cleaver had an illegitimate child. The moment played over and over in my mind, but I enjoyed the repeat.

I liked kissing her. It wasn't the most amazing kiss of my life, but it had felt so right. My lips tingled to do it again. I wanted to feel her smooth skin, smell her soft coconut scent, and have more than just a quick peck on the cheek.

I wanted so much more.

I drove to practice lost in a love haze, nearly running over our Cameron in the parking lot. Hitting him would have been an impressive feat. Cameron was six foot three and three hundred pounds of pure muscle. He would have done more damage to my car than I would have done to him.

"Hey, you're not on defense today," he joked as I got out of my car. "Your mind here? Coach has us running plays before it gets hot."

I nodded. I needed to make a good showing today. I needed to prove not only to myself but to Natalie and Ellie that I was good at this. If I was making Natalie lose sleep, then it better be worth it.

I knew it was going to be a rough practice when my wrist brace decided to pop off in the middle of warm-ups. I bent down to pick it up, and somehow my cleat got tangled in my shoelace. Down I went, a six-foot-four heap of grace and dignity sprawled on the field.

"Nice, Callahan!" Marcus shouted from across the field, his voice dripping with the kind of sarcasm usually reserved for bad reality TV. "Maybe next time, try falling in the end zone—might help us score more points."

"Thanks for the advice, *Coach*," I muttered, brushing turf crumbs off my pants. My wrist throbbed as I tightened the brace back on. I was determined not to go to the medical tent to sit yet another practice out. Sitting out wasn't in my vocabulary. Well, unless it involved sitting out of wind sprints. Then I suddenly became fluent.

"Let's focus up!" Cameron yelled, jogging toward us with his usual calming air, like a human mediation app. "We've got plays to run. Marcus, dial it down. Dylan, you good?"

I gave him a thumbs-up with my non-injured hand, which earned me a skeptical raised eyebrow. Cameron had a knack for seeing through BS, especially mine.

Meanwhile, Franklin shifted back and forth on his feet, anxious to run. Every muscle in his body vibrated with energy, making his movements jerky. I could already see a multitude of false starts in his future. He might have gotten away with some of that in college, but it wouldn't fly in a real NFL game.

"Franklin, do you have to pee?" Marcus asked, standing to his full height. "Or are you just excited to give Callahan a friendship bracelet for the concert later?"

Apparently, Marcus had noticed Franklin's movements as well.

Franklin blinked. "Uh, no, sir?"

"Then stop moving and get your ass on the line!" Marcus growled, daring anyone else to breathe wrong. I wished the offensive coach wasn't busy talking with the defensive coach and letting us run the plays. I could have used a little grownup intervention today.

I leaned over to Cameron. "Marcus seems fun this morning."

Cameron sighed. "He's stressed. Something about a girl."

I rolled my eyes. "He needs to figure it out then. I'm not letting my love life ruin the game."

Cameron raised an eyebrow. "Nah, you're just dying of a broken wrist."

"Ouch, man." But he was right. For a moment, I wondered if he suspected something more, but he didn't give any indication he knew about my daughter or my nanny. I needed to make sure I didn't give him any reason to suspect the bags under my eyes were from my daughter waking me every two hours. Let them all believe it was my wrist and only my wrist.

We lined up for the next drill, Marcus becoming more annoyed with every second. I was supposed to run a quick out route. Easy. I jogged to the line, gave Franklin a wink to loosen him up and set my stance. Cameron snapped the ball.

The thing about having a bum wrist is you don't realize how much you rely on it until you're trying to catch a rocket pass from a quarterback who throws like he's mad at the world. The ball hit my hands and ricocheted off like I was wearing oven mitts.

"CALLAHAN!" Marcus exploded, throwing his helmet on the ground. "Are you even trying?!"

"Not sure if you noticed," I shot back, shaking my wrist, "but I've got this little thing called an injury. Maybe try throwing it less like a bazooka?"

James, the left tackle snickered.

"Maybe try catching it like a professional athlete!" Marcus snapped, glaring at James.

Before I could fire off a witty retort, and I had a really good one queued up, Cameron stepped between us.

"Hey!" he barked. "Both of you, cut it out! We're supposed to be a team, not an episode of Housewives."

Marcus glared at me. I glared back. The coaches didn't notice a damn thing. Franklin looked like he wanted to crawl under a tackling dummy. He needed to work on going to the outside. He was faster than most of the guys on the D-line and could get past them as long as he didn't get stuck. The kid was good, he was just used to college ball.

"Can we just run it again?" Franklin piped up, voice small. "I think I can get it this time."

Marcus let out a long-suffering sigh but nodded. "Fine. But if you screw it up—"

"Enough threats," Cameron interrupted. "Run the play."

We lined up again. I flexed my wrist, gritting my teeth against the dull ache. Cameron snapped the ball, and Marcus dropped back, scanning the field. Franklin took off like his cleats were on fire. This time, I got caught up in the defensive line. Franklin was open, but instead of running into the end zone, he tripped over his own feet and face-planted at the five-yard line.

The field was silent for half a second. Then Marcus groaned, Cameron shook his head, and Franklin rolled over, arms outstretched like a tragic Shakespearean hero.

"Did I at least get the first down?" Franklin asked, his voice muffled by the turf.

"First down?" Marcus snapped. "You got a face full of dirt."

Cameron helped Franklin up while I jogged over, patting the kid on the shoulder. "Hey, rookie. Next time, catch the ball, then face plant. It hurts the same, but at least you get the score."

Franklin gave me a sheepish smile. "I'll work on it."

Marcus stomped off, muttering something about retirement. Cameron clapped his hands. "Alright, huddle up. We're running it again until we get it right."

I groaned but jogged to the huddle. My wrist was killing me, I couldn't catch the ball, my quarterback was perpetually annoyed, and our rookie running back might've been allergic to success.

But at least I had kissed her.

17

LAKE HOUSES ARE THE BEST

What's it called when a hospital runs out of maternity nurses?
A midwife crisis.

NATALIE

"WHAT ARE YOU DOING HERE?" Dylan asked, sleep heavy in his voice. Surprise, not accusation, tinged his tone.

I tried not to stare at the thin pajama bottoms clinging to his hip bones and leaving very little to the imagination. He wasn't wearing a shirt, which made it even harder for my eyes to stop looking at him. He was all muscles and bare skin. Lots and lots of bare skin.

"I, uh..." I forgot how to speak. There was just so much bare skin and those pajama pants were showing the line of his hips, keeping my mind very firmly in inappropriate territory.

"My eyes are up here," he teased. "Did you forget that today's my day off?"

I closed my eyes and sighed. At least I could think when I wasn't looking at his gorgeous body that was very much off limits.

"Yup. I forgot. I'm so sorry for waking you up on your one day to sleep in." I quickly turned to head back to my apartment, silently cursing myself.

"Natalie," he called out. I froze when he said my name, my cheeks flushing as I couldn't help but smile. I turned slowly to face him again. "I was going to make some breakfast. You want some? Ellie should be up soon and I know she'd love to see you."

I wished I had the self-control to pretend to need to think about it, but I didn't. I practically sprinted back to his apartment. He chuckled as he closed the door behind me as if even he had noticed how quickly I had returned.

"I just need to put on some better cooking clothes," he said, padding down the hallway toward his bedroom. "I'll be right back. I just put the coffee on and there's lots."

I did manage to have enough self-control to wait until he was in the bedroom before I went to the kitchen to pour a cup of coffee. It probably helped that I had already had one cup today, but Dylan's coffee was better than mine and who was I to say no to coffee.

He returned a few moments later, dressed in basketball shorts and a well-worn baggy t-shirt. Even then, he didn't look like a regular guy. He still had too much athletic build and easy movement, but at least I wasn't openly gaping at his muscles anymore.

"I heard the weather is supposed to be gorgeous today,"

I said, pouring him a cup of coffee and handing it to him. "I was actually thinking I might take Ellie out for a walk before I realized you'd be home, but we could still go."

His face brightened and then fell. "That sounds amazing, but the DNA results haven't come back in yet. I can't risk being seen in public with an infant, even if you're the one holding her. The press will assume the worst and drag you into it."

I shuddered thinking of the headlines. I'd be labeled a single mom gold-digging an NFL player, or that I was the mother of his child that no one knew about. Either way, I'd be in the spotlight and that wasn't something I was quite ready for.

"Is a DNA test supposed to take this long?" I asked, sipping on my coffee.

He shrugged, the motion easy even on his broad shoulders. "The lawyers say it's all going to plan."

"And how do you feel about it?" I pressed, watching him.

He leaned against the counter, cradling the coffee mug in his large hands. He stared into the dark drink for a moment before answering. "I'm not sure. I love her though."

The sweet admission made me smile, although I tried to hide it in my own coffee mug. He grinned as he caught my smile.

"I can honestly say that I have never felt this way about another woman before," he continued. "She's needy and clingy, but..." He paused, glancing toward the bedroom where I assumed Ellie was still sleeping in her crib. "But I hope she's mine."

To say that my ovaries were on fire would be an understatement.

"What if we go to my aunt's lake house?" I blurted out.

He raised an eyebrow waiting for me to continue.

"It's on a private lake," I explained, gaining steam as the idea grew in my mind. "There's a small pool and a beach. We can bring sandwiches and make a picnic out of it and get to enjoy our day off and the great weather. The house has showers even so we don't have to be sandy for the trip home."

I was rambling, but I desperately wanted him to say yes.

"Wow, a house that has showers..."

"We can have a day out without worrying about anyone seeing us," I continued, ignoring his teasing. "And I think the water and sunshine will be good for the baby."

He sipped at his coffee, appearing to give my idea consideration.

"Well, if it's good for the baby, who am I to argue?" he finally said, setting down his mug on the counter. "I will just need some help with this car seat. I think you need an advanced technical degree to install it."

I laughed, thrilled that he had agreed. I then realized that I had not shaved for at least a couple of days. At least I had a swimsuit I knew looked good on me.

With a laugh, he continued. "Plus, it will give us a chance to use the swim diapers I bought!"

* * *

THE DRIVE to my aunt's lake house took less than an hour. The cottage-style home was a staple of my childhood. It had three bedrooms, three baths, an outdoor shower, a pool, a hot tub, and lake access. My aunt's husband had been rich. Ridiculous level rich, but they'd never had kids. He'd died when I was four so I didn't remember him, but I did remember my aunt letting my not-rich family use the lake house for summer vacations.

My dad had loved it here. It was one of my favorite places on the planet.

I sighed with pleasure as we spilled out of the car and into her gravel driveway. The smell of trees and water filled my lungs, replacing the heat and smoke of the city. Somehow, out here, the humidity felt cleaner and sunshine less intense, yet somehow more welcoming.

"Wow, this is nice," Dylan whistled as I keyed in the numerical lock to let us in.

"My aunt is the reason I can live in our building," I explained, pushing the door open. "She owns my apartment. She owns most of the building to be honest, but she lets me live there as long as I pay the dues and fees."

He nodded, as if he had been wanting to ask how I could afford to live in such a nice building but had been too polite to say anything.

"She doesn't have any kids so she likes to help out her nieces and nephews when she can," I continued. "I try not to ask her for too much because she's already given me a lot."

Dylan easily hefted the car seat onto the kitchen counter where Ellie gurgled and cooed at him.

"You ready to swim?" he asked her, bending at the knees so his face was in line with hers. She reached for him, her chubby hands missing by miles but making him smile at the effort. He unclicked her from the seat and set about changing her diaper and putting on the now useful swim diapers.

I headed out to the pool to take off the pool cover and lay out towels. My aunt had a house cleaner and pool cleaner come by weekly, so the pool sparkled in the sunshine. The lake glittered just beyond the pool, inviting us with darker water and a sandy beach. I figured Ellie should try out the pool first since the water would be cleaner and warmer. We could wade in the lake after. When she was bigger, we could take the kayaks and go find the creek where all the turtles liked to congregate.

When she was bigger.

I was already planning on having Ellie stay in my life. I swallowed hard. I wasn't sure if I was invited to stay in her life once the DNA results came back. I wasn't really sure where I stood in Dylan's life other than as his nanny, and that wasn't a long term position. Neither one of us had said a word about the kiss, and I didn't want to bring it up and ruin things. Today was supposed to be a nice relaxing day at the pool.

"Cannonball!"

I turned, ready to yell at Dylan that babies shouldn't be doing cannonballs into the pool, but instead saw him knee-deep in the pool holding onto his daughter and dipping her toes under the water. Ellie shrieked with delight, kicking her feet and splashing the water.

I tried not to stare at his muscled bare chest and the absolutely adorable little girl in his arms. She was so tiny compared to him, yet he was absolutely at her mercy. He could have been an advertisement for having children because I was ready to purchase the whole kit.

"Come on in, the water's great," Dylan called out to

me. He looked up, the sun highlighting the strength of his face and making his eyes sparkle as he grinned at me.

I reached for my shirt, lifting it up over my stomach before getting self-conscious. Was he going to like what he saw? I swallowed hard, the butterflies going hard in my stomach but I stripped. I might have made sure to pop my chest and roll my shoulders a little, but that was just because it was comfortable, not because I wanted him to notice.

But notice he did. I saw his eyes focus on me and even from this distance, I could see his pupils dilate. He licked his lips as he looked me up and down.

Heat blossomed in my chest and core at the idea that he thought I was sexy. I liked it, and I did saunter to the pool stairs in order to join him.

"Can you teach a baby to swim?" he asked, lowering Ellie into the water, but keeping a firm grip on her. "Do they have baby swim lessons?"

I nodded as I slid into the water and stood on the second step of the pool with him. Even though the water was warm, I could still feel his heat radiating off of him into the water.

It was distracting. I needed to focus on the baby, but all I could see was his muscles and bare skin.

Get a grip, I told myself. *Be a professional.*

As if swimming with your boss in a private pool with his illegitimate daughter was professional in the first place.

Ellie giggled and kicked her legs, helping to bring me back to the task I was supposed to be doing. I focused on her, doing my best to ignore the well built arms holding her safely in the water.

Together we lowered her into the water. She flailed

with her balled fists, frowning at the water as she tried to figure out exactly what was going on. Dylan chuckled, the sound low and deep as he watched her try to figure out this new thing in her world.

She was too little to do more than just hold and wander around the shallow end of the pool. The water was warm and the sun hot, so I wasn't too worried about her getting chilled. Ellie giggled and babbled, wriggling her entire body in the new sensation of being surrounded by water.

"I think she likes it," I said, grinning as I watched her chubby arms flail. Her tiny eyebrows alternated between heavy thinking and joyful surprise. Dylan murmured his agreement, dipping her down low into the water so it came up to her chest. Ellie's eyes watched everything, trusting in the ever present security of her father keeping her safe from all harm.

"I think she's going to sleep like a rock after this," Dylan said with a laugh after we "swam" around for a good twenty minutes.

"Here, let's see if she can float," I offered, holding out my arms to him. He hesitated, unsure of what I was going to do to his daughter. "I promise I won't let her go," I added.

He gave her to me, his shoulders relaxing when she smiled up at me and flailed her arms happily in the water. Carefully, I maneuvered her onto her back, cupping her head in my hand so that she couldn't sink but her body could float out in the warm water. At first, she wasn't sure about the new position, especially since it meant her head was getting wet, but after a moment, she let out a long breath and her entire body relaxed.

"There you go," I whispered, letting her float gently in

the warm water. Every muscle in her face relaxed, her arms and legs splaying out as she gave me her absolute trust that I would keep holding her head and keep her from going under.

"I wonder if this reminds her of when she was in the womb," Dylan said thoughtfully, his dark eyes focused on his daughter. "She looks so peaceful."

I watched as her eyes started to blink slowly, growing heavier and heavier with every flutter downward.

"I guess this would be the ultimate water bed," Dylan remarked. I glanced up at him to see him grin at me. "Can it be my turn next?"

"Only if you don't require a diaper change after," I teased. He snorted a laugh, making Ellie stir but not wake.

"We can wrap her up in a towel and put her in the baby pen," I offered. I'd set up the travel crib on the patio near the hot tub.

"And then hot tub for us?" He grinned. "Sounds great."

He crossed the pool in three strokes, his strong muscles propelling him through the water. I tried, and failed, to not stare as he hefted himself out of the water and up onto the patio deck. Water streamed down his bare chest in tantalizing designs, curving around his well-defined pecs and abs. I forced myself to look away when the rivulets of water surged toward his low slung swim trunks.

He grabbed a towel and waited for me to tow the sleeping infant to the stairs. Carefully, although I was pretty sure she was tired enough to sleep through a hurricane, I cradled Ellie into my arms and then handed her into the waiting towel. As if he had done this a thousand times, he had her swaddled in the towel. She sighed in contentment but did not wake.

I climbed out of the pool, wondering if Dylan was watching the water slide down my body the way I had stared at him. He carefully placed Ellie in the travel crib and sat on the edge of the hot tub. I joined him, sitting next to him. I could have sat on the opposite side of the tub, but I didn't. I couldn't help it. I wanted to be close to him. I could pretend to justify it that I wanted to be nearer to Ellie, but I knew the truth.

I wanted to be next to him.

I wanted to touch him.

I knew it was a bad idea and I decided I didn't care.

I was going to have this moment.

18

HOT TUBS ARE H O T

What is a football player's favorite dessert?
Any given sundae

DYLAN

PLEASE KEEP SLEEPING, I silently begged, glancing over to the sleeping child. *Please, please, please.*

It wasn't that I didn't enjoy every second of my daughter's smiles. I did. Seeing her swim today and experience the water for the first time was magical. I could relive that moment over and over in my mind a million times and never have it grow old.

But, I wanted a little bit of time with Natalie. Alone. No baby between us, no bottles, no exhaustion, no talking about sleep schedules.

Just me and her.

Alone.

And I just needed Ellie to sleep so that I could have that.

"I think she might sleep for a week after all that activity," Natalie joked. She sat on the edge of the hot tub, so close that we were almost touching. I was feeling hot, and it wasn't because of the steaming water we both rested our feet in.

"Do you think we might be that lucky?" I replied, looking everywhere but at her. It was hard. She was gorgeous in her swimsuit. The dark blue two-piece wasn't something that anyone would advertise as sexy, but it accented her features subtly, making me want to look closer. It was a demure swimsuit that covered all the important bits and would be more than acceptable at a local pool, but I couldn't tear my eyes away from her soft curves and smooth skin. My fingers itched to untie the strap at the back of her neck and see what goodness she was keeping to herself.

"The break is nice," she agreed. She flashed me a quick smile before sliding into the water. The tip of her ponytail drifted lazily in the water as she submerged herself to her chin, sighing with contentment.

"You've been doing a great job with her," she said after a quiet moment. The praise made me want to puff out my chest, but I just shrugged.

"She's worth it," I told her. I slid into the water with her, feeling her eyes follow my every motion. "And I couldn't do it without you."

She opened her mouth like she was going to contest that, yes, yes I could do this on my own, but we both knew that was a lie. I was still trying to figure out diapers and formula and safe sleeping practices. "I'm glad I could help."

Anticipation thrilled in my stomach, the butterflies beginning their dance of excitement. I'd thought I'd gotten over butterflies in my stomach by playing for crowds of thousands, but Natalie made new butterflies. Desire filled my bones.

It was time to take my shot. I could feel that it was time.

"So, about the other day..." she began, but I cut off her words with a kiss.

The back of her head slid into my palm as I kissed her, our bodies pressed close together in the water.

She didn't hesitate. She didn't freeze. She didn't pull away.

She kissed me back, her mouth opening to let her tongue out to explore the edges of my mouth. I couldn't have stopped the low moan that escaped out of me if I'd tried. She tasted like summer sunshine and lemonade. Warm moonlight and sweetness.

I wanted more of her. I *needed* more of her.

She slid her arms around my neck, pulling me and continuing the kiss. Warm water trickled down the back of my neck as she threaded her hands into my hair, making sure that I couldn't escape her. Not that I wanted to. I never wanted to leave her sweet mouth, never wanted to stop feeling her tongue on my lips, her body pressing into mine.

Slowly, she pulled back, her eyes big as she looked at me. Her arms were still wrapped around my neck and I realized that her legs were now wrapped around my waist. She bit her lower lip, a blush staining her cheeks.

"So…" She grinned at me. "I think I might have a crush on my boss."

"Is that so?" I grinned back at her, threading my fingers into her wet ponytail and pulling her into me again. "I think your boss is into it."

I pressed my lips to hers again, savoring the softness and warmth. Her fingers traced patterns on my neck, sending shivers down my spine despite the heat of the water. The jets bubbled around us, creating a private cocoon of warmth and intimacy.

"I've wanted to do this since I accidentally kissed you," I murmured against her mouth. She smiled, her eyes sparkling with mischief.

"Me too," she whispered back. "I kept telling myself it was unprofessional."

"Very unprofessional," I agreed, trailing kisses along her jaw. She tilted her head, giving me better access to the smooth skin of her neck. "Completely inappropriate."

"Totally wrong," she said with a tiny little moan, her fingers threading through my hair. The gentle tugging sensation made my scalp tingle pleasantly. "There's a power imbalance here that raises serious ethical questions."

I pulled back to look at her face, taking in her flushed cheeks and bright eyes. The water droplets on her skin caught the sunlight, making her glow. Her ponytail had come loose, tendrils of hair curling around her face.

"You know, we're kind of in the middle of nowhere," I said as I stared into her eyes. "Maybe we could ignore the ethical implications just this once."

She closed her eyes and made a happy moan. "Just this once," she agreed.

"You're beautiful," I told her honestly. She ducked her head as she smiled involuntarily, but I caught her chin with my finger, bringing her face back to mine. "I mean it."

She opened her eyes and I saw true happiness. She opened her mouth as if to answer, but was at a loss for words. Instead, she leaned in and kissed me again, soft and sweet. Her legs tightened around my waist as she pressed closer. I wrapped my arms around her, holding her against my chest as our kisses deepened.

A splash of water hit my face as Natalie pressed closer. We both laughed, breaking apart for a moment to catch our breath. She rested her forehead against mine, her eyes closed and a content smile on her face.

"We should probably check on Ellie," she whispered, though she made no move to let go of me.

I glanced over at the travel crib where my daughter still slept peacefully, her little chest rising and falling in steady rhythm.

"She's fine," I assured her, stealing another quick kiss. "Still sleeping like an angel."

Natalie hummed happily against my lips, her fingers tracing patterns on my shoulders. I loved the way she felt in my arms. The water swirled around us, creating a peaceful backdrop to our stolen moment together.

Our kisses became more passionate and urgent, my hands sliding down her back, feeling the warmth of her skin under my fingertips. As we took a break for air, she looked into my eyes, a mix of desire and vulnerability that made my heart race.

"Are you sure about this?" I asked, my voice low and husky.

I didn't need to bother. She had already made up her

mind. She smiled, a soft, sweet smile that made my heart swell with happiness. "I want this," she said firmly. "I want you."

With that, she leaned back in, her lips meeting mine once more. This time, our kiss was slower, filled with the promise of something deeper and more intense. I gently move my hand up her back, grabbing on the string tied around the back of her neck, and pulling on it slowly enough that she could stop me if she wanted to.

She didn't stop me, but when the two ends of the string finally came free, she backed away from me. Her hands went to the cups of her bikini top, holding it in place as I watched.

She bit her lip, as if still unsure what to do. I brushed my fingertips lightly down her back, making her shudder with pleasure. Her hands dropped away, and with them, her bikini top.

Her breasts, now bare, fit perfectly into my hands. I caressed them, feeling the weight and warmth of them against my skin. She moaned softly before pressing herself closer. Our bodies entwined in the water, the swirl of the jets around us creating a sensual, soothing background.

"Oh, hell yes," she whispered, her voice barely audible over the sound of the hot tub jets. Her hips danced against me, a slow and sensual rhythm that seemed to pulse through my very being. I ached to be set free. To fill her. To have every inch of her.

"Natalie..." I breathed, my hands tightening on her hips as she continued to grind against me. My cock throbbed under my swim trunks. Our bodies were slick with water, the heat of the hot tub only adding to the intensity of our connection.

She looked up at me, her eyes hooded with desire. "Mm hmm?"

"You feel so good," I groaned, the pressure against my shorts becoming almost unbearable. Every movement she made sent waves of pleasure coursing through me, making me want her even more.

Her smile widened, and she leaned in close, her breath hot against my ear. "Do you want me?" she whispered seductively.

I couldn't resist. I took her hand, placing it under the water and on my cock so she could feel how much I wanted her. She moaned, sliding her hand under my waistband and stroking my length.

I shuddered, my lungs unable to take in oxygen with how damn good her touch felt. I couldn't believe this was happening. Just moments before, we'd been playfully "swimming" with Ellie, and now here we were, lost in our own passionate world. The contrast was exhilarating.

"You're so beautiful," I said again against her lips, my hands roaming over her bare skin, feeling every curve and contour of her body.

She moaned softly, her hips gyrating against mine as she pressed herself closer. Our bodies were entwined, our hearts beating in sync as we danced in the water.

The sounds of our passion filled the air, mingling with the soothing hum of the hot tub jets. It was a heady mixture that only served to heighten our desire for one another. We were lost to one another, drowning in our own ecstasy as the world around us faded away.

But even as we reveled in the pleasure of our shared moment, a small voice in the back of my mind whispered a warning. This was dangerous territory we were treading, and the consequences of our actions might not be so easily ignored.

I tried to push the thought away, determined to savor every second of this forbidden romance. The feel of Natalie's body against mine was too intoxicating, too exhilarating to resist.

But the gnawing feeling kept coming back, and I knew that I wouldn't be able to perform without asking.

"Hey, just how cool was your aunt, anyway?" I asked

Natalie broke away from the kiss with a confused look on her face. "Um… why are you asking me that?"

I immediately knew I could have phrased it better. I didn't know what she thought I meant, but I knew I better clarify quickly.

"Did she store any… condoms?"

Natalie looked at me like I hadn't spoken English.

"It's just that, you know. I kind of got myself in this mess by being irresponsible, and as much as I love Ellie, I-"

"Quiet," Natalie said, leaning in and kissing me to shut me up. "I'm on birth control, and I've seen the kind of man you are. I trust you."

My heart skipped a beat. *I trust you.* Plenty of women had wanted to fuck me, but nobody had ever told me they *trusted* me.

It was the ultimate libido-enhancer, and I felt myself getting even harder. I moved my hand down Natalie's back, moving my hand over her ass and down between our bodies. I moved her bikini bottoms to the side slightly, loving the slight gasp of pleasure she made at my touch.

"Natalie," I said softly.

The look in her eyes said it all. She was ready for

anything. And as I moved her bikini bottoms more to the side, I knew that we were about to connect on a whole new level…

…until the baby started to scream at the top of her lungs.

We both froze, as if by not moving the baby might magically go back to sleep.

She did not.

She continued to scream, angry that not only was she not in the water, we were not holding her.

With a groan of displeasure, Natalie pulled away from me, slipping through the water and out of my reach to help my daughter.

I watched Natalie spring into action, grabbing a towel and wrapping it around herself before rushing to Ellie. My little girl's face was scrunched up and red as she wailed. Natalie lifted her with practiced ease, cradling her against her chest.

"Shh, shh, it's okay sweetie," she cooed, swaying back and forth. "Did you have a bad dream? Everything's alright."

I climbed out of the hot tub and grabbed my own towel, trying to get my racing heart under control. The sight of Natalie comforting my daughter made something warm bloom in my chest that had nothing to do with desire.

Ellie's cries started to soften as Natalie paced the deck, humming softly. She looked over at me with a shy smile. "She might go back down. We could…" She glanced toward the cabin. "The bedroom's right there."

I ran a hand through my wet hair, considering. "What if we went back to my place instead? She's got her own crib there, and we wouldn't have to worry about her waking up in a strange place."

Natalie's eyes lit up. "That's... actually a really good idea. We could take our time, not rush anything."

"Exactly." I stepped closer, pressing a kiss to her forehead. "No pressure, no hurry."

Ellie had quieted to little hiccuping sobs now, her eyes already drooping again. Natalie smiled down at her. "What do you say, sweet girl? Want to go home?"

As if by magic, Ellie seemed to nod her head, right before drifting back off to sleep.

"Get your clothes back on," Natalie said. "I'll lock the place up before we go."

I wanted to stick around and see her when she dropped that towel, but I just nodded and started getting dressed. I knew that, if I kept playing my cards right, I'd get to see plenty soon enough.

19

———

DRIVE FASTER

Be kind to nurses. They will eventually see you naked.

Natalie

I couldn't remember a time the drive home from the lake took this long. Every minute sitting next to him, not touching him, not feeling his kisses was torture. Sure, I put my hand on his leg, but I didn't want to distract him while he was driving, so I didn't do much more than just rest my hand there. It was difficult knowing what pleasure was just inches from my fingers.

I stared out the window, watching the trees blur past as we drove. My skin still tingled where his hands had touched me, and my heart wouldn't slow down. Every time I glanced over at him, I caught him stealing looks at me too. The electricity between us was almost visible, crackling in the small space of his car.

Ellie slept peacefully in her car seat, completely unaware of the tension surrounding her. I envied her peaceful expression. My own thoughts were a whirlwind of desire and uncertainty.

What if he regretted it? What if, once we got back to reality, he decided this was too complicated? The way he'd kissed me felt real, but doubt has a way of creeping in during quiet moments.

His hand found mine on his leg, threading our fingers together. The simple touch sent shivers up my arm. When I looked at him, he smiled – that warm, genuine smile that made my insides melt.

"You're thinking too hard," he said softly, keeping his eyes on the road.

"How can you tell?"

"I can practically hear the gears turning." He squeezed my hand. "Talk to me."

I took a deep breath. "I just... I hope you don't think this was a mistake. The hot tub, I mean."

He glanced at me, his expression serious. "Natalie, I've wanted you since that first day you walked into my home. The only mistake was waiting this long to tell you."

My heart skipped. "Really?"

"Really." He lifted our joined hands to his lips, pressing a kiss to my knuckles. "And just so we're clear, I plan to show you exactly how much I want you as soon as we get home."

The promise in his voice made my whole body flush with heat. I squeezed his hand, unable to stop the smile spreading across my face. "Drive faster."

He laughed, the sound rich and warm. "Patience, beautiful. We've got all night."

All night. The words echoed in my head, filling me with anticipation. I settled back in my seat, still holding his hand, watching the miles tick by that separated us from his house.

He pulled into the apartment's garage, my heart racing with anticipation. As soon as he cut the engine, I was out of the car, gently unbuckling Ellie from her car seat. He grabbed the diaper bag and led the way to the elevator. I kept sneaking glances at him the entire ride up, wishing that three neighbors hadn't decided to ride up with us.

Once inside his apartment, we moved in perfect sync. I cradled Ellie while Dylan prepared a bottle, testing the temperature on his wrist before handing it over. We settled on the couch, Dylan holding Ellie while I draped my arm around his shoulders.

"She's got your eyes," I murmured, smiling down at Ellie.

Dylan chuckled softly. "Poor kid."

I elbowed him gently. "Don't say that. Your eyes are beautiful."

Our gazes met, and for a moment, I forgot how to breathe. The intimacy of the moment - feeding his daughter together - felt more intense than our heated encounter in the hot tub.

When Ellie finished her bottle, we moved to the changing table. Dylan grabbed a fresh diaper while I expertly cleaned and changed her. Our hands brushed as we worked together, sending little sparks of electricity through my body. It felt like we had been made to work together like this.

"There we go, all clean," I cooed, lifting Ellie into my arms. We cuddled on the couch again, this time with Ellie nestled between us. Dylan stroked his daughter's soft hair, marveling at how perfect she was.

"You're amazing with her," I said softly to Dylan.

He smiled, a slight blush coloring his cheeks. "She makes it easy. She's such a good baby."

We sat in comfortable silence, watching as Ellie's eyes began to droop. When her breathing evened out, we shared a look of understanding. Carefully, we stood and set her in the pack-and-play. We would be using the bedroom and I didn't want to accidentally wake her.

With Ellie safely asleep, I turned to Dylan. The hunger in his eyes mirrored my own, and I knew the moment we'd been waiting for had finally arrived.

He grabbed my hand and led me out of the room. We didn't stop at the living room for a drink, or pretend to turn on the TV. He led me straight to the bedroom.

And his eyes never left mine for even a moment.

I watched as Dylan pulled his shirt over his head, revealing his toned chest. My breath caught in my throat at the sight of him. He stepped closer, his eyes dark with desire, and my heart raced in anticipation. He was so big and strong that I felt tiny with him in this room.

I liked it. I liked that he felt so powerful and big because I knew he would always protect me. There was no danger in him, just desire.

As his lips met mine, I caught the faint scent of chlorine from the hot tub still clinging to his skin. It didn't matter - if anything, it only heightened my arousal, reminding me of our heated encounter earlier. I wanted that again.

I wrapped my arms around his neck, pressing my body

against his as I returned his kiss with fervor. The stubble on his jaw scratched my skin, but I wanted it. My fingers tangled in his hair, still damp from the pool. I had to stand on my tiptoes, but he made sure to lean so I had easy access to him.

Dylan's hands roamed down my sides, leaving trails of fire in their wake. I arched into his touch, desperate for more contact. He kissed me like he'd never tasted anything as delicious as my lips in his life.

I tugged at his lower lip with my teeth, eliciting a deep groan from him that sent shivers down my spine. His hands slipped under the hem of my shirt, his warm palms skimming across my bare skin.

"Natalie," he breathed against my lips, his voice husky with need.

I responded by kissing him harder, pouring all of my pent-up desire into the action. My hands explored the planes of his chest, tracing the contours of his broad muscles. The heat of his skin beneath my fingertips was intoxicating.

Dylan backed me up until my legs hit the edge of the bed. We tumbled onto the mattress, our bodies inter-twined, never breaking the kiss. The heavy weight of him pressed me into the soft bedding, but he didn't crush me. He made sure I was protected under him, and I reveled in the feeling of being surrounded by him.

His lips left mine to trail kisses along my jaw and down my neck. I tilted my head back, giving him better access as I gasped for air. Each press of his lips against my sensitive skin sent jolts of pleasure through my body.

Panting for more, I ran my nails lightly down his back, feeling the muscles flex beneath my touch. Dylan shuddered, pressing himself closer to me. The evidence of his arousal pressed against my thigh, making me ache with want.

My hands found their way to the waistband of his shorts, my fingers dipping just beneath the elastic. Dylan's breath hitched, and he pulled back slightly to look at me, his eyes searching mine.

"Are you sure?" he asked, his voice barely above a whisper.

In response, I pulled him back down for another searing kiss. There was no doubt in my mind. I wanted this, wanted him, more than I'd ever wanted anything.

"As you said," I said in between kisses. "The only mistake was waiting this long."

My words seemed to ignite something within Dylan, and he kissed me harder and faster, as if he couldn't get enough. His hands were all over me, feeling every inch of my skin. His touch was like fire, spreading warmth and desire through my body.

In one swift motion, he pulled my shirt off over my head, my white cotton bra the only thing between us. I shimmied out of it, breaking our kiss just long enough for me to feel the cool air kiss my nipples before Dylan's lips touched them. As he kissed one, I arched my back, my body straining for more contact.

His lips were gentle but insistent, and he moved from one nipple to the other, peaking them into his mouth and flicking them with his tongue. My breath came in ragged gasps. I couldn't help but grasp his head with both hands, pulling him closer. He nipped and teased, obviously enjoying how it made me writhe beneath him.

He was so strong, so powerful, yet he was only using

that strength to keep me safe. He was holding back, making sure he didn't overwhelm me. I could feel his heartbeat, faster and stronger than mine, and it sent waves of exhilaration through my body.

He nipped at my throat before soothing the sting with a kiss. The small gasp of pleasure that left me only made him grow harder between my legs. He chuckled softly, pleased with himself.

Dylan's hand slid down my stomach, his fingers tracing a path southward that set my skin on fire. I gasped, my body tense with anticipation as I felt him reach the waistband of my shorts.

His fingers dipped beneath the waistband of the fabric, and I moaned softly, my body writhing against his touch. I couldn't help but rock my hips, trying to get him to touch more of me. I moved to pull the shorts off, but he held me in place.

Strong, yet gentle.

Keeping one of my hands pinned to the bed, he tugged the shorts just low enough to expose the lacy waistband of my panties. He kissed down my chest, down my stomach, down to the top of my panties, not daring to go any further.

I lifted my hips up and started to pull my shorts down, but he stopped me again. His firm grip let me know that he was in charge, and I laid back and let him take control. One kiss to the bare skin right below my navel and he slid my shorts down my legs, leaving me bare but for the pretty pink panties I had carefully chosen this morning.

He paused, admiring me. A cocky smile, but a pleased one, filled his face. A man had never looked at me like that before. Like I was everything he had ever wanted. Like he craved me. Like I was perfect. He licked his lips like he was a hungry man about to feast.

Dylan kissed his way back up my legs. His lips were warm and soft against my skin, contrasting with the scratch of his stubble, and every touch sent a shiver down my spine. He moved with a slow, deliberate pace, taking his time to savor every inch of me.

When he reached the bottom of my panties, he paused. I could feel his breath against my thighs, and I knew that he could feel how wet I was. I wouldn't need the lube he'd accidentally purchased. My heart was pounding in my chest, and I found myself struggling to breathe.

I wanted this. I'd never wanted sex this badly in my life. I'd always thought it was just that sex was fun, but not that great. Now I realized it was because no one had ever looked at me the way Dylan did. No one made me feel the way he did.

As Dylan began to kiss all around the bottom hem of my panties, I felt a moment of panic. I couldn't help but worry that I still smelled like the hot tub, and I didn't want him to be turned off. But before I could say anything, he lifted his head to look at me.

"Are you okay?" he asked, his voice low and husky.

I froze. "It's just... you know... the hot tub... and you don't have to... do that."

He laughed, a low laugh that told me he didn't care that I smelled like chlorine. "Stop me if I really make you uncomfortable," he said.

I nodded, unable to find the words to express how I was feeling. Dylan must have sensed my apprehension, because he pressed a gentle kiss to my leg before continuing on his journey up my body.

When he kissed my inner thigh, just next to where the panties started, I gasped. It felt so good, so intense, that all my doubts and fears melted away. All that mattered was the connection between us, the passion that burned so brightly.

Just as I was relaxing into the sensation, Dylan placed his tongue against my pussy, through the fabric of my panties. I moaned, my body convulsing with pleasure. Every thought in my head swirled, my legs widening, wanting more of his touch and tongue.

His fingers slipped under the sides of my panties, and I lifted my hips to help him remove them. He hummed his approval at what he saw before leaning forward and kissing the top of my pussy. He settled himself between my legs, making himself comfortable as he began to taste me.

I surrendered myself to him, allowing him to explore my body with his lips and tongue. Each touch sent waves of pleasure crashing over me, and I felt myself getting closer and closer to the edge.

He gripped my hips as I panted, so close to release. He looked up at me with a mischievous grin, his eyes sparkling with desire.

"Do you want to come right now?" he asked, his voice a low growl.

"Yes," I moaned with a quick nod. "Keep going."

"Tell me what you want," he commanded.

"Lick me," I replied. "I want you to keep licking me and tasting me."

The smile he flashed me was feral before leaning forward again and devouring me for my pleasure.

He licked at my clit, keeping a steady pressure as he

moaned softly, as if I were the most delicious dish he had ever savored. My mind became foggy with lust. I reached down and grabbed Dylan by his hair, not letting him leave.

My legs started to shake. The orgasm building inside of me was huge and threatened to drown me, but I wanted more. I needed to crest the final wave and his licks and nibbles were climbing me higher and higher until I was teetering on the edge of a cliff. And then, just as I was about to fall into glorious oblivion, Dylan stopped. I looked down at him, confusion clouding my senses, but then I felt it - a single finger pressing gently against my entrance.

My eyes widened as he slowly pushed it inside me, stretching me in a way that was both intimate and overwhelming. He curled his finger, feeling for that spot deep inside me that would send me soaring. As he pressed down, his tongue flicked back against my clit, and I lost myself to him.

The orgasm was unlike anything I had ever experienced before. My body shuddered and spasmed, every muscle contracting as my pleasure peaked. I felt as if I was being torn apart, yet somehow, I was still whole. The sensation was overwhelming, the intensity almost too much to bear. I clawed at the sheets, my body writhing and bucking as I rode out the wave of ecstasy.

But just as I began to come down from that first incredible high, Dylan shifted his position. He added another finger, filling me even more, and kept that same relentless pressure on my clit. It was too much, and yet, it was not enough. My body craved more, and Dylan was more than willing to give it to me.

The second orgasm hit me like a freight train. My

muscles clenched around his fingers, my body twisting and contorting as I cried out in pleasure. I felt as if I was falling, my senses swallowed by an cloud of bliss.

By the time my legs finally stopped shaking, I was beyond reasoning. I needed him to fuck me. I needed him inside me, to feel him fill me completely.

"Please," I whispered, my voice barely audible. "I need you now."

My words were desperate, my voice trembling with desire. Dylan looked up at me, a smile on his face, and slowly removed his fingers from my pussy.

He stood up, his erection straining against his boxers. I reached out, my fingers tracing the outline of his cock through the fabric. I could feel his heat, his desire, and it only intensified my own. I looked up at him, my eyes filled with longing.

Dylan nodded, his own desire evident in his eyes. He removed his boxers, revealing his thick, gorgeous cock. My heart raced at the sight of it, and I knew that I was ready.

He positioned himself at my entrance, his cock teasing me with how close he was to giving me what I wanted. I took a deep breath, my body preparing for the moment I had been craving. And then, with one powerful thrust, Dylan claimed me.

I nearly came just from that first thrust. He moved slowly at first, savoring the sensation of being inside me. I felt him hit that spot deep within me, the one he had been searching for with his fingers, and I moaned, shifting my hips to give him better access.

He picked up the pace, his thrusts becoming more forceful, more intense. I met each one with equal ferocity, my body moving in perfect sync with his. I could feel another orgasm building, but this time, it was different. It was deeper, more intimate.

He was so strong. His body moved with such ease that I knew his panting was from lust, not from working too hard. He held onto my hips, groaning whenever I shifted my weight to take more of him.

And I wanted all of him.

It was so easy to fall off the cliff of orgasm with him inside me. It was so easy with his muscles flexing and the way he looked at me.

My back arched again, and I felt my pussy clench down on his cock as he continued to thrust inside of me. I gripped the bed sheets and held on for dear life as that cock continued to piston inside of me, spreading me open.

"Lie down on your side," he commanded, tracing a finger down the curve of my breast. He pulled free of me, letting me roll onto my side.

I felt his muscular body lie down behind me, and he guided his cock between my legs. I was shocked at how wet I was down there, and how easily he slipped back into place like he belonged inside of me.

Dylan's hands moved from my legs to cup my breasts in his warm grasp. The sensation of his skin against my nipples made me gasp, and I arched my back, pressing myself into his touch. His hard chest pressed against my back, his hands cupping my breasts as our hips moved in tandem.

"Oh, God," I breathed, my voice barely above a whisper. "You feel so good."

Dylan's breathing grew ragged, his chest heaving as he found the rhythm that he needed.

He groaned, and his body began to shake even harder.

I could tell that he was giving it everything he could, and that his eruption would rock us both to our cores. Most of all, I knew that he was close.

"Natalie…" My name was a prayer on his lips.

"Don't stop," I begged, matching his increasing tempo. "Don't pull out. Don't stop. I want it. I want you."

He moaned, tucking his chin into my shoulder and kissing the skin there. His strength wrapped around me, consuming me and protecting me at the same time. I didn't want it to ever stop, except I craved feeling him lose himself to me.

I wanted this big strong man to lose control. I wanted to be the cause of it.

My name came whispered again, this time breathless and guttural as his body began to shake. His breathing grew ragged and every muscle in his body tensed.

And then, with a powerful thrust, he came apart inside of me.

The sensation of him filling me was overwhelming, and I cried out in pleasure, feeling his orgasm as if it was my own. My body shook around him, pleasure and lust vibrating through both our bodies as if they were the same creature.

Dylan held me close, his body shuddering as he pounded into me again and again, continuing to fill me. Even when I knew he had to be done, I didn't want it to stop. I didn't want this feeling, this bliss, to ever stop.

We lay there for a moment, our bodies tangled together, basking in the afterglow. His heart pounded a steady rhythm against my back, his arms still wrapped around me and my breasts in his hands.

He kissed my shoulder.

"Stay the night," he whispered, still six inches deep inside me.

I nodded. "On one condition."

He put three small kisses on the top of my shoulder. "Anything."

I smiled, turning my head to look at him.

"We do that again."

His grin lit up the room. "As you wish," he said. "I can't wait to taste you again, and again and again."

I chuckled, the sound low and rich. "I don't know if I can go that many times," I teased.

The cocky grin was back. "We'll see."

20

———

A WALK IN THE PARK WITH A GOAT

"Nursing is not a career… it's a post-apocalyptic survival skill."
—*Unknown*

NATALIE

I WOKE up in a strange room with a very warm, very large, very muscular arm draped possessively over me.

And I'd never felt happier.

My body ached in the most delicious way, and I had a feeling I would be walking crooked for at least the first half of the day, but I felt deliriously happy.

"Don't leave," Dylan mumbled, his face buried in his pillow.

"I don't have any clothes here," I whispered to him. "And I want to brush my teeth."

"Don't care. You still taste good to me," he replied, his eyes still shut.

I kissed his cheek. "I'll bring back breakfast."

One eye cracked open. "Burritos?"

I nodded. "Do you like the bacon or the chorizo?"

"Chorizo, extra green salsa." He didn't move his arm to let me up though.

I kissed his cheek again and slid out of bed, he groaned as he lost touch of my skin, but that half-open eye followed me with a hunger that had absolutely nothing to do with breakfast burritos.

I threw on my clothes from the day before and quickly slid out of the bedroom. I paused at the crib, making sure that Ellie was still fast asleep. We'd both woken up once during the night to take care of her, but it was easier with a partner. Plus, being able to slide right back into bed afterwards and snuggle up to Dylan made the getting up feel worth it.

Penelope brayed softly at the bathroom door as I walked past, but I didn't let her out. All she wanted to do was sit on the recliner and watch *Supernatural*. She was going to burn through all the seasons at this rate, and I wasn't sure she would be okay doing a rewatch. It was better to let her sleep in for a little bit longer. I didn't bother to put on shoes as I peeked out the front door and scampered back to my own apartment in the world's quickest and easiest walk of shame.

I brushed my teeth, did a very fast shower so that I felt clean and sexy, threw on comfortable weekend clothes and then ran downstairs. Since it was a Monday, the burrito cart was out front of our building. I ordered three, all with extra green salsa before heading back upstairs with a friendly wave to the front desk worker.

I headed back upstairs, humming the entire way up the elevator. When I walked back into Dylan's apartment, he had coffee going and a now awake baby in his arms. They both smiled when they saw me, making my heart suddenly feel too big and wonderful for my body.

A girl could get used to this.

"I have the day off," Dylan reminded me. "And so do you."

"I don't think my aunt will mind if we go back to the lake house..."

He grinned, his eyes lighting up. "I was thinking of a date."

I stopped with my coffee cup half way to my mouth. "A date?"

"Yeah, I know we're kind of doing everything out of order here. A kid, sex, then a date, but..." He shrugged. "Can I ask you to dinner tonight?"

My heart sped up and words failed me as nerves hit for the first time. I'd already slept with the man. I was already taking care of his child and his goat, but a date sounded... serious. I swallowed hard.

"Who will watch Ellie?" I asked, remembering that he didn't want to be seen in public with his daughter yet. Hopefully, the DNA results would be in soon, but I understood his need to keep the paparazzi away from this story for the time being.

"I already asked Alex. He said yes."

I raised a skeptical eyebrow.

"I have to pay him double." Dylan sighed and rubbed his forehead. "I had no idea how expensive kids were."

I laughed at his expression, knowing that I had heard many a parent lament the cost of a good babysitter.

"So, are you in?"

I didn't hesitate this time. "Yes. What do I need to wear?"

"If I said nothing..." He looked me up and down appreciatively.

"Then it wouldn't be a date. Dates take place in restaurants or bowling alleys," I informed him.

"Then it's a good thing I have reservations at La Chez."

I almost dropped my coffee mug, which would have been a true tragedy.

"You got reservations at La Chez?" I repeated. "Isn't there a six week waiting list?"

He grinned and shrugged nonchalantly. "Not when you're a world famous NFL player."

"Oh. I guess that does come with some perks," I agreed. I swallowed hard. At least I did have a dress that was appropriate for that nice of a restaurant. It was technically an old bridesmaid's dress, but luckily the bride had chosen something that could actually be worn again.

"I'll pick you up at six," he said, then paused. "Although, you are welcome to stay here until it's time to get ready. We'd love to have your company."

Ellie gurgled that she too would like me to stay.

I grinned. "I would love that. Thank you."

* * *

"I REALLY HOPE you aren't wearing that to La Chez." Alex looked me up and down, his face judgmental and unimpressed.

I was still in my comfy sweats and t-shirt, my hair piled up mom-style on the top of my head. I didn't have an ounce of makeup on my face and I smelled liked I'd spent the day taking care of a baby that liked to blurp milk onto my shirt, no matter how many burp clothes I put on my shoulder.

"You just have no sense of fashion," I informed him, striking a model pose. "I'm told this is all the rage in Paris."

"Yeah, for zombies," Alex retorted with a sniff and a wince at my smell. I knew it wasn't that bad. He was as bad as a little brother.

"Good thing you're here early then," I said, sticking my tongue out at him. "Watch me leave a mess and come back as Cinderella."

"Don't forget the pumpkin. Your goat will love it," Alex said, walking past me and into the apartment to flop on the couch. He looked around the apartment. "Where's my cutie-pie date for the night?"

"Your date is currently sleeping off her latest bottle," I said, picking up my things to return back to my own apartment. "Dylan's in the shower."

"You should join him." Alex wrinkled his nose again. "You really smell like baby barf."

I rolled my eyes at him, but he didn't see it. He was too busy hunting for the remote control to change the TV channel.

"I wouldn't change the show," I warned him. "Penelope only likes *Supernatural*. You may not like the results of watching something else."

"Penelope is a goat. She will adapt," Alex replied, holding up the remote victoriously as he pulled it from between two couch cushions. "Maybe she'll even like my show better."

"Good luck," I warned with a shrug and headed back to my apartment to get beautiful.

I didn't make it out of the door before I heard Alex shouting at Penelope to get off of him. I shook my head but didn't stop walking. He could figure out what to do with the goat. I needed to get ready.

Luckily, I was just high maintenance enough to know how to look good, but low maintenance enough that I could do it fast. Well, relatively fast. I did minimal makeup, but took my time with a smokey cat-eye look. I didn't bother to curl my hair, instead opting for a fancy-looking, but easy to do, french twist. My dress was dark red and strapless, with a slit up the thigh that made my legs look long and model-like.

I knew that I should probably wear heels, but I knew if I did I would be able to walk about three feet before they hurt my feet or I face-planted into a wall. So, nude flats for the win. I did not want to visit my workplace with an injury because I chose to wear inappropriate sexy shoes.

I double checked that I had indeed pulled off a Cinderella-worthy transformation and checked my watch to see I had minutes to spare. Just enough time to add some gold jewelry to make everything sparkle. Oh, and spray on a little bit of fancy perfume my aunt had bought me in France last year.

I finished the final touches just as the doorbell rang. I schooled my face into what I hoped was seductive and opened the door to see Alex with a baby on his hip and Dylan's front door hanging open.

"Where's Dylan?" I asked, looking up and down the

hallway. A roll of toilet paper decorated the hallway now, looping up and down the hallway in a messy pattern. It looked like an entire roll of paper towels had also been flung around as decoration for a terrible party.

"He's chasing the goat."

I slowly turned from the toilet paper mess to look at Alex. "What happened?"

"So... Penelope did not like my TV show..." He hefted Ellie up on his hip, looking everywhere but at me. "And so she threw a fit. I didn't know goats could throw temper tantrums, but she did. She got the toilet paper and..." He motioned to the mess in the hallway.

"And then?"

"And then she snuck onto the elevator. I don't even know how she did it, but that goat knew what buttons to press to make the door open!" he exclaimed. His cheeks were flushed and his voice had a tinge of panic rising with every word. "Dylan went after her, but..."

"I'll go help Dylan," I said, suddenly very glad I'd gone with the flats rather than the heels. "You clean this up and watch Ellie. I'll help Dylan catch Penelope, and then we can head out on our date once we have her."

I hit the elevator button and rode down, noticing that the paper products were not in the elevator. At least Penelope was nice enough to leave them all upstairs in the hallway.

"I told him not to turn off her show," I said under my breath, walking quickly through the apartment building's lobby. It was busy with evening traffic, everyone coming home from work and preparing for dinner, I hurried toward the front door where I could see Dylan's silhouette against the darkening sky outside.

"Dylan? Did you find her?" I asked, hurrying to join him on the sidewalk.

"Not yet." He turned to face me and stopped, going completely still. He looked me up and down, opened and closed his mouth twice, and then finally said, "Wow. You look amazing."

I blushed at the compliment, but before I could tell him how handsome he looked in his suit with his hair brushed back, Penelope tried to walk into oncoming traffic. "There she is!" I shouted. We both moved to get her out of the street, but she saw us coming and decided that we needed to play chase.

Without another word, we both took off after the goat. My feet slapped against the pavement as I tried to keep up with Dylan, who was surprisingly fast for someone in formal wear, but then I remembered that he did this for a living while wearing pads.

Penelope was nimble, weaving between pedestrians and dodging hot dog carts with the agility of a seasoned New York cabby. She bleated defiantly as she led us on a merry chase through the busy streets, drawing bewildered looks from passersby. Some people cheered us on, while others just stared as if seeing two people in formal wear chase a goat was a totally normal part of their day.

Maybe it was normal in Nebraska.

She slowed at a corner, deciding if she wanted to head into the park or down the alleyway. Both were good options for her- the park was full of grass and open spaces, but the alley had a trashcan full of restaurant leftovers.

"Penelope, come here," I called, making the clicking noise my aunt made when she took her up the elevator to the rooftop. "Come here, baby girl. I will get you all the cabbage you want if you come here."

Penelope took a small step toward me. Dylan moved off to the side, obviously setting up a play. I wondered if he was going to tackle Penelope like he was a linebacker instead of a tight end.

"That's it, girl..." I coaxed, squatting low and holding my hand out to her. I suddenly realized that I didn't bring her leash. I didn't have a halter, a rope, or anything to walk her back home with. I hoped that Dylan was wearing a belt or the walk home was going to be very interesting.

A car honked, probably because a man in a suit was about to tackle a woman in a dress talking to a goat. It was lucky no one had called the police on us yet. Unfortunately, the noise spooked Penelope and she bolted for the park. We both sighed and took off running.

Dylan, slightly ahead, glanced back with a grin. "I can't believe this is happening. You know, I did not have chasing livestock through the city on the agenda for our date tonight."

Somehow though, that seemed to fit with our lives in a way that made me feel happy.

"There's a first for everything!" I called back, laughter bubbling up from deep in my chest. Despite the insanity of it all, I felt a strange sense of joy. I wouldn't want to be chasing a goat down with anyone else. I definitely would have preferred to be eating a fancy meal at a fancy restaurant, but this wasn't awful. It wasn't a bad time, but the only reason it was good was because it was with Dylan.

We chased her deeper into the park, running along the walking paths in our dress clothes and passing people walking their dogs and pushing babies in strollers. Dylan was crazy fast, but I managed to keep up. I did have practice chasing patients down the halls, so this felt surprisingly familiar.

We both spotted the goat stopping to take a drink from the decorative fountain in the middle of the park. It was a huge cement fountain, the kind that kids threw pennies in to make a wish and Penelope was up on the sitting space, her head lowered as she took a deep drink.

Dylan and I slowed, not wanting to spook her again.

"Okay, so you distract her, and I'll… tackle her?" Dylan suggested, clearly unsure of his own plan.

I laughed again, shaking my head. "Distract her with what? My charm?"

"Couldn't hurt to try. You are quite charming."

"You're the one with goatskin experience," I countered.

He turned, clearly confused. "Goatskin?"

"Isn't that what they call the football?" I asked, suddenly pretty sure that wasn't one of the nicknames for a football.

"Pigskin," Dylan corrected me with a laugh. His shoulders shook as he tried to keep the laughter contained. "I play the pigskin."

"Same difference." Rolling my eyes but still smiling, I gingerly approached the fountain. I was so close I could almost touch her. "Penelope," I cooed, trying to sound soothing. "Why don't you come down from there and—"

Before I could finish, Penelope let out a triumphant bleat and jumped into the water, splashing water everywhere and all over me. My squawk of surprise made her jump again, this time out of the fountain and directly into Dylan's knees.

"Watch out!" I shouted, but it was too late. The goat

barreled into Dylan's legs, sending him stumbling backward into a nearby bench with an undignified *oof*. It was a tackle fit for the NFL.

"Are you okay?" I asked, trying to keep my giggles contained as he lay flat on his back in the dirt.

Penelope stood just off to the side, munching on a patch of grass like this was a completely normal thing to do.

"I'm just really glad Coach didn't see that," Dylan grumbled, rolling to his side and getting up. He had dirt all down his back, across his knees, and his hair was a mess. I had a feeling I didn't look much better.

"Well," I said, looking down at my water-splattered dress, "I don't think we're making it to the restaurant."

Dylan chuckled, reaching over and smoothing a huge strand of hair out of my face. I could feel my hair falling out of the up-do and catching in the late summer wind. "Probably not."

We stood there for a moment, catching our breath and trying to process the absurdity of it all. Finally, Dylan turned to me with a sheepish grin. "We can still do dinner. Maybe somewhere where they serve goat?"

I laughed, knowing that he was joking. Although, I did know a kebab place that made the best lamb. That probably counted.

Dylan slipped off his belt, and I let my eyes watch the movement, suddenly hungry for something that had nothing to do with food. With a smooth and easy motion, he had his belt wrapped around Penelope's neck like a leash. She didn't balk or bleat. She let us catch her easily now that she had eaten some grass and had some fountain water. She walked docile alongside us like a very strange pet dog as we exited the park and returned to the apartment.

Alex snapped to attention as we entered the apartment, relief and then horror crossing his face as he saw us march the goat in.

"What happened to you guys?" he asked, his eyes wide as he looked us over.

"We have decided to order in for the night," I said.

21

JUST LIKE REAL PARENTS

Reporter: Coach, what do you think of your team's execution?
John McKay: I'm in favor of it.

Dylan

"Alex, you watch the baby," I said to my assistant. "Natalie and I will be cleaning up. You are also responsible for answering the doorbell for the food."

"Roger that, boss," Alex said, apparently realizing that Natalie was in no mood to joke around.

I pulled two glasses from the cabinet and poured Natalie and I each a shot of whiskey.

I'd had NFL games with less running and tackling than I had tonight. I could already feel the sore spot on my back where I'd hit the ground. It was easier to hit the ground with pads on. Hurt less.

Natalie accepted the drink with two hands, taking a long sip of whiskey and sighing with pleasure. Alex watched her, apparently figuring out that our goat chase had worn us both out.

It didn't help that I hadn't had a full night of sleep all week. I felt like I could curl up on the couch and pass out, but I wanted to spend time with Natalie. I wanted to take her on a fancy date, but her wet dress and my muddy suit were not going to allow that tonight.

It was time to change plans.

Alex turned the TV to *Supernatural* and turned up the volume. He settled with Ellie on the couch and Penelope went to her easy chair. She did not look like she'd just ran several miles and bathed in a fountain. She looked like she'd just had a wonderful outing and was incredibly pleased with herself.

Damn goat.

Natalie followed me into the bedroom, closing the door behind us.

"So, should we just order Chinese food then?" I asked.

"Now wait just a minute. I'm sure I can get the mud off this dress," Natalie said, rubbing at the fabric. "Well, some of it anyway."

"Even if you could, my suit needs a full trip to the dry cleaners," I said, picking a rather large piece of grass out of the fabric.

Natalie pouted and crossed her arms in front of her chest. "When are we going to get another chance to go to La Chez?"

"Anytime we want," I said. "Well, that is, until that goat ends my football career early."

Natalie's pout didn't go away. "She didn't hit you that hard."

"I don't know," I said. I winced as I took a shoe off. "I might need you to take a look. You know, as a medical professional."

The teensiest weensiest hint of a smile crossed her lips. "Oh, really?"

"Not only did those horns connect with my legs, but she also knocked me flat on my ass. And you know how important my ass is."

Now she cracked a real smile. "How can you play football with a broken ass?"

"Exactly, that's what I'm saying!" I said.

"I suppose I better check out your ass," she said. She stepped toward me.

"Well, while we're doing that, I might as well have you check out my whole body."

"I can already see your muddy hands," she said. "And your hair is a mess. I'm going to say that practice is over and it's time to hit the showers!"

I grinned. "Yes, ma'am!"

I nodded, my eyes following Natalie's hands as she carefully unbuttoned my jacket. Her fingers brushed against my chest as she slid it off my shoulders. The fabric was stiff with dried mud, and it made a soft crunching sound as she set it aside.

"Arms up," she instructed, and I complied, letting her pull my dress shirt over my head rather than struggle with the buttons. Her touch was clinical, but I couldn't help the way my skin tingled wherever her fingers grazed.

She knelt down to untie my shoes, and I steadied myself with a hand on her shoulder. As she worked the laces, I noticed a smudge of dirt on her cheek. Without thinking, I reached down to brush it away.

Natalie looked up at me, a small smile playing on her lips. "Thanks," she murmured, before returning her attention to my shoes.

Once my shoes and socks were off, she stood and hooked her fingers into the waistband of my pants. "These are a lost cause," she said, shaking her head as she helped me step out of them.

Now in just my boxers, I felt oddly vulnerable. Natalie's eyes roamed over my body, but her gaze was analytical rather than appreciative. She frowned as she noticed the bruises forming on my legs from where the goat head butted me.

"Turn around," she instructed, and I did so, wincing slightly at the twinge in my back.

I heard her sharp intake of breath. "Oh, Dylan. Your back..."

"That bad, huh?"

"You're going to have quite the bruise," she said, her fingers ghosting over what I assumed was a tender spot on my lower back. "You might need a massage later, but for now, you just need to clean up."

I made an exaggerated sigh. "I suppose if I must clean up, at least I'll have you to help me."

She laughed. "We really are doing this all backwards," she said. "I was really looking forward to our date tonight."

"Look, let's just take a quick shower together, and then we can go out and do whatever you want, as long as it doesn't require a suit."

She did a once-over of my body, settling on the bulge in

my underwear for a few extra seconds. "Alright, I guess that sounds like a good deal. Unzip me."

I walked toward her and she turned around. I could smell the perfume that she put on for me, now tainted by the smell of mud and goat. Still, as I unzipped her dress and watch it fall away, revealing a black bra and thong, I found I could ignore all of that.

She turned around and caught me staring. "Go turn on the water, or we'll never leave this apartment."

As much as it pained me to turn around before she was completely naked, I did as she said. I was still checking the water before she pressed her body up against me. I faced her and stared at her naked breasts, and she gave me another once-over.

"You can't get in with your underwear on," she said. She dropped to her knees, grabbing my briefs and pulling them down. My cock sprang out, hard as a rock and pointed directly at her face. She grabbed onto it and caressed it a little bit. "Oh yeah, this definitely needs to be cleaned off."

I put my hands behind my back, sure that she was going to start to suck it, but instead, she just stood back up and got in the shower. "Time's a wastin'," she said as she took some of my soap and began to lather herself up using my shower poof.

I couldn't believe my eyes. She hummed as the water sluiced down her body, not a care in the world as she scrubbed the mud off of her perfect skin. She looked back at me, then ran the shower poof over her breasts. Every inch of her was slick with soap and water.

"Are you coming or what?" she asked.

I jumped in the shower, and my hands were on her

immediately. I ran my hands all over her body. As if she was immune to my charms, she used the shower poof to get the mud off of me while I touched every bit of her that I could. Her skin was slick with soap and water, making her feel even more incredible under my fingertips.

She made sure to gingerly dab at my legs, then moved around to my ass. She kneaded the flesh with one hand as she worked the poof over me with her other hand.

When she got to my cock, she put the shower poof down and put extra soap in her hands. With both hands, she massaged my cock, jerking me off. Her touch was gentle but firm, just the way I liked it. With one hand, she moved down to my balls, lathering them up and making them all slippery as well.

I leaned against the shower wall, closing my eyes and letting out a soft groan. "Natalie," I whispered, my voice barely audible over the sound of the water.

She looked up at me and smiled, her eyes sparkling. "Just relax," she said. "Let me take care of you."

And so, with the water cascading down on us, she continued her sensual massage. Soon, I regained my senses, touching her softly. I explored her body, working my way up her stomach to her breasts, then kneading them and enjoying how they felt all wet and soapy.

All the while, she took care of me in the most intimate way possible.

My heart felt lighter than it had in months. I felt cared for, not just desired. I was *wanted.*

She rose to her toes, pressing a kiss to my lips. The taste of soap and water mingled with the heat between us. I could feel her heart beating faster, matching the rhythm of my own. My hands roamed over her wet, soapy body, exploring every curve and contour as we explored the other's mouth.

As our kiss intensified, I began to thrust at her, pressing my cock between her legs. She let out a soft moan, her fingers digging into the skin of my back as she moved against me. The water cascaded around us, creating a soothing background noise that droned out the rest of the world. We were alone here. Just the two of us.

Natalie broke the kiss, her eyes filled with desire as she looked up at me. "I want you inside me," she whispered, her voice barely audible over the sound of the water.

"I want you," I said, unable to say any more with all my blood out of my brain and in my dick.

"But I need you to be fast," she said, her face stern. "I still need to be wined and dined. I am a lady, even if I'm not dressed like it anymore."

"Do I look like the kind of guy that likes to give a wham, bam, thank you ma'am?" I asked sarcastically.

"If you're quick now, we can have a second round later," she said, somehow being a tease and a sexpot at the same time.

I just nodded. She made sure to rinse my dick off completely, the water washing away the soap. Then, with a gentle grip, she stood on her tiptoes and guided me to her entrance. Her fingers traced the length of my cock before finally guiding me into her.

Every muscle in me relaxed and tightened at the feel of her warmth and wetness as I pushed against her, the head of my cock barely entering her. Her eyes closed, and she let out a soft sigh, her body tensing as I continued to push forward.

As I slowly slid deeper into her, her sighs turned into

moans, our bodies moving together in a slow, sensual rhythm. The water splashed against us, mingling with the sounds of our love making.

I held her close, our bodies pressed together as I thrust into her. I could feel her heart beating faster, her breaths coming in short gasps as she responded to each movement.

Suddenly, she stepped back, making me gasp with the lack of her around me. She just flashed me a grin, grabbed her wet hair, threw it over her back and turned around. Then, she got back up on her tiptoes, showing me that delicious ass of hers with a welcoming wiggle.

I grabbed onto her hips and took her from behind, causing her to yelp a little bit. I loved this view of her. Her wet hair slid down her back with water trickling down to her fabulous ass. It was hot as hell. Soon we were in a fantastic rhythm, and I knew I wouldn't last long.

I leaned forward, cupping her breasts in my hands and leaning down to her ear. "I'm gonna come," I said through gritted teeth.

Her response was immediate, a soft, desperate moan echoing in the shower enclosure. "Please," she begged, her body writhing under my touch. "Please come inside me."

I let out a low groan, unable to resist her plea. With a final, powerful thrust, I drove myself deep inside her wet body. The sensation as the first spurt shot out of me was was incredible, so intense that it was almost over-whelming.

As I came, I experienced an incredible release, a rush of pleasure that surged through my entire body. I felt every muscle tensing, every nerve firing, as the pulses of my orgasm reverberated deep inside her. I gripped her hips even tighter as I pumped deeper and deeper inside of her.

The warmth of my release filled her, our bodies becoming one in that moment of pure, unadulterated pleasure. It was an intimate bond, a connection that transcended words.

After several long moments, I slowly pulled out of her, my body still tingling from the aftershocks. I watched as her body continued to convulse, the last remnants of her own orgasmic release shuddering through her.

We stood there for a while, just catching our breath, enjoying the shared warmth of the shower. Eventually, wordlessly, we began to wash up, the water washing away the evidence of our passionate encounter, along with the remainder of the mud from our wild goat chase.

As we stepped out of the shower, she wrapped herself in a towel, her eyes sparkling with contentment.

"So, what'll it be tonight?" I asked. "We can go bowling, or I heard there's a new axe throwing place a few blocks away."

For a moment, I thought she was going to suggest we continue our plans for the night, but instead, she surprised me.

"Can we just order Chinese food?" she asked, a shy smile crossing her face. "We can send Alex home and stay in with the baby."

"Oh, is throwing an axe not your style?" I asked. "There's an escape room that I've been meaning to try."

She kept smiling as she shook her head. "I just don't really feel like going out anymore for some reason," she said as she wrapped her arms around her tummy, obviously still in her sexual afterglow.

I smiled, feeling a sense of relief wash over me. Despite our earlier exertions, the thought of spending an evening indoors, curled up with her and the baby, was incredibly appealing.

"Of course," I agreed. "We can do that."

And so we sent Alex home, and settled in for the night. As we sat on the couch, the baby snuggled between us, I reached for the remote. With a sigh, I turned on another episode of *Supernatural,* even though I couldn't care less what happened to Sam and Dean today.

Cradling Ellie, Natalie laid down next to me, resting against my shoulder. She threw her legs over mine. As I leaned down and kissed the top of her head, I heard her give a happy sigh.

We watched the show in comfortable silence, our bodies entwined, our heartbeats synchronized. This wasn't the night we had planned, but it was so much better.

And, after the way she had refused going back out, it was no surprise to me to hear her snoring softly instead of the promised "second round". And I barely made it past when Dean figured out who the real monster of the week was.

My last thought was how we were like a couple of tired parents instead of a couple of new lovers, and that that was just fine by me.

22

FOOD IS LOVE

If you ever want to get punched in the throat by ER staff, just say the words "Sure is quiet around here" in the middle of their shift.

NATALIE

"AND THEN EVERYTHING WENT ALL FUZZY," the kid on the gurney told me. He shrugged, his eyes fading out for a moment before he refocused back to me. "At least the cheerleaders all came to the sideline when I fell. They're pretty."

He smiled, his eyes going blank as he remembered the pretty girls all looking at him. At least the pain meds were working.

"So you got hit on the field during a high school football practice," I repeated. "You hit your head and you hurt your knee."

He nodded lazily. "The medicine is making the knee feel a lot better. I bet I could go home now." He started to get up to his feet.

"Oh no you don't," I quickly said, putting my hand on his shoulder and keeping him on the gurney. "We loaded you up with some pretty good drugs."

My patient frowned. "I'm not supposed to do drugs. I don't think my mom will be happy with me."

"You have permission to take these drugs," I reassured him. "These are okay drugs."

"Oh." His face relaxed out of the frown, but he still looked unhappy. "I feel funny. I don't think I like drugs."

"Sorry about that," McKenna, the EMT replied as she gathered her supplies to return back to the ambulance. "Poor guy was not a happy camper on the way here. His knee is pretty messed up."

"I don't like camping," our patient agreed.

"I called his mom," McKenna continued, ignoring the puppy dog eyes the teen was giving her. "She said she would meet us at the hospital."

"Can you stay, pretty lady?" our patient asked, smiling at McKenna. "I like your uniform. And you gave me drugs."

I arched an eyebrow at her. "He seems a bit young for you."

She rolled her eyes and blatantly stole the pen off my computer cart.

"Everyone likes me after I make the pain go away," McKenna replied. She smiled at the teen boy. "Good luck, Kid."

He smiled at her, the joy in it wavering as soon as she left the room.

"I'm not going to be playing football for a while, am I?" he asked softly, looking down at his leg. We had it hidden under a blanket, but it was already swelling and didn't look good.

I sighed. "Probably not. This looks like a pretty decent injury. And you banged your head really hard. We're going to run some more tests to make sure you're okay."

He nodded slowly, as if the motion required effort. "Man, this sucks. I was having a great season."

He slumped back on the gurney, tears starting to trickle down his face.

"You okay?" I asked, stopping the charting to put my hand on his arm.

"I just... I thought I could go pro, you know?" His voice grew thick with tears. "I was supposed to start this Saturday. I was supposed to play. I'm really good." He looked at me with suddenly wild eyes. "Can you fix it? Can you make it so I can play?"

Hope shone behind fear-filled eyes.

I wanted to lie to the kid. I wanted to tell him that through the miracle of modern medicine, we would have him out the door with a band-aid and some pills and that everything would be fine.

But his knee was bent in a completely unnatural position. He had a concussion that was bad enough to require a CT scan.

I couldn't predict the future, but I had a sinking feeling that this kid's football hopes and dreams were over. If he was lucky there wouldn't be lasting damage, but given the severity of his knee, I suspected he would have future pain and issues with it as a result of this accident.

All for a stupid game.

Why Dylan liked this stupid sport was beyond me. Was it really worth risking the ability to walk without pain to smash into another person and try to steal their ball?

Before I could say anything that I might regret, the curtain pulled back and a woman with the same soft brown hair as the boy ran in. She wrapped her arms around him, kissing his head and yelling at him that she was so glad he was okay.

"The doctor will be in shortly," I told them both, wanting to get out of the room. I didn't want to answer the mother's questions about the severity of the injury. I didn't want to destroy the hopes and dreams of this kid. Sure, there was a chance he would come back from this game and go pro, but the odds were not in his favor. Besides, I needed to go find the doctor to get his orders. It would be nice when I was a nurse practitioner and could just order the CT scan myself and save us all time.

I didn't even make it three steps before a trauma alert went off and two staff members sprinted past me toward the ambulance bay.

It was going to be a long night.

How's your night going, gorgeous?

I glanced around the nurses station, making sure that my boss wouldn't see me checking my personal phone. I'd been running like crazy all night and my feet hurt. I finally found a little time to sit and chart in between codes and injuries. I wondered if it was a full moon because we seemed busier than usual.

But Dylan's text made me smile and feel a little lighter.

What are you doing awake? I texted back, seeing that it was a little after four in the morning.

Ellie thought it was a good time to stare at the moon, came the reply. Then I remembered he had a newborn.

I wish it was you keeping me up, the text continued. *I'm going to be dreaming of the feeling of your body for a long time.*

A happy flush washed over me.

So, how's your night going? he asked. I imagined him standing in the kitchen wearing just his pajama pants, cradling Ellie as she sucked down a bottle.

It's been busy. I didn't get to the cafeteria and they're closed, so I'm going to see if I can steal some graham crackers and jello for dinner.

I thought about some of the meals I'd eaten with Dylan and my stomach grumbled. I'd forgotten to bring my lunch and the hospital cafeteria was only open from midnight to two. It opened again for breakfast at five, but that felt like a long time away.

I tucked my phone away, not wanting to get caught. Besides, I had so much charting to catch up on I needed to focus or I would never leave in the morning.

Ten minutes later, I stood up from the nurses' station and stretched, feeling my spine pop. My stomach gurgled again and I wished there was something better than pilfered graham crackers or a stale bag of chips from the vending machine on the second floor.

"Uh, Natalie?" Sherri, my charge nurse waived to get my attention. I turned, already mentally preparing for a lecture or a new patient. Instead, she surprised me. "You have a visitor."

"At almost four in the morning?" I asked but secretly hoped it was Dylan. I would need to strangle him for bringing a baby to the ER and exposing her to germs, but I liked the idea of getting to see him.

"They're in the lobby," Sherri replied. "And good job tonight."

I thanked her and headed out to the lobby where I stopped dead in my tracks. It was not Dylan in the waiting room, but Alex. Alex with two plastic grocery bags and a very grumpy expression.

"Did you know that nothing good is open at three in the morning?" he informed me as I approached him.

"What are you doing here?" I asked. "Are you okay? What's wrong?"

"Other than my boss waking me up before the butt crack of dawn to bring his girlfriend dinner? No. I'm fine."

"You brought me dinner?" I asked, taking a closer look at the various containers stashed under his arm. My stomach growled.

"Do you have a break room or someplace I can set this down?" he asked, shifting his weight uncomfortably. He glanced around the waiting room, noticing that the three visitors and the security guard were all watching him. If they were half as hungry as I was, it was a miracle they hadn't jumped him for the food in his hands. I could smell melty cheese and taco spices from the bags.

"This way," I said, scanning my badge and bringing him back. I waved at my charge nurse and pointed to my stomach. She nodded and pointed to the board. The message was clear: it's okay to eat because it's calm right now. If it gets busy, you come out.

The break room was tucked off in a back corner of the ER. We had a coffee machine, a fridge from the late eighties, and six old plastic chairs from the same time frame. Only two of the chairs were comfortable and they were both tucked under a very worn Formica table in the center of the room. There were no windows in case we wanted to escape. No expenses were spared for this part of the hospital.

McKenna stood at the empty coffee machine, looking annoyed. It had been a crazy night for her too.

Alex thrust out the plastic bags. "It's my mom's salsa, enchiladas, and a couple of tamales."

"Did you say tamales?" McKenna interrupted, walking up behind me and resting her elbow on my shoulder. She gave me a gentle push. "You know you're sharing, right?"

"I will bite you if you touch my food," I growled at her, twisting away from her and guarding my now precious food bag like an angry dragon.

She laughed and winked at Alex. "Don't get between a girl and her food," she told him. "I was going to grab an energy drink from the vending machine upstairs. The good one. Do you want anything?"

I shook my head, my mouth already salivating for the food. The first bag held various plastic containers along with a Ziploc baggie filled with homemade tortilla chips. I popped open the lid to the first container and breathed in the scent of tomatoes, peppers, and cilantro. I moaned with delight as I I took a chip out of the bag, dipping it into the fresh pico de gallo. My entire body, not just my mouth, did a little happy dance as the food filled me with warmth.

"Alex, where did you get this? It's so good!" I said, settling down at the table and opening the container to the enchiladas. They were cold, but they tasted so good I didn't care. The nursing commission should just be glad I wasn't snarfing this food with my bare hands. I was barely managing to eat it like a human being.

"My mom. She grew up in the States, but *mi abuela* insisted that she learn how to cook," Alex explained. He leaned against the wall, watching me eat and glancing at the door leading out to the hallway.

"She is amazing," I mumbled through a mouth full of food. "Does she give lessons?"

"Only when she's mad," Alex replied. "This stuff was from dinner. If she found out I gave it away, she'd kill me."

I stopped eating. "Alex, I don't want to get you in trouble..."

"No, no." He frantically shook his head. "She'd only be mad because this isn't her best. This is *leftovers*, not the stuff she gives to guests. She'd be so embarrassed to know you were snarfing what she made without thinking."

I happily continued stuffing my face. "It's still amazing. She can give me leftovers anytime."

"Don't tell her that," Alex said with a wince. "But my usual three A.M. restaurant is closed for repairs and there was nothing else open. So you get what was in my fridge."

"And I am so incredibly grateful," I told him, still stuffing enchilada into my mouth and trying to savor the taste before adding more. It was so spicy and good.

"Nat, they are out of the orange kind, so I let Sherri know. She says they'll restock the vending machine tomorrow," McKenna said popping her head into the break room. I noticed she kept her orange energy drink carefully hidden behind the wall.

I nodded, my mouth too full of food to say anything else. She laughed and headed off to the nurses' station to probably fill out paperwork and steal our pens.

"Who's that?" Alex asked, his eyes following her out the doorway.

"Who, McKenna?" I swallowed my bite and grinned at him. He stared after her, mouth open. "She's single, you know."

I was rewarded with his face turning a fabulous shade of crimson. He started stuttering and couldn't complete a sentence denying that he was interested.

"She's cool. She likes football and video games. You two would get along," I said, finally slowing down on inhaling my enchiladas enough to manage complete sentences.

"Now you're just being mean. She's way out of my league." Alex glanced wistfully at the doorway again.

"You brought me food at four A.M. The least I can do is play wing-man," I replied, popping another chip loaded with salsa into my mouth. I tried to savor it. It was about to be my last. "I'll even try not to be obvious."

Alex narrowed his eyes and crossed his arms. "I don't believe you."

I sighed and picked up the delicious container of home-made salsa.

"I want you to know how much I want to eat this. It's the best salsa I have ever had. I want it very clear to you that this is not too spicy. It's perfect. I'm doing this for you." I put the lid on the salsa and gave it a fond, but sad, little pat before standing up. I took a step out of the break room and saw McKenna at the Nurses' station filling out paperwork using the hospital pens. "Hey, McKenna. You like spicy stuff, right?"

The girl perked right up like I'd said magic words. Paperwork and pen forgotten, she hurried back over to the break room to join me.

"This salsa is too spicy for me," I lied, making a disgusted face. "Alex made it himself. You want it?"

Alex's eyes bounced between me and McKenna as he nervously swallowed.

"Salsa?" McKenna grinned and grabbed the container from me with gusto. She slid into one of the plastic chairs at the table and stole my chips to try out the salsa. I made sure to give Alex a look that said *"look how much you owe me."*

"Oh man," McKenna groaned. "This is really good stuff."

"Yeah..." I gazed longingly at the salsa. "You should know that Alex delivers this stuff. You should get his number."

"You deliver fresh salsa?" McKenna asked, her eyes going to Alex and suddenly seeing him in a new light. She fluttered her eyelashes at him.

"Yeah. *Mi abuela* taught me how to make it, so it's super authentic," Alex replied, managing to sound smooth.

"Alex works for my neighbor," I explained to McKenna. "Usually, I love his salsa, but for whatever reason, it's just not doing it for me tonight. My loss is your gain, though."

"I would love to get more of this," McKenna said, biting her lower lip. Food was her love language.

Alex's chest puffed out just a little bit and he grinned at her. "I also make really good tamales."

I made sure to hide the container with tamales a little deeper in the plastic bag before tucking it into the staff fridge. I was willing to give up my salsa, but the tamales were not for sharing.

"Well, I have to get back to patients," I said, washing my hands and making sure I hadn't left a mess. "McKenna, will you make sure Alex makes it out of the ER?"

"Yeah, I can do that." McKenna didn't look at me, but she grinned at Alex.

I left the two of them in the break room to flirt.

23

―――――

DO I HATE FOOTBALL NOW?

The best way to gain more yards is advance the ball down the field from the line of scrimmage."
-John Madden

DYLAN

"CAN you just catch the fucking ball for once?" Marcus screamed at me. Anger vibrated off every inch of him as he ripped the helmet from his head and stomped down the field in my direction. Cameron moved to stop him, but Marcus gave him a death glare that made the entire team shrink away.

I bent and picked up the ball from the grass. It had slipped through my fingers yet again. *I'd caught it.* I'd caught it, but I hadn't been able to hold onto it. I felt the bumps on the ball against the tips of my fingers, rough and grippy. I should have been able to hold onto it. There was no reason why the damn thing should have flown out of my hands and into the grass.

Yet there it was.

"Do you want a fucking interception?" Marcus was beet red as he got up in my face. I had a couple of inches on him, but his anger had me shrinking away. "Are you trying to be the worst in the league? Are you trying to get kicked off the team?"

He slapped the ball out of my hands as if to show just how easy it was to get the ball away from me. My wrist twinged as it twisted with the momentum and I winced.

"If your wrist is still that fucked up, I don't want you playing," Marcus announced, his voice now low and dangerous. Disgust twisted his features as he looked at my empty hands. "Get your act together, Callahan."

He stalked off before the coaches could come out and break up the fight that was clearly brewing. I just stood there like an idiot.

I didn't know what Marcus's problem with me was. He hadn't said more than two words to me since the accident last season. I knew he'd come to visit me in the hospital. He'd sent flowers that were the first thing I'd seen when I'd woken up from surgery, but I hadn't seen him.

He was avoiding me and yet could find the energy to scream obscenities at me when I failed.

"Fuck this," I whispered, rubbing at my injury. It ached more than usual today. This last catch had hit my hand funny, bending my wrist. Maybe that was why I'd dropped it. This damn wrist. This damn injury. Hate, anger, shame, fear, and panic started to well up in my chest.

Why couldn't I get past this? It was just a broken bone. I'd broken bones before. I'd given my body to the game harder than this one injury. I had a dozen concussions and probable brain damage that was worse than this stupid wrist injury.

Yet this was what was going to ruin me.

"Go cool down and hit the showers," Coach yelled at me from across the field. I realized that Marcus had left the field which meant that we couldn't run plays anymore. I was alone on the field. I sighed, feeling defeat weigh my shoulders. I nodded to Coach. I didn't need to have him go over ball catching procedure with me again. We'd already run drills for two hours today to help me practice.

It obviously wasn't working.

I wondered if the practice field could just swallow me whole. I could live underground here and finally get some sleep.

But I would miss Natalie. I was glad she didn't follow football or know anything about the game. She'd be so disappointed in me if she knew how badly I was doing at practice while she watched my daughter. My daughter should be ashamed of me too. A tight end that can't even catch a ball was not a good father figure.

I walked slowly off the field toward the locker rooms.

A couple of kids on the berm watching practice yelled down to me. "Hey! Callahan! Can we get your autograph?"

My mood brightened slightly. Two boys, probably in middle school or high school whooped with joy as I climbed up the grass to where the visitors were allowed to watch the preseason practices. We usually had a pretty good sized crowd, but it was the end of the day so only the die-hard fans were left watching.

The boys eagerly held out the hats they'd gotten today as entry gifts. They'd already gotten dozens of signatures and there wasn't much room for me to sign the baseball caps, but I managed to find a space and add my name to the group.

"Thanks. This will probably be worth a ton when you're traded," one of the boys remarked, carefully stowing the cap in his bag.

My stomach dropped.

"Yeah, my dad says we shouldn't have even bothered. You're going to end up homeless and broke with the way you're playing," the other boy remarked. "He says your sponsorships are going to start drying up."

His friend elbowed him hard in the gut.

"Oh, sorry. Thanks for signing the caps, Mr. Callahan," the first boy said, glaring at his friend.

"You boys keep watching the team," I said, my voice sounding distant and far away.

The two boys walked away, leaving me dumbfounded.

Homeless and broke. I wasn't too worried about that actually happening, but if I kept playing this badly, the kid was right. The sponsorships would dry up. We'd had a big meeting about financial literacy every year since I'd started playing professionally. It wasn't uncommon for players to blow through their NFL money, and once they weren't playing, there wasn't anymore coming in. A lot of players really did end up broke and homeless, or barely scraping by.

I couldn't do that to my daughter. She deserved

someone who she could look up to. Someone that could provide for her.

My hand ached and I looked down at it, rubbing the scar lines.

I didn't bother going to the showers. I just threw on my clothes and left. The car was hot and sticky, the leather seats squeaking with my sweat. I let the car cool down for a moment before pulling out to drive home, letting the radio wash over me. My lawyer still hadn't emailed me the results to the DNA test. It was still early, but the fact that it wasn't done yet still made me anxious.

I fiddled with the radio, needing something to calm my nerves. Nothing good was playing so I flipped through the channels pausing only when I heard my name.

"Callahan just isn't playing like he used to," the radio voice proclaimed. It was one of the regular announcers on a local sports show. I'd met him a few times and he was a decent guy. "If he keeps this up, the team is going to trade him."

The words were an eerie echo of the day.

"Inside sources say that the owners of the Omaha Twisters are considering a trade. He just isn't worth the money so far this season. Technically, he's still out on medical leave, but he's just not showing his potential at these preseason practices. If he plays this weekend, we'll see if they keep him. If he doesn't play, I'd trade him. He's just too much money for not enough play."

My shoulders slumped low enough they could press the car's brakes.

"There's apparently an offer from the Chicago Bears, but it would be a fraction of his current salary," the radio continued.

"That may end up being a bad deal for the Bears!" the other announcer replied. The two men on the radio laughed like it wasn't my life on the line.

I couldn't move up north. I'd lose Alex. He'd never leave his family, even for me, and I couldn't ask him to. And Natalie? She had her job and school here. Besides, she'd only known me a month. It would be stupid for her to chase me across the country at this point. And what about Ellie?

I hit the radio button off with a little more force than necessary, my breathing harsh in the stuffy silence of the hot car. The owners *should* trade me. I was a liability at this point. Not an asset.

Maybe I should just quit while I was ahead. I still had enough fame to get some sponsorships. It might be enough.

But I wouldn't be happy. I loved this game. I loved playing. If I quit now, I would forever regret it. I wasn't ready to quit. Besides, I didn't know how my world would make sense without football. Football was how I knew it was summer. Football was how I celebrated holidays. Football was all I knew, and if I gave it up, I might as well crawl into a grave and throw on some dirt.

I revved the engine, gunning my car out of the parking lot and onto the highway.

I didn't have a plan. I just needed to get home to someone who could make me feel like it might end up okay.

24

BE CAREFUL WHICH LUBE YOU CHOOSE

The best part about working in the ER isn't saving lives. It's the unlimited access to the blanket warmer.

-Unknown

Natalie

"Dance party!"

I spun Ellie around as music blared from Dylan's expensive speakers. Penelope was still upstairs with my aunt, so I didn't have to worry about her delicate ears or stepping on her as Ellie and I danced and spun. Ellie giggled, her little hands gripping onto my shirt as we dipped and ballerina twirled to the beat. It wasn't graceful. It wasn't pretty, but it was fun and it felt good to move my body.

"Shake it, baby!" Dylan wolf-whistled. I turned to see

him standing at the door, a grin on his face as he watched the baby and I get our groove thang on.

I stuck my tongue out at him but kept shaking my money maker. I wasn't about to stop. It was a good song.

When the song ended, I hit the volume to the speakers and brought Ellie over to him. She gurgled and cooed, snuggling into his chest like she'd missed him all day.

"Nice moves," Dylan said, giving me a sweet kiss on the cheek. He smelled like sweat and dead grass, making me wrinkle my nose when he got close.

"You stink," I informed him. I was surprised that Ellie didn't object to snuggling up next to him, but she was already giving him happy sleepy eyes. A bottle and she would be out, which made me hopeful for a wonderful evening. I didn't have to leave for work until eleven since I was only taking an eight-hour shift tonight, so I could stay with Dylan and Ellie until they went to bed. As much as I would have rather stayed and watched my two favorite people sleep, I needed to get my student loans taken care of.

"Want to shower with me?" He grinned, a mischievous sparkle in his eyes. "You could wash my back. I can wash yours."

"My, what a gentleman," I replied, fluttering my hand like a fan and affecting a terrible Southern belle accent.

He laughed, heading to the kitchen to make Ellie her bottle. With a push of the button and a whir of the machine, he had a bottle in his daughter's mouth. She sighed dramatically as she chugged on the formula.

"Starving my kid, huh?" he teased, raising an eyebrow at me and winking.

"Yup. It's the only way to keep her from growing up

and attending college and leaving us with nothing to do except debate *Supernatural*," I replied, leaning against the back of the couch and smiling at him. He was such a big man and Ellie was so tiny in his arms that it was hard to believe she was his. It wasn't hard to believe that he loved her, though. He cradled her carefully to him, watching her every move and making sure that she was safe and well cared for.

He smiled down at his daughter. "I swear she's grown just in the past week. She'll be taller than me in no time."

I scoffed. The man was well over six feet. She wasn't even two feet at this point.

"I bet she'll be smart," I said, coming to join him in the kitchen. "She looks like a reader to me."

"And math. She's going to be good at math, I can feel it," he agreed.

Ellie didn't pay any attention to either one of us. She was focused entirely on getting the contents of her bottle in her belly before she fell asleep. Her eyes were getting heavy, but she was determined. She sucked down the last of the bottle and let out a little burp.

"Such a lady," I commented, making Dylan chuckle. He carefully put her on his shoulder and expertly burped her as if he had done it her entire life. She was out like a light in his arms in no time. He winced slightly as he maneuvered her back into the traditional baby hold.

"You okay?" I asked, watching his movements for more signs of discomfort.

He sighed. "I got hit pretty good at practice today. My shoulder is feeling it. Nothing a little hot water and Icy Hot won't fix."

"I can help with both those things," I replied.

"I would like that very much." He grinned at me. "Will you turn on the water while I put her down?"

I hurried to the shower and started the water, letting the steam fill the room. I could hear Dylan softly whispering dreams of wishes to his daughter in the other room before he joined me in the bathroom. I rose to my tiptoes and kissed him, he wrapped his arm around me, but I saw him wince with the motion.

"Into the shower with you," I commanded, dropping back to my heels and pushing away from him. "Now."

"I'm fine," he said, wincing as he shrugged.

"Sure. And you can prove that to me after your shower. Get in the hot water. Did you take some meds yet?" I crossed my arms.

"Yes, Doctor." He rolled his eyes, but he didn't protest more as he got into the shower. His movement was slow and careful.

I absolutely snuck a peek of him. Good Lord, the man was gorgeous. He was pure muscle and masculine power. I could see he had worked hard today. He had bruises forming on various parts of his body, turning his beautiful skin into shades of purple. I frowned, knowing that while this was part of being in the NFL, I didn't have to like it. Bruises, scrapes, and injuries were standard for practice. How could you expect to play at the top level if you didn't practice at the top level?

I still hated seeing purple bruises appearing on his shoulders and hip.

"I'm guessing you're not going to join me," he said, peeking his head out of the shower to pout.

"No, because I am being your nurse instead," I replied. I raided the medicine cabinets, searching until I found the tube of menthol muscle cream. I knew the tingle of this stuff well. It would help relax his muscles and increase blood flow to help him feel better and heal the aches and bruises quicker.

"You know, they pay people a lot of money to take care of me," he replied. I turned in time to see him step under the water and rinse the soap out of his hair. Bubbles danced down his skin, gliding along every line of muscle. I momentarily forgot how to speak as I looked at his soapy body.

He chuckled and made sure to turn so that I had an even better view.

I took the opportunity to stare as he made sure to rub soap across every glorious inch of him.

"Yeah, but they aren't going to take care of you like I will," I finally managed to get my mouth to spit out the words.

"Is that so? I like it when you take care of me." He turned off the water and stepped out of the shower. He put the towel on his head first, drying his hair before draping the towel around his shoulders. I noticed because it left every inch of his body very visible. And aroused.

Apparently, I wasn't the only one getting turned on by watching him touch himself.

"To the bed with you," I commanded.

He grinned. "Yes, ma'am."

He turned and sauntered to the bed, giving me a very, very nice view of his ass.

He flopped onto the bed, groaning as he hit the mattress. I followed behind, carrying the tube of menthol muscle creme and figuring out where I wanted to start his massage.

"What hurts the most?" I asked, stopping at the bed and admiring the view of his bare backside.

"I have something you can rub," he mumbled, his face in the pillow. I smacked his butt. "Okay, you can do that last. My shoulder and hip need attention first. I took a rough hit at the end of practice."

I evaluated his naked body and decided that I did not need pants. To give the best massage possible, I took them off. And my shirt, because I didn't want to get it dirty. My bra and lacy panties stayed on because I was a professional, but skin-to-skin contact was a known healing technique that I wasn't about to waste.

It just wasn't one that I was going to use in the ER anytime soon.

I got up on the bed, straddled his waist, and squeezed some of the menthol cream medicine onto my hands. The minty scent filled the room and made my fingers tingle. I put the cap back on the tube and set it on the nightstand.

"I don't think I've ever gotten a massage quite like this," he said, his face still in the pillow. He reached his hand back and caressed my bare calf. "Not that I mind."

"Shh." I put my hands on his shoulders and began working the medicine into his skin. His shoulders were boulders of tension. I worked on the muscles with my fingers, careful to avoid the forming bruises as best I could but making sure they got medicine put on them.

He groaned with pleasure, and I would have stripped out of my pants and climbed him like a tree if I wasn't already on top of him. "Don't stop," he moaned as I worked one of the knots in his shoulder.

"That's what she said," I whispered, making him laugh. Still, he groaned again as I hit the right spot right by his shoulder blade and dug in with my knuckles, working out his tension with my hands.

I loved having my hands all over him. The minty scent and tingle of the medicine barely bothered me as I let myself find his sore spots and made him groan with pleasure as I worked out his kinks. I loved touching him. I loved that I could make him feel this good and I wasn't even naked yet.

His shoulders slowly relaxed under my hands as I worked his muscular back. Slowly, he turned from marble back into human flesh. I worked the menthol cream into his entire back, shoulders to butt, working every muscle. He was so strong that I could find every muscle in his back like he was in an anatomy textbook. I traced the long muscles of his back all the way down to his very fine ass. There was barely an ounce of fat on him, everything about him was lean and strong.

I licked my lips and kissed the top of his shoulders, the menthol medicine making my lips tingle.

And that's when he rolled over.

"And now for the happy ending," he purred, looking up at me with dark eyes. I could feel his excitement between my thighs, pushing and straining upward. He reached up, cupping my breast through my bra. My heart sped up and the ache between my legs grew insistent. Heat coursed up and down my spine, promising the pleasure I knew he could deliver.

I leaned forward and kissed him, his hips rocking to find release against my thin panties. I wanted him. I ached to feel him fill me like I knew he would. I wanted to feel him come undone inside of me. I wanted to come undone around him.

He slid one finger under my panties, watching me with knowing eyes as he found the spot that made me gasp. He smiled then, slow and cocky as he began to work his magic. My head fell back, rocking my hips against him. His thick length pressed against my entrance, straining against the thin fabric, his finger flicking a beat that matched my heart rate.

"I need you," I gasped, feeling my body start to tremble. It had never been this easy before. He could barely touch me and I was ready to climax. He tightened one hand around my hip, the other still flicking my clit to drive me crazy.

I saw the tube of lube that he'd accidentally bought sitting on the nightstand. "Do you think we could use some of that lube that you bought with the rest of the baby supplies?" I asked, batting my eyelashes a little bit. "Might as well get some use out of it."

He reached for the nightstand and the bottle of lube, that cocky smile the only thing I could focus on. The lube would make everything easier. I wanted to have him inside me when I came. I clung to the thought, that it would feel so much better with him deep within me that I just kept climbing up the mountain of pleasure.

He poured the lube onto his fingers, ready to make me even slicker for him to slide into. He was so big and hard, and I appreciated the little bit of extra help to make him fit easier.

"Please," I whimpered, rocking my hips and pulling my panties to the side to give him easier access. He reached down and froze millimeters away from my skin.

"Stop," he whispered. "Don't. Move."

I didn't listen. I rocked my hips and he pulled his hands away hard.

I looked down and saw his horrified expression.

And the bottle in his hands.

The bottle that wasn't lube.

No. It was the menthol muscle cream.

"I think we need to shower, now," he said, swallowing hard. "This stuff is not good on sensitive areas."

I could already feel an unwanted kind of tingle in my groin. I'd been rubbing my inner thighs against him while giving the massage. The minty tingle was creeping closer to the apex of my thighs and I did not think it would end in a world-ending orgasm.

We both bolted for the shower, the scent of menthol trailing after us like bad perfume.

He slammed on the water. He shifted from foot to foot.

"You okay?" I asked, stripping from my clothes.

"Let's just say I'm really glad I didn't get more on me. This is not the sexy massage ending I had in mind." He tested the water and jumped under the spray, reaching for soap. I followed right behind him.

The warm water washed over both our bodies, but it did not give relief from the tingly sensation growing on my skin. He handed me the bottle of body wash and I poured a huge amount onto my hands and started lathering.

"Well, at least I'll smell like you," I teased, soaping up my legs. The tingles started to slow.

He put his hands on my breasts, soaping my skin with suds. My skin grew slippery under his fingers which he seemed to enjoy. "Oh yes you will." He kissed me, pinning me against the tile wall. "You're not getting out of this that easy."

"*I* wasn't the one who grabbed the wrong bottle," I protested. Our bodies were slick with soap now, sliding against one another in the steam of the shower. I loved the way his muscles felt like this, pressing against me, yet sliding past.

He silenced me with a kiss, sliding his hands up and down my soapy hips. I wrapped one arm around his shoulders and reached for his cock with the other. Soap made him slippery, but he groaned as my fingers slid up and down his shaft. My fingers slid up and down, gliding on the soapy water and feeling him swell in my grip.

I loved the sound he made. A low sound of raw desire, a sound of pure pleasure, and a sound that I had caused.

His fingers trailed down my stomach and then slipped between my thighs, still slick with soap. "Let's clean you off," he whispered.

He stepped away from me just enough to grab the handheld shower head. The main shower head stayed on, keeping the room steamy and hot. He flicked a dial and the handheld came to life, spilling hot water onto my body. He moved the dial again, turning the sprayer from a gentle rainfall into a single jet of water. And then he pointed that stream of water right at my clit.

White hot pleasure seared through me at the pulse of hot water pressing into my clit. The steady pressure of the hot water ratcheted my climax, pushing me over the threshold of pleasure in seconds. The world stopped and it was only his hand on my hip that kept me standing as my body spasmed against the shower head.

"That's it," he purred, keeping the water directly on

my clit. He had that cocky smile again, the one that said he was enjoying this almost as much as I was, as he watched my body rock with pleasure. "I love watching you."

"...need you," I whispered, not wanting the pleasure to end, yet wanting him inside me more. I couldn't form complete sentences anymore. The very essence of my being ached to have him inside of me, to feel him give this pleasure to both of us.

His body covered mine, the handheld sprayer left to dangle to the side as moved to fill its place. I ran my fingers down his thick length, looking up at him as I moved him to the right spot. I gasped as he filled me, pushing himself to the hilt until I couldn't fit any more of him inside of me. I loved the low breath of pleasure that came from him, the small involuntary shake of his body as he found his way into me.

His hips rocked. I was still coming down off my orgasm, so every inch of him sliding in and out was an exquisite torture threatening to push me over into oblivion yet again.

"Natalie..." he gasped, his arm braced against the shower wall. Water beaded on his skin, running in rivulets down his arm muscles and joining with the water on my own skin. I nodded, wanting him to find his release in me.

His body shook with effort, his hips rocking, his breathing hard. I braced against the wall, loving the way he filled me and made me want to explode right along with him. I could feel it when he lost himself to me. The feeling of him finding so much pleasure that he couldn't contain himself any longer filled me with a feeling of power. I loved that I could do this for him. I loved that I could make this big strong man shiver and groan. I loved that he wanted me more than anything on the planet.

I loved that he was mine.

Panting, he smiled and wiped the water off my cheek.

"The water bill is going to be outrageous if you keep this up," he teased, kissing my cheek. "If you had wanted a shower that badly, you could have just asked."

I slapped his chest. "*You're* the one that grabbed the wrong bottle!"

"You're the one that put the two bottles in the same place!" He laughed and shook his head. "I'm just glad it wasn't worse."

"Yeah. Just because I have work tonight does not mean I want you to be my patient," I replied.

"But then we could live out one of those *Gray's Anatomy* or *ER* TV show episodes. I'll put on a lab coat and pretend to be a doctor and you can meet me in the supply closet for our secret romantic tryst." He grinned at me like he could already see the episode airing in his head.

"No. Please no." I gagged a little. "Not unless you want to live out the fantasy where I come to the locker room and..."

"Nope," he cut me off. "We can skip that fantasy. You do not want to be in that locker room."

We both laughed.

"How's your shoulder?" I asked as we got out of the shower.

"Would it be terrible if I asked you to put some more medicine on it?" he sheepishly asked.

I double-checked to make sure I had the right bottle this time.

25

WORST DAY OF MY LIFE

"Three or four plane crashes and we're in the playoffs."
-John McKay

DYLAN

YESTERDAY'S PRACTICE SUCKED. Today's somehow sucked more.

First thing, Coach pulled me aside and reminded me what was at stake. I would have preferred yelling to the calm disappointed tone. Marcus made it clear he wanted nothing to do with me and had started to refuse to throw the ball to me. It didn't matter if it was a simple run drill or just getting the ball to the next guy, if the ball was in his hands, he wasn't putting it in mine.

I couldn't blame him. I couldn't seem to hold onto the ball to save my life. The damn thing was made like a bar of soap. I could catch it, but the moment I tried to hold onto it, it slipped away from me.

"You need to use your body," one of the trainers, Sara, whispered as I sucked down water after yet another failed drill. "Cradle the ball into your chest. You're too busy protecting your wrist and not the ball."

"Of course I'm protecting my wrist," I snapped at her. "It hurts."

Luckily, she didn't take offense to my tone. Sara frowned at me. "Medical. Now."

She pointed to the building and I didn't object. The lure of air conditioning beckoned. I didn't want to be out in the hot sun and fucking it up for everyone to see. I let my coordinator know that I was headed to the medical area to work on my wrist. He didn't say anything, but marked something down on his notepad.

It was probably a recommendation to trade me. They should. I was a liability at this point.

Sweet cold air blasted my face as Sara led the way to the room near the locker room. Once again, I was glad that we held preseason practices at our practice stadium. It meant that we had all the equipment we could ever want and the familiarity of home.

"Go ahead and drop the pads," Sara said, washing up her hands. "You'll need to ice it. Then I'll wrap it. I want to see you tomorrow so I can wrap it properly for practice." She walked over to me, holding out her hands for my wrist. I offered it and she turned it with gentle fingers, feeling the stiffness and seeing where I winced. "Yeah, you need a better wrap. This brace is shot. You need more support."

I stopped paying attention as she mumbled about the

different wraps and braces and which one would work better. I let the ice bath fill. I could just ice my entire body and my wrist. Plus, it was an excuse not to return to practice. There wasn't much left, but I didn't want to be out on the field making a fool out of myself anymore for the day.

I hid in the medical room until I was sure that everyone had left. I didn't want to face Marcus. I didn't want to face Coach. I didn't want to see a single fan.

I wanted to curl up in a ball and let the ice turn me into a Popsicle. A Popsicle didn't have worries or concerns. Popsicles didn't care about DNA tests. Everyone liked Popsicles. Popsicle fans didn't hate them.

I made sure I didn't turn the radio on for the drive home. The last thing I needed to hear tonight was how much I sucked at practice today and just how cold Chicago could be in the winter with the lake effect. I didn't want to think about a possible transfer, or even worse, no transfer. With the way I was playing, there was a very good chance no team would want me. I had absolutely no idea what I would do then.

Probably die.

At least coming home made me smile. Ellie snuggled into me like I was her favorite person and Natalie kissed me like I had just won the Super Bowl.

"How was practice?" she asked, packing up her things. She had to work a full shift tonight, so that meant she had to be out the door by six thirty. I hated days like this. I wanted to have a nice leisurely shower with her and then a delicious meal. I wanted to curl up on the couch with her and watch reruns of old TV shows. I wanted to put Penelope in the bathroom, Ellie in her crib, and make Natalie whimper my name until we were both too exhausted to move.

That would have made my day better.

"It was rough," I replied, playing with the wrap on my wrist. Sara had been right. The new wrap did help make my wrist feel better, but it felt like it was too little too late. My career was going down the tubes and I didn't know how to fix it.

Natalie stopped for a second and made sure I knew I had her complete attention, even though I knew she was already running late. "I'm sorry, Dylan. Is there anything I can do?"

"Call in sick?" I asked hopefully, giving her a little kid smile. She smiled sadly at me and shook her head. "Eh, it was worth a shot."

"I'll make sure to bring breakfast burritos in the morning," she promised, slinging her bag over her shoulder. "That way tomorrow will be better."

I smiled at her. It felt good to have her on my team. It felt good to have someone to rely on, someone that had my back no matter what. Even running late, she made sure to make time for me.

I was falling hard for her, but even more, I wanted her on my team permanently. She made everything feel possible, even when the rest of my life felt impossible.

She kissed me and the baby before leaving the apartment.

Even with the baby gurgling, the goat bleating, and *Supernatural* on in the background, the house felt too quiet. It felt empty without her in it. I gave serious thought to calling her and telling her to come back. If I called the ER, would they let her come home?

I sighed. I wouldn't do that to her. She loved her job as much as I loved mine.

"Well, Ellie Girl," I said to my daughter. "How about some films? You want to help your old man not lose his job?"

Ellie just drooled, but I took that as a solid yes.

I settled into the couch with my phone. I didn't dare change the channel off *Supernatural* and risk the wrath of Penelope until bedtime. She liked to watch a few episodes in the evening and then retired to the bathtub, with a strict bedtime of eight P.M. on the dot. Until then, I watched the plays on a tablet. It wasn't convenient, but I could hold Ellie and watch the screen so it wasn't too uncomfortable.

"Franklin is looking good," I told my daughter, watching some of the run plays. "He's a rookie from Florida, but the kid has skill." I paused the film, rewound, and watched the way he caught the ball. I realized I wasn't looking for tips on how to do it. Instead, I was analyzing and figuring out how he could do it better. He was fast off the line, but his running form needed improvement. A few modifications, and he would be faster and able to catch anything Marcus threw at him.

Franklin reminded me of myself only a few years ago. I'd needed a mentor when I started. I was now in the position to be the mentor, which made me feel old, but powerful at the same time. I had knowledge this kid could use. Franklin could be better than me, and for the first time in a long time, that wasn't intimidating. It was exciting. I could get him there.

I just had to take him under my wing and teach him.

Ellie batted at my phone, accidentally making the

picture of Franklin grow larger on the screen. I was going to help him.

"Should I be his daddy too?" I asked her, immediately hating with every fiber of my being how that sounded. I needed to be a mentor, not a father figure to a man only five years my junior. I laughed at the idea. Marcus would absolutely make fun of me, but he'd probably help me out with getting the kid better. I zoomed the screen out to Marcus throwing the ball.

I stared at the video, not watching it but finally truly seeing it. It had been a long time since I'd stopped watching just my film trying to fix my catches. I had been so focused on my own issues the past few months that I honestly couldn't remember the last time I'd cared about anyone else on my team.

Even Marcus.

"Marcus..." I sighed.

Ellie gurgled a question at me.

"Yeah, I don't know why he's so mad at me. He hasn't said two words to me since the accident, but..." I paused and re-watched the video. Marcus paused before throwing the ball at me every time. I switched videos. He hesitated before throwing it, again and again and again. It looked like he didn't want to throw it to me, like he would rather throw it anywhere else. I was sure that wasn't helping my catch rate.

It didn't used to be that way.

"I should talk to him," I said to Ellie. I should talk to Coach about it too, but I owed Marcus the chance to explain.

"Thbubs," Ellie replied.

"You're right," I conceded. "I should talk to both of

them. I miss having Marcus around. I miss hanging out with him. He and I used to watch this shit together, I mean, this *stuff* together."

"Akda," Ellie agreed. I smiled at her.

"I will talk to Marcus tomorrow. I should have talked to him a long time ago, but..." I sighed again. "I'm going to make sure you are better at communicating than I am."

Ellie did not say anything. She was staring at the lamp, her eyes getting big as if it were the most interesting thing in the entire universe. I didn't mind. I laid her down in the pack-n-play next to the couch, her eyes glued on the lamp as I went back to the tablet to keep reviewing the tape.

I woke up a few hours later with a kink in my shoulder the size of Alaska. I was getting old. I could remember sleeping all night on a threadbare futon with pizza stains and waking up feeling like a million bucks. Now, I slept two hours on an expensive leather couch and woke up unable to turn my head.

The *"Are you still watching?"* screen glowed blue on the TV. Penelope raised her head and glared at me as I stood and rubbed at my neck muscles. It was clear that she did not appreciate that no one had tucked her in or at least hit the "yes" button to continue the show for her. She bleated an annoyed sigh as she hopped down from the recliner and trotted over to me for head pats.

"Sorry," I mumbled, scratching her forehead. She closed her eyes, enjoying the pets and possibly forgiving me for missing her bedtime rituals. Ellie fussed from the floor, letting me know that she too was awake. I reached down and picked her up, wondering what could have woken all three of us up. She snuggled into my chest, smacking her lips. I figured she was probably getting hungry, so I moved to the kitchen, Penelope trailing behind hoping that I might give her some cabbage in the process.

That's when the fire alarm went off. Lights flashed and the alarm screeched horribly through the room.

Penelope bolted for the front door and safety, but unfortunately, I was in her way. She crashed into me, taking me out at the knees and sending me flying through the air with a baby in my arms. It was like being hit by the world's smallest linebacker.

Time slowed. The world spun out of my control as my feet flew into the air.

Without thinking, I cradled Ellie into my chest, using every inch of my hands to keep her pressed safely into me. I protected her with my body, my weak arm, my hands, everything I had. I twisted in the air so that she wouldn't land first, it would be me who would take the brunt of the hit. I was going to hold onto her and keep her safe if it killed me.

We landed with a thud, my good arm taking the impact, the rest of my body shielding my daughter and protecting her from the fall. It didn't matter though. Ellie started screaming, her pouty face pressed into my shirt.

My heart sank like a stone. I didn't see any blood, but that didn't mean there wasn't an injury. Every stat I'd ever heard my entire football career about head injuries swirled and mixed in my mind in a terrifying nightmare. The fire alarm stopped. The lights no longer flashed and the alarm didn't even chirp. A message popped up on my phone that a neighbor had triggered the building's alarm system but that it was all clear.

The world was fine, even if Ellie wasn't.

Penelope stood in the kitchen, staring at the fridge like she was waiting for her cabbage, the fear of the alarm gone as quickly as it had come.

But panic filled my bones. My daughter was screaming.

I had to get Ellie to the ER. I had to get her there now.

26

THE LAST PATIENT I WANTED

Knock Knock
Who's there?
HIPPA
HIPPA who?
Sorry, I can't tell you that

NATALIE

"DON'T YOU JINX IT," I warned McKenna, pointing my pen at her in a semi-threatening manner.

"What?" She raised her hands innocently and shrugged. "I was just going to say it looks like you're having a nice--"

"Don't jinx it!" I yelled at her.

Sherri poked her head out of the room.

"If you say a quiet or nice night, I will call your supervisor and report you," she threatened before pulling back into the curtained area. "I will not have you ruining my ER with your nonsense."

"Sheesh, you guys are no fun," McKenna mumbled, but at least she didn't say it was quiet.

Which of course meant that all hell came crashing down.

I could hear the baby screaming in the waiting area, the sound gaining volume as the triage nurse quickly whisked the patient into the back. I was next up for a patient, so I chugged some coffee, grabbed clean gloves and waited for them to come through the patient doors.

My heart plummeted.

It wasn't just any baby.

It was my baby.

Well, I considered her mine.

Dylan was pale and shaking. He wasn't wearing shoes as he ran toward me.

"I fell! She fell!"

Every syllable was a death beat as I ushered them into a bay.

"Call pediatrics!" I shouted to Sherri as Dr. Wood jogged to join us with a concerned look on his face.

"Put her on the gurney," I told Dylan. My emergency calm voice took over. I let years of ER training take over, despite the fact that I wanted to run and scream. "Don't take her out of the car seat. We'll look at her in there first. Tell me what happened."

Dr. Wood was beside me, checking pupil reactions, feeling her head as I tried to steady my hands and get the story out of Dylan.

"The fire alarm went off and Penelope bolted. She

knocked me over. Ellie was in my arms and we fell," Dylan said, desperation and guilt in his voice as he watched Dr. Wood inspect his daughter. Tears ran down his face. "I put her in her chair and drove as fast as I could. Please, please, make her okay."

The terror in his voice nearly broke me. I grabbed his hand, holding it, trying to keep both him and me grounded.

"So she wasn't in the car seat when it happened?" Dr. Wood asked, flashing a light in Elsie's eyes. Ellie screamed her disapproval until Dr. Wood handed her the flashlight pen.

"No, she was in my arms when we fell," Dylan explained. "I put her in the car seat to get her here."

"Okay, so the car seat isn't a part of this. Did she hit the floor?" Dr. Wood asked, carefully feeling Ellie's head. "Did you land on her at all?"

"No." Dylan shook his head emphatically. "I took the hit. I tried to protect her, but she started screaming."

"So she landed on you?" Dr. Wood clarified, his hands still gently probing the baby. "Not the floor?"

"I made sure she landed on me," Dylan promised. His entire body shook with fear. "Just make her be okay."

Dr. Wood smiled at him. "She'll be okay."

"What?" The world went wobbly for a moment, and I had to hold onto Dylan and the gurney so my knees didn't give out.

"Look, she's already stopped crying," Dr. Wood said, smiling at the little girl. "I think she just had the scare of her life. Didn't you? I'd be screaming too if I was suddenly flying through the air."

Ellie gurgled at him waving her arms around.

"We can run some tests, but I don't feel any injuries. She's not vomiting, no irritability, no soft or hard spots that aren't supposed to be there," Dr. Wood continued. "I'd say she's fine."

"She's okay?" Dylan's voice was breathless and he held onto my hand like he might fall over.

Dr. Wood undid the car seat straps and pulled Ellie out of her cars eat. He ran his fingers over her neck and spine, tickled her tummy, and watched her giggle.

"As long as she keeps this happy attitude and doesn't develop any bruises, I'd say she's good. You're welcome to stay here under observation for a while if you'd like," Dr. Wood replied.

"I would..." Dylan let out a slow breath. "Are you sure she doesn't need x-rays?"

"We don't like to x-ray babies this little unless it's absolutely necessary," Dr. Wood explained. "Since she's not showing any signs and you said yourself she never even touched the floor, I'd rather not give her any radiation."

"Thank you," Dylan said to Dr. Wood, but he squeezed my hand. I felt like I might pass out now that I knew that Ellie was safe. I was still doing my own nursing check on her once I had her in my arms, but I trusted Dr. Wood enough to believe him. I just needed to make sure with my own skills.

Dr. Wood handed Ellie to Dylan. She happily curled up in his arms, as if she knew that he was still her safe person. She wasn't afraid of him falling again, or if she did, she knew he would catch her.

"If you have any questions, I'm sure Natalie here can answer them for you. I'm going to go grab some more coffee." Dr. Wood shook Dylan's hand, gave me a professional nod, washed his hands and left the room.

"She's okay…" Dylan whispered, sinking into a chair next to the gurney. I pulled another one next to him, needing to sit down myself. "I don't think I've ever been more terrified in my entire life."

"You and me both," I replied.

"I thought you did this for a living," he teased me, giving me a gentle shoulder nudge with his own shoulder.

"Yeah, just not with my own child," I replied and then froze. "I mean, a child that I know personally."

My face went hot and I looked everywhere but at Ellie and Dylan. Me and my big mouth. I'd known the man and his daughter for a week and was already calling her mine.

He didn't say anything but reached his hand out to hold mine.

We sat there in the ER room, holding hands and watching Ellie suck on her fingers in the bright fluorescent light. A heart monitor somewhere beeped smoothly and regularly.

"I heard there was a baby that fell?" A woman in dark blue scrubs and a white doctor's coat asked, stepping into the room. She smiled at the two of us. "I'm Dr. Lang, the pediatrician. I came down as soon as I got the call."

"The more doctors that look at her, the better I will feel," Dylan replied, standing up to put Ellie on the gurney for Dr. Lang to look at. He relayed the same story of the fall and Dr. Lang repeated most of Dr. Wood's questions to get the same answers.

"I agree with Dr. Wood," Dr. Lang said after looking at Ellie. "She's a gorgeous little girl and I don't think she took any of the hit. How are you doing, Mr. Callahan? That kind of spill can cause damage."

Dylan was rubbing absently at his injured wrist. He stopped as soon as the doctor saw him doing it.

"I didn't tell you my name," Dylan said, eyeing her carefully.

"What can I say? I'm a huge fan," Dr. Lang said with a smile. "I went to C State, so I have been cheering you on for a long time."

Dylan sighed, but was apparently mollified by the mention of his alma mater. He let the doctor look over his shoulder and wrist.

"You're going to get a bruise on that shoulder, but it won't be anything new. I think your football skills are what saved both you and the baby," Dr. Lang said. "I'll let you relax and we'll get you back home as soon as you're ready to leave. Good luck in the next game. I'll be cheering for you."

She flashed Dylan a smile and left the room.

"Do you think she'll tell anyone that I have a baby?" Dylan asked, watching the curtain sway from her departure.

"Nope." I shook my head. "Dr. Lang is a professional. She won't even tell people that she met you in the ER. That might kill her, since you're her favorite player, but she won't say a word."

"I'll make sure to send her some tickets." Dylan relaxed a little bit. He picked up Ellie, cuddling her close to his chest and smelling the top of her head.

"You did really well, Dylan," I told him. "You protected her."

He gave a dry laugh. "Must be all those football drills finally paying off."

I raised an eyebrow at him. "You mean like holding onto the ball and protecting it at all costs?" I motioned to his injured arm. "And not hurting yourself in the process?"

He lifted his eyes from his daughter, but only to glare at me. "You're trying to make a point but I have too much adrenaline in my system to see it."

"Treat the ball like you just did your daughter," I said. "Pretend the ball is Ellie and you won't drop it anymore."

"Like it's that easy," he mumbled.

"Why not?" I crossed my arms. "You know you can do it now. Your body knew what to do when your brain was too busy to realize it."

Dylan sighed. "You sound like some sort of terrible TV shrink."

"I thought I sounded like a football coach," I replied.

"You weren't nearly loud enough to be a coach," he replied, flashing me a smile. "And you didn't mention giving it 110%."

I stuck my tongue out at him and he gave me a real smile in return.

"You did a good job," I repeated.

"You're sure she's okay?" he asked, his voice steady but full of a quiet fear that I felt deep in my bones as well.

"Yes. Two doctors confirmed it," I told him, as much for his sake as for my own. I frowned. "I guess I should be asking if Penelope is okay."

"She was just standing in the kitchen when I left. She didn't seem fazed at all by it." Dylan shrugged.

"Wait, you just left her in the kitchen?"

Our eyes met and we both imagined a horror scene of Penelope loose in the apartment without anyone to reign her in. Or turn on *Supernatural*. Nothing would be left if someone didn't check on her and put her in the bathtub to go back to bed.

"So should I call Alex, or should I skip straight to 911?" he asked with a slight grin.

27

IT'S ALL COMING TOGETHER

We didn't lose the game; we just ran out of time.
-Vince Lombardi

DYLAN

"CALLAHAN!" Coach's voice boomed out across the field. I winced as I hustled over to the sideline where he stood with his clipboard.

"Yes, Coach?"

"I don't know what changed, but you're like a new player today," he informed me. He tapped on the clipboard. "Thirty-four catches today and you haven't dropped a single one. That is literally a 110% improvement over the rest of the week."

I believed him. I caught every ball today. Today, the ball stayed in my arms.

Did I imagine the ball was Ellie?

Yes. But there was no way I was telling Natalie that.

"Franklin also tells me that you gave him some advice," Coach continued. He leveled a look at me that had me swallowing hard. "Good job."

How long had it been since I'd heard those words from Coach? Weeks? Months? A flush of pride washed over me and I felt taller than I had in days.

"However," Coach continued, and the warmth disappeared. "You and Marcus need to work things out."

I nodded, even though that was the last thing I wanted to do. I did not want to talk to Marcus. I wanted things to just go back to the way they were before the accident. I wanted things to be right in the world again. I didn't want to sit and have tea with Marcus and discuss our feelings, even though I knew that it would probably help.

"So you and Marcus are running laps," Coach informed me. He pointed with his chin toward the track where Marcus was fixing his shoelaces. "Get going. You both can come back when you have things fixed. If that means I keep the lights on for you, then we'll take the extra electric bill out of your pay."

I stared after him for a minute while he walked away from me. With a huge sigh, and absolutely no desire to run or talk, I headed to the track.

"So." Marcus didn't look at me.

"So." I didn't look at him.

We started a light jog. The afternoon sun was brutal, but at least the breeze made it tolerable. Our feet were rhythmless on the ground, both of us out of sync with the other.

"How's your wrist?" Marcus asked after a quarter mile.

"Fine." I held up the uninjured one. "No problem."

He scoffed and for a minute I thought I might have made him smile, but it was gone and we jogged in silence for a bit.

"It's fine," I said. "It hurts, but I think I figured it out. I had a fall last night. Nearly ended up in the ER, but I kept the thing I was holding safe. And my wrist didn't snap again."

"The ER?" Marcus stopped running and grabbed my shoulder. "Are you okay, man?"

The concern in his face made my heart stutter. He cared. He still cared. He didn't hate me.

"Yeah, I'm fine," I assured him. "I *almost* ended up in the ER." I still didn't want to tell him about Ellie yet and there were too many fans, too many reporters around that might hear something worse than some friendly banter that was all over the radio talk shows anyway.

"I did notice you could catch today," Marcus said, releasing me. We started jogging again, but it felt lighter now. Our steps were still out of rhythm with one another, but every third step we seemed to match up.

"You know these injuries get in your head." I stared at the rust-colored track as we ran, not looking at the world going by. "They make you believe that you'll always be hurt. That it's always going to be like this. That it will never get better."

"Do you blame me?" he asked.

The question forced me to stop and stare at him. It took him a few steps to realize that I wasn't moving. He turned and wiped sweat from his brow and squinted at me. He looked calm, but he was bouncing his leg. He only did that when he was crazy nervous.

"For what?" I asked. "Throwing me the ball? Doing your job?"

"It was a bad pass..." He looked away from me. "If I hadn't thrown it..."

Suddenly things clicked into place. He'd thrown the pass that had gotten me injured. Did he blame himself? Was that why he never came to the hospital? Was that why he was always so angry when I couldn't catch the ball? Because he blamed himself?

"Your job is to throw the ball, my job is to catch it," I replied. I took a step to him, putting my hand on his shoulder this time. "I never blamed you. Ever."

"You can't catch because of me." His leg bounced.

"I can't catch because I'm an idiot," I replied. "I'm working on that. You can't fix my stupid."

A hint of a smile flashed across is face for just a moment.

"They're going to trade you and it's my fault. I threw that pass. And now..." He looked away from me, squinting into the sun.

I tightened my hand on his shoulder. "No, it's mine. You threw that pass. You didn't cause the hit. You didn't make me drop any balls this season unless you suddenly got telekinetic powers that I don't know about. And they aren't going to trade me."

His eyes came to meet mine and the last six months of us not talking, not hanging out, not being friends, seemed like the most stupid thing in the world.

"You sure? You're playing like shit. I'd trade you."

"Thank you for that vote of confidence." I pushed his shoulder this time and he grinned at me.

"I don't want you to leave the team," he said quietly as

we settled back into our jog pace. This time, our feet fell at the same time, running together in cadence.

"I don't want to move," I confessed. The fear of it tightened in my stomach and then loosened. Talking to Marcus made it feel real and yet better at the same time. I glanced over at him. "Maybe throw me some good balls?"

"I only throw good balls," he informed me. "I can't help it if you can't catch a cold."

This time, the joke made me laugh. There was no malice in his words, just the teasing of a friend.

We circled the track.

"We good?" Marcus asked.

"We're good," I promised. "But we should probably do a few more laps just to make Coach happy. He's watching us and I would hate for him to think he could solve all our problems in under a mile."

"I can yell at you," Marcus offered.

"You'll have to catch me first." I picked up my speed, smiling at the string of curses coming from the friend behind me.

* * *

THE REST of practice felt good. I caught the ball. I kept the ball. I got hit, but I didn't let go.

Marcus asked where the hell I'd been on vacation for this past month. It felt good to have him talking to me again.

I stopped to have Sara re-wrap my wrist before heading home. Unfortunately, as head trainer, she had several athletes in front of me. I decided not to be the prima dona athlete and let the others go ahead of me. As much as I wanted to get home to Natalie and Ellie, I knew they were okay tonight. I texted Natalie that I'd bring home food tonight for us. She gave me a huge thumbs up emoji. I was quickly learning that her stomach was the best way into her heart. Give that girl food or caffeine and she was a happy camper.

"Hey man, how long for the trainer?" Franklin asked, coming to stand beside me. He had his arms crossed across his chest, and an uncomfortable look on his face.

"No idea, but probably a little bit. Why? What's up?"

Franklin glanced around, as if taking stock of the other players nearby.

"It's my nipples," he whispered, leaning forward. "It's the jerseys or the heat or something, but.. I'm getting rubbed raw. I was hoping the trainer might have some ideas on how to help it other than wearing band-aids like some sort of cheap stripper."

It took everything I had not to laugh.

But, this was my chance to be a mentor. The fact that he was willing to ask something this personal meant he trusted me and I didn't want to let him down.

"I actually have something that will help," I said, an idea popping into my head. "It's this nipple cream. It's usually for new moms, but it works really well on soothing nipples."

Franklin raised a skeptical eyebrow. "Mom nipples? How'd you find out about it?"

"I had something similar. It was recommended to me," I lied. "I'll bring you a tube tomorrow."

Franklin smiled, his shoulders relaxing. "Thanks, man. I really appreciate it."

I smiled back at him, the fabulous feeling of being a

good teammate filling my chest. "It's nothing. You've been doing good this week. Keep it up."

He gave me a nod and left the treatment area, his steps light and confidence up. It felt good.

My phone buzzed in my pocket. Alex's name popped up on the screen.

"What's up?" I cradled the phone to my shoulder.

"So, there's a problem," Alex informed me. I glanced around, making sure that no one could hear my conversation.

"And?"

"The DNA test didn't work," Alex said.

"How does a DNA test not work? Is Ellie an alien?" I asked.

"No, but you probably are," Alex replied. "The lab thinks the sample got too hot or something. It wasn't a good sample. They need a new sample."

Anger and annoyance flared hot, but I kept my cool. "So we'll have to wait how long to find out if she's my daughter?"

"A week. But the new test will be at your place tonight," Alex promised. "They said they'll expedite it."

"They better." I would strangle someone if they didn't.

"You got it, Boss," Alex promised. He was quiet for a moment, not hanging up the phone.

"What else?" I rubbed at my temples. Maybe I should just head home? My wrist wasn't that bad today.

"I talked to my cousin. She and her husband both signed the NDA and passed all the background checks. They're interested in adopting. They'd love to adopt your daughter if that's what you decide." Alex's voice went soft. "They're good people. She'd have two older brothers.

Two loving parents. They have enough money they are comfortable, but not so much that she'd be a spoiled brat. They have a good school. They have a big family. It's a great life for her."

My chest tightened to the point that I found it hard to breathe. I stood up and moved to a different spot in the room.

"Thanks, Alex. I'm not ready to decide yet," I said, my voice coming out flat.

"No problem. You should wait for the DNA test anyway," Alex quickly agreed. "I just wanted you to know that it's a valid option."

"Thanks."

A hollow ache filled my chest as I hung up the phone. The fluorescent bulbs flickered slightly overhead, the lights turning on in the building as the sun set outside. It was later than I realized and I was suddenly exhausted.

"You're my last patient," Sara called to me, motioning me to her. "Let's look at your wrist and then we can both get home."

She showed me a couple of exercises and stretches that she wanted me to start doing several times a day to help strengthen and support my wrist.

"Let me walk you to your car," I offered when we finished. Everyone else had left for the day, so ours were the only cars left in the parking lot other than the custodians. It was a safe neighborhood, but I would want someone to walk Natalie out if she were here late. Heck, I would want someone to walk me out if one of the linebackers was available.

"Sure, that would be great," she said with a smile as she grabbed her bag. We stepped out of the building and into the late summer air, the sound of insects buzzing all around in the grass.

It was a quiet summer evening until it wasn't.

"Hey, Callahan!" An angry voice called. "You can't catch for shit!"

I looked up, thinking it was Coach or Marcus giving me a hard time, but it wasn't. It was a fan. A young man, probably late twenties wearing a dark hoodie and shorts stomped over to us. Instinctively, I moved to block Sara from him, pushing her back into the doorway of the building.

"I lost the spread because of you," the man shouted, getting up and into my face. His breath smelled of bad whiskey and worse decisions, but his hit to my shoulder was strong enough to send me back a step. Unfortunately, it appeared the door back inside had locked behind us so there was nowhere to get away from him.

"Man, I'm sorry," I said, raising my hands to show I meant no harm. "I'm working on it. I got some things--"

"You're working on it?" He said the words so hard that spit landed on my cheek. "I lost my mortgage because of you! My wife left me because of you! My life is in shambles and it's absolutely your fault!"

He pushed me again, but this time I was ready and he didn't get any motion from me. I needed to keep Sara safe in the doorway.

"Listen, I'm sorry about all that," I told him, keeping my voice low and calm like I was soothing a wild animal. "But this isn't going to help."

"Is this the bitch that's distracting you?" He pointed at Sara who flinched when he noticed her.

Damn. I had hoped he wouldn't see her.

"She's just a trainer here doing her job," I said, moving to block him from her more. "She's not the problem here."

"Like hell, she isn't!" The man lunged past me, taking a swing at Sara's head. Once again, everything moved in slow motion. I saw the punch fly through the air. I felt my body trying to move, but I couldn't move that fast. Superman couldn't have moved fast enough to catch him.

Luckily, Sara must have had older brothers because she grabbed his arm and slammed him into the wall in a move that would have made Bruce Lee proud. She screamed like a teenage girl while doing it, but the move was still bad ass. I grabbed him by his sweatshirt and pinned him into the building.

Was I a little rougher than I needed to be? Was he going to have some serious bruises? Probably.

Did I care? Not even a little bit.

I was pissed. The guy was lucky I wasn't pummeling him into the ground and on his way to meet Natalie in the ER. I wanted to destroy him. I wanted to let the anger burst from me and put him in the ground, but Sara was screaming at security to get over to us. The guy stopped resisting after I made it very clear that if he so much as breathed in a way I didn't like, he was going to not only find his head in the brick, but that he also would have a dislocated shoulder.

Security took him from me, taking him to a waiting police car.

"You okay?" I asked Sara, rubbing at my sore wrist.

She fixed her ponytail. "That was not the evening I was expecting. How's your wrist?"

"Fine." It didn't hurt any more than it usually did.

Sara rolled her eyes and held her hands out so that she could look at it.

"The cops will be here in a minute. I'll re-wrap your wrist," she said, inspecting her work. The wrap had become loose in the scuffle. She looked up at me. "Thanks for saving me."

"You did a pretty good job of saving yourself," I replied. "You could have taken him."

She laughed. "Tell the other players. I can use all the street cred I can get."

"I'm just glad you're okay," I told her. For a moment, I imagined she was Natalie. Or worse, Ellie. What if she had been carrying Ellie when that guy came over and got aggressive? I didn't want to think about it. I didn't want to think about what could have happened to her, or what I might have done to the guy to protect my daughter.

"This stuff happens," Sara said, waving a hand dismissively. "Fans are crazy."

That didn't make me feel better. The idea of anyone coming after Natalie because of my fame made my stomach turn. It was a real wake-up call that I had famous people problems. Problems that I did not want my child or wife to have to deal with. Problems that Natalie and Ellie didn't deserve to have.

Natalie was a grown-up. She could make her own decisions, but Ellie? I thought about the family Alex had lined up. Two older brothers. No famous dad. No stalkers. Was that a better option for a small girl?

"You okay?" Sara asked, touching my arm. "You look like you are thinking some dark thoughts."

"Just rattled," I said with a false laugh. "Don't tell the guys."

She nodded as if she understood but there was no way she could. There was no way she could know I was questioning my abilities as a father to protect my child or if I was the right person to raise her.

And now I had to talk to the cops again. And I'd be late with dinner.

Red and blue flashing lights filled the scene, blinding me with their brightness. Cops spilled out of the cars and I wasn't sure if it good luck or bad luck that I recognized one of them.

"Oh. Hi, Officer Brown. How nice to see you again."

28

PLAY BALL!

*"Sometimes I have to remind myself around my non-nurse
friends not to talk about bodily functions."*
—Unknown

Natalie

"LET'S GET READY TO RUMBLE!"

The entire stadium vibrated beneath my feet as I
followed the man in a black suit in front of me. The game
was about to start.

My first NFL game and I was going to be watching it
from the good seats.

I was of course late and had missed all the pregame
festivities. Alex was watching Ellie and he'd had more
questions than I'd prepared for. I was pretty sure that he
was going to do fine with her, especially since I told him

just to call McKenna if he needed anything. A baby was a perfect excuse to ask her to come over and help him out.

I grinned to myself as I walked past concrete arches leading out to a packed stadium. Sunlight streamed onto the seats and the grass, the afternoon game off to a start with perfect weather. I tugged at the hem of the jersey with Dylan's name emblazoned on the back. He'd given it to me to wear, along with the tickets to the VIP area. I felt like a pretender. A fraud. I wasn't a fan.

But I did want to see Dylan at work. He loved this stupid game so much, so it was the least I could do to come and watch him do it.

"Ma'am, this way." The man in the black suit motioned me into a very swanky area. The sound of the crowd dimmed slightly as I stepped inside. Huge TVs lined the walls of a space bigger than my apartment. People in jerseys similar to mine lounged comfortably on sofas and nibbled on the buffet along the far wall.

I'd never been to an NFL game, but I had a feeling this was not the typical experience.

The man in the suit nodded to me, pointed out the amenities, and informed me that if I wanted anything, anything at all, to just pick up the white phone and ask.

I grinned as I looked around at the world I had just walked into. A girl could get used to this kind of service.

I walked over to one of the huge windows overlooking the field and got a little bit of vertigo. The stadium was so much bigger than it looked on TV. Thousands and thousands of people filled the stands, packing it full of color and sound. Below, I could see the players lining up, getting ready to slam their bodies together and give out concussions.

I mean, score touchdowns and have a good time.

"Hi."

I turned to see a young woman with the most gorgeous curly hair I'd ever seen smiling at me.

"Hi." I tugged on the bottom of my jersey, wondering if it was obvious that I didn't belong here. I wasn't a true fan.

"I'm Annette," she said, holding out her hand with a smile. "You look new here."

She shook my hand, clearly waiting to find out more about me.

"Oh, I'm a guest of Dylan Callahan. I'm his neighbor," I added lamely when I realized that I was in a very elite room and should probably explain why I was there. "I'm Natalie."

She smiled. "I was told to find you. Alex did mention he was sending a rookie to me," she took a swig of her beer and smiled widely. "I just figured it would be one of his bros and not someone who might actually be capable of conversation."

"I must say, I'm shocked to learn Alex knows someone who can speak in complete sentences," I said. "Although, I guess Dylan speaks in complete sentences most of the time."

My brain went to a dirty place where Dylan couldn't speak complete sentences because of the pleasure coursing through him. I swallowed hard and pretended to look out at the field like I understood what was going on out there.

"So, how do you know Alex?" I asked, looking for Dylan out on the field.

"We hang out at a lot of these games," she explained.

"You have season tickets?" I asked. I wondered what she must do for a living to afford tickets like these.

"Kind of. Marcus Johnson is my brother," she explained. "I know a lot of the team because of him."

"Oh, the quarterback, right?" That was one of the few names I recognized and actually understood the position they did.

"Yup. So you're the *neighbor*, huh?" She looked me up and down, a wicked gleam in her eye. "Where's Alex? He never misses a game. Said it was one of the few perks of the job. And they always give out multiple tickets to family."

"He's at home." I nearly said blurted out that he was watching Dylan's daughter, but managed to catch myself. "He has to watch one of his nieces. He couldn't get out of babysitting."

It was kind of true. Dylan was like a brother to Alex.

"Too bad, but I'm glad it's not his grandma," Annette said, looking back out at the game below us. "Seems like Dylan's finally found his mojo again. I was sure he was going to be benched this game, but he's out there and doing a decent job."

"What?" I followed her gaze to see Dylan out on the field. He looked focused. Calm. He carried himself with confidence.

I realized that the huge Jumbotron TV overlooking the field was watching him too. There he was, larger than life up on the screen. He looked really good in his pads, too. They made his broad shoulders even more masculine and the skin tight pants made his butt look amazing. Plus, I knew that what was underneath was just as good as what was on display.

"Oh. Wow." I swallowed hard, staring at his image on the screen.

"Yeah, just *neighbors*," Annette muttered under her breath, looking over at me and shaking her head. I wiped at the drool on my chin from staring at Dylan.

Below us, the teams formed two groups. The crowd was screaming but I had no idea what was going on.

"Isn't this the part where they huddle up and talk about… what are they talking about?" I asked, wanting to change the subject.

"Plays," Annette said. "They're figuring out what they're gonna do next. Cameron usually decides, but Marcus is the one who yells it out."

"Oh. " I nodded, pretending to understand, but my mind was racing. I mean, how did they talk about what to do?

"Hey, you go left buddy and I'll throw you the ball but don't get tackled, okay?"

I thought of all the little diagrams of x's and o's Dylan kept studying. How he could keep that in his mind while literal linebackers were after him was rather impressive.

They lined up. The center guy tossed the ball through his legs to Marcus. Marcus did not give the ball to Dylan. I had no clue what was going on, but the crowd cheered.

The announcer boomed something about a first down and rattled off names of players, but I was still lost. They lined up again.

The ball was snapped, and Dylan started running. Fast. The quarterback pulled back, looking for someone to pass to. Suddenly, the ball was flying through the air toward Dylan, and I felt my stomach flip. He reached up, caught it with perfect ease, and then—WHAM—he got slammed into by what could only be described as a human freight train. They both went down, hard.

I gasped and instinctively clutched the railing of the window. "Is that normal? He's okay, right? Please tell me he's okay." I looked to the sideline, watching the medics and staff not react to the hit.

"Yeah, totally normal," Annette replied casually. She sipped at her drink. "That wasn't even that hard of a hit. And he got a first down, so he's happy."

No wonder he ached when he got home. This game was brutal. The guy that hit him was huge, and Dylan was not a small man.

Dylan popped back up like nothing had happened, giving the other guy a slap on the helmet. How was he so calm? Was he too calm? Could he be hiding a concussion? I should've checked him for signs of disorientation this morning. Did his pupils look uneven during breakfast? I'd been so focused on Ellie that I hadn't thought to give him a mental health check for baseline.

"Hey, relax," Annette said, noticing my wide-eyed panic. "Dylan's tough. He can handle it."

"I know he's tough," I sighed. "But he's not invincible. You guys think he's made of steel or something, but I'm the one who's going to have to nurse him back to health when his ACL snaps like a rubber band!"

"Because you're his *neighbor*," Annette added. "And that's totally what *neighbors* do. Nurse each other back to health."

I gave her a flat look and crossed my arms. "We're friends too."

She didn't look like she believed me.

"Would you like a drink? We get free booze up here," Annette offered, motioning to the bar on the side of the room. "You seem like you could use the drink."

"That would probably help," I admitted. I attempted a smile. "Although, I will warn you, I am a friendly drunk. And I will probably still be freaking out about Dylan's bones."

That made her laugh. "After that hit last season, we're all freaking out about Dylan's bones." She grinned slyly at me. "But I think you're the only one jumping them."

I opened my mouth but she just laughed. "Right, I forgot. You're just *neighbors*."

"It's still really new..." I mumbled.

"Don't worry. I won't say a thing," she promised, guiding me to the bar.

The game went on, and with each hit Dylan took, I felt my blood pressure rise. One minute he was blocking some guy twice his size, and the next, he was diving for the ball like his life depended on it. I kept calculating in my head how long it would take to get him into a neck brace if anything went wrong.

Annette kept feeding me cold beers and answering questions about the players and the game.

"That's Franklin. He's a rookie this year, but he's pretty good. He's got a pet cat named Bob," Annette informed me. "And the big guy to the right of Marcus, that's Bob. Well, really he's Robert Huxley the Third, but everyone calls him Bob. He does not appreciate that he shares his name with a cat." She leaned forward, whispering like she was sharing a secret. "Probably because everyone likes the cat more. He smells better after the games."

I giggled, my eyes still glued to the field. I actually found myself rooting for the other team to have the ball because that meant the defensive line was on the field instead of Dylan. Unfortunately, the Twisters were the better team and our offensive was out more than I would have liked.

I also got to see just how athletic Dylan was. I'd seen him up close and personal, but seeing him in action was a whole new world. He could run. He could jump. He could catch the ball. He could hit other guys.

And I found that I really liked it. I really liked watching him outrun players. I liked watching him figure out what the other team was doing and how to put himself in the best spot for Marcus to throw the ball. He was smarter than everyone out there. He wasn't the fastest, but he knew how to use his speed and agility.

It was hot.

What was not hot was watching him get hit. That part I hated. That part scared the crap out of me and had me running mental nursing diagnostics every time the other team touched him.

Then came the moment I had been dreading. He caught another pass—clean, perfect—and then out of nowhere, two guys collided into him from opposite directions, like a tight end sandwich, with Dylan as the unfortunate filling.

I screamed.

"Oh my God! Oh my God, is he—" I grabbed Annette's arm, spilling her beer.

"He's fine," Annette assured me, way too calmly for my liking.

"Fine?!" I squinted at the screen, trying to see if Dylan was moving because I couldn't see it on the field. He was moving, but in my head, I was diagnosing him with at least four different injuries: concussion, fractured ribs, dislocated shoulder, and possibly a torn meniscus for good measure.

But, to my shock, Dylan just stood up, brushed himself off, and jogged back to the huddle like it was nothing. Not even a limp. How could he walk after that hit?

"Does he know what his spine looks like right now?" I groaned, sinking back into a chair. "I don't think he's aware of how fragile vertebrae are."

"You should tell him that after the game," Annette joked, but I was only half listening. The game was coming down to the final minutes, and Dylan was back on the field, lining up for one last play.

"Please don't get hit again. Please don't get hit again," I whispered, my hands clasped like I was saying some sort of football-related prayer.

The ball was snapped, Dylan ran his route, and—thankfully—someone else caught the pass. No hit. No collision. No ER visits tonight. I exhaled for the first time in what felt like an hour.

"You doing okay, *neighbor*?" Annette asked.

The final whistle blew, and we officially won. The entire stadium erupted into cheers, throwing pizza crusts in the air like confetti, but I just sat there in a daze, trying to calm my racing heart. I felt like I needed medical attention after watching that.

"So, what do you think?" Annette asked, finishing off her beer and grinning at me.

"Is it always this exciting?" I asked, looking out at the stadium. The place was pandemonium, but a happy cheerful pandemonium. Everyone was happy. Strangers were clapping one another on the back. Friends were laughing. People were holding doors and helping one another down the steep stairs.

"Yup. You should see when we get to the playoffs. It's intense." Annette looked out at the stadium. "The guys will be in a good mood tonight. And, your *neighbor* had a great game."

She said neighbor like it was a naughty word.

"I think he finally figured out how to catch the ball," I said with a grin. "I will take full accolades, as his *neighbor*. I definitely helped. I'm very good with balls."

Annette laughed and slung her arm over my shoulder like we were the best of friends. "I hope you come to more games. You're way more fun than Alex, but don't tell him I said that."

"I promise to absolutely tell him that," I teased her, making us both laugh.

I realized why Dylan loved this game. The fans and the energy of the game was fast and loud. There was joy and competition. It felt like a family I didn't know I had, but as long as I had on this jersey, I was a part of it. It felt good to be here.

I could feel the memories being made all around us. The friendship, the comradery, and even the good-natured teasing. It felt amazing to be a part of something this big.

My phone buzzed with a text. It was Dylan. I stepped away from Annette to read it, but she was already singing out of key with another watcher to the song playing overhead.

"How'd I do?"

I smiled, shaking my head. *"You almost gave me a heart attack. Do you even feel pain?!"*

"Not when I know you're watching ?"

Ugh. He was insufferable. But also kind of adorable.

"Stick around. I'll have someone come get you and I'll drive you home," he texted.

"You are cheaper than surge pricing, so you got it," I replied, ending the message with a wink face.

I didn't understand all the stats or the plays, but I understood one thing—I was proud of him. Even if he was currently giving me gray hairs.

I sat down in a chair and nursed my beer. I knew that Dylan had to talk to reporters, and his coach, and shower, and change. He probably would get his wrist looked at, so I had plenty of time before he was ready. I didn't mind waiting. I watched the people hugging and laughing. I watched the little kids riding on their dads' shoulders and waving to strangers. I watched couples, families, and friends, all smiling and cheering to the music blaring overhead.

On the Jumbotron, key plays flickered across the screen. I winced as Dylan caught the ball, but got smushed in the process. Everyone seemed fine with it since he scored. I might not know football, but I knew one thing: I would need a stronger stomach if I were going to keep dating an NFL player.

And possibly a subscription to a meditation app.

29

ANOTHER CHANCE AT DINNER

What do you tell a nurse when she administers an injection
painlessly?
Good jab.

N ATALIE

"W OW," Dylan said as I opened the door to my apartment.

I wasn't used to him coming to my apartment since I usually met him at his. This felt formal and strange, but in a good way. It felt like a real date.

We were going to celebrate tonight. He'd had his first win of the season on Sunday. Today had been a good day at practice. We had a lot to celebrate.

I'd left Ellie with Alex at Dylan's place a little over an hour ago. Alex had agreed to take Ellie for the whole night, provided that he got tomorrow off. Tuesdays were

Dylan's day off, so he could watch her. I didn't have to work tonight, so I had a feeling I would happily be helping him tomorrow.

But tonight, the night was ours. And Dylan looked like he was excited for the night.

"Wow yourself," I said. "I'm glad you got the suit dry cleaned in time."

He shrugged. "Alex is truly a miracle worker," he said. "I'm glad you have more than one dress."

I smiled and did a little turn. The dark green dress was probably the second best dress I had. I had picked it up during a girls' trip to Las Vegas, and I had never found another one like it.

I couldn't help but blush under Dylan's appreciative gaze. His eyes traveled slowly from my low heels up to my face, lingering on the way my dress hugged my curves. I'd decided to risk the low heel tonight because there was no way I was chasing a goat again.

"You look absolutely stunning," he said, his voice low and warm. I felt a flutter in my stomach at the intensity of his stare.

"Thank you," I replied, smoothing my hands over the silky fabric. "You clean up pretty well yourself."

Dylan grinned, adjusting his tie. "I do try. I've got a surprise for you."

"Oh?" I raised an eyebrow, intrigued.

"I managed to get us reservations at La Chez again," he announced proudly.

My jaw dropped. I had thought after the evening of chasing a goat around the city that my dreams of the new French restaurant were over. "What? No way! How did you pull that off?"

"It's Monday, remember? They're not as busy at the beginning of the week. Besides, it's good business to be seen serving local celebrities."

I laughed. "So you're a celebrity, huh?"

"*Local* celebrity," he repeated. "Are you going to be okay being gawked at?"

"They're not going to be gawking at me if you're the local celebrity," I said.

He gave me another once-over. "Have you seen yourself in this dress?"

I blushed. "Well, La Chez is booked solid for months. If I get to eat there, I guess I'll deal with a few extra eyes on me."

* * *

As we drove to the restaurant, I found myself stealing glances at Dylan. He looked incredibly handsome in his suit, and I couldn't help but feel a little thrill knowing that he had gone to all this trouble for me.

"So, how are you feeling after the game yesterday?" I asked, remembering the brutal hits he had taken.

Dylan flexed his shoulders. "A little sore, but nothing I can't handle. How about you? I heard you were quite the nervous wreck in the box."

I groaned. "Annette told you about that, huh?"

"Marcus might have mentioned something during our workout," he said with a grin. "I think his exact words were 'your neighbor was ready to scrub up and play nurse on the field.'"

"I wasn't that bad," I protested weakly.

Dylan reached over and squeezed my hand. "I think

it's sweet that you were worried about me. But I promise, I'm tougher than I look."

"You'd better be," I muttered. "Because I'm not sure my heart can take watching you get tackled like that every week."

He smiled, but the smile faded away. I knew he was thinking of his injury last season, and I was sorry I had brought it up.

We pulled up to the valet stand at La Chez, and Dylan came around to open my door. As I stepped out, I caught him staring again.

"What?" I asked, suddenly self-conscious.

He shook his head, a soft smile on his face. "Nothing. I just can't get over how beautiful you look tonight."

My heart skipped a beat at his words and the unguarded expression on his face. As we walked into the restaurant, hand in hand, I couldn't help but think that maybe, just maybe, this time our dinner at La Chez would be perfect.

"Your waiter will be wif you soon, but no need to worry about ze menu," the maître d' said in a French accent that I figured must be authentic. "We have a seven-course meal prepared for you zis evening. Would you like ze standard wine pairing or somezing else?"

"The wine pairing will be great," Dylan said as he pulled my seat out.

Before I could sit down, the maître d' grabbed the chair next to him. "Ah, monsieur. I wouldn't be doing my job if I let you seat mademoiselle."

"This is so fancy," I mouthed to him. He hid his smile as he hopped back and surrendered the chair magnani-mously. I smiled and sat in the chair while Dylan sat across from me at the small table in the middle of the dining room. Dylan was right; all eyes were on us.

As we settled into our seats, I couldn't help but feel a flutter of excitement. The atmosphere was intimate and romantic, with soft lighting and the gentle clink of silverware against fine china. Dylan reached across the table and took my hand, his thumb tracing small circles on my skin.

"I'm glad we finally made it here," he said softly. "After everything that happened last time—"

"Let's not jinx it," I cut in with a laugh. "I'd rather not chase any more farm animals tonight."

Dylan chuckled, his eyes crinkling at the corners. "Fair enough. Although I have to admit, you looked pretty adorable chasing that goat. I did not realize how practical that thigh high slit could be."

I was about to retort when I noticed a young man approaching our table. He looked nervous, clutching a napkin in his hand.

"Excuse me," he said, his voice barely above a whisper. "Dylan Callahan?"

Dylan hesitated for a moment, his eyes flicking to me apologetically before turning to the fan. "I am, yes."

The young man's face lit up. "I'm such a huge fan! Would you mind signing this for me?" He held out the napkin and a pen.

I could see the conflict in Dylan's eyes. He was always so gracious with his fans, but I knew he wanted this night to be just about us. After a moment's pause, he nodded and took the napkin.

"Sure thing. What's your name?"

"Jason," the fan replied eagerly.

Dylan quickly scribbled his signature and a brief

message on the napkin before handing it back. "There you go, Jason. Thanks for your support."

Jason beamed, clutching the napkin like it was made of gold. "Thank you so much! You're the best tight end the team's ever had! I'm never trading you off my fantasy team!"

As Jason walked away, I could see other diners starting to take notice. A few were whispering and pointing in our direction. Dylan shifted uncomfortably in his seat.

"I'm sorry about that," he said, reaching for my hand again. "I hope it doesn't ruin our evening."

Before I could respond, the maître d' appeared at our table, looking flustered.

"Monsieur, Mademoiselle," he said, bowing slightly. "I must apologize for zis interruption. It was not our intention to allow zis to happen."

Dylan waved him off. "It's alright, really. We haven't even started eating yet."

The maître d' shook his head adamantly. "Non, non. It is unacceptable. I assure you, I will personally see to it zat no one else interrupts your meal zis evening. You have my word."

I couldn't help but smile at the man's earnestness. "Thank you, that's very kind of you."

As the maître d' bustled away, presumably to ward off any other potential autograph seekers, Dylan and I shared a look of amusement.

"Well," I said, raising my water glass in a mock toast. "Here's to an evening free of interruptions, farm animals, and anything else that might try to come between us and this seven-course meal."

Dylan laughed, the tension in his shoulders easing as he clinked his glass against mine. "I'll drink to that."

The waiter returned moments later with two flutes of golden, bubbling liquid. "To start your evening, we 'ave a light champagne cocktail with a twist of lemon and a splash of elderflower liqueur. Bon appétit!"

I took a sip and felt the effervescence tickle my nose. The delicate balance of flavors danced on my tongue - the crisp champagne, the subtle sweetness of elderflower, and the bright citrus notes. It was the perfect way to begin our meal.

"Oh, this is lovely," I said, savoring another sip. "What do you think, Dylan?"

He nodded appreciatively. "It's excellent. Light and refreshing - just what we need to kick things off."

As we sipped our champagne cocktails, the waiter returned with a beautifully arranged platter of hors d'oeuvres. My eyes widened at the array of delicate bites before us.

"For your hors d'oeuvres course, we have a selection of amuse-bouches," the waiter explained. "We have a goat cheese and fig tartlet, a smoked salmon blini with crème fraîche, and a duck confit crostini with cherry compote."

I couldn't help but let out a small gasp of delight. "They all look amazing!"

Dylan grinned at my enthusiasm. "Well, don't let me stop you. Dig in!"

I picked up the goat cheese tartlet first, marveling at how such a tiny morsel could be so intricately crafted. As I bit into it, the creamy tang of the goat cheese melded perfectly with the sweet fig. I closed my eyes, savoring the explosion of flavors.

When I opened them again, I caught Dylan watching me intently, a soft smile playing on his lips.

"What?" I asked, feeling a blush creep up my cheeks.

He shook his head, still smiling. "Nothing. I just love seeing you enjoy yourself."

I felt a warmth spread through my chest that had nothing to do with the champagne. "Well, you'd better try some of these before I eat them all," I teased, pushing the platter towards him.

As we worked our way through the hors d'oeuvres, I found myself stealing glances at Dylan. He seemed more relaxed now, the earlier tension from the fan interaction melting away. I loved how his eyes crinkled at the corners when he laughed, how his hands moved expressively as he talked about his latest game strategies.

Before I knew it, the platter was empty and the waiter was clearing it away. He returned moments later with two elegantly plated dishes.

"For your next course, we have a pan-seared sea bass with a lemon beurre blanc sauce, served with asparagus tips and fingerling potatoes."

The aroma wafting up from the plate was heavenly. I picked up my fork, eager to taste this new creation.

"This looks incredible," I said, carefully cutting into the perfectly cooked fish.

As I took my first bite, I couldn't help but let out a small moan of appreciation. The fish was buttery and flaky, the sauce adding just the right amount of brightness to complement it. The asparagus was crisp-tender, and the potatoes were seasoned to perfection.

I looked up to share my delight with Dylan, only to find him watching me again, his own food untouched.

There was an intensity in his gaze that made my breath catch.

"You haven't touched your food," I pointed out, my voice coming out softer than I intended.

He blinked, as if coming out of a trance. "Sorry, I just... I can't seem to take my eyes off you. The way you're enjoying everything, it's... captivating."

I felt my face heat up again, but I held his gaze. "Well, you should eat too. It's absolutely delicious."

Dylan nodded, finally picking up his fork. As we ate, we fell into easy conversation, discussing everything from our favorite childhood meals to our dream vacation destinations. I found myself laughing more than I had in ages, feeling completely at ease despite the fancy setting.

As I finished the last bite of my sea bass, I realized that for the first time in a long time, I wasn't thinking about work, or Ellie, or any of the million other things that usually occupied my mind. In that moment, it was just me and Dylan, enjoying each other's company over an incredible meal.

"You know," Dylan said, leaning in slightly, "I've been looking forward to this all week. Just you and me. No goat, no baby, no distractions."

I smiled, feeling a flutter in my chest. "Me too. It's nice to have some time to ourselves, away from... well, everything else."

He reached across the table and took my hand, his thumb tracing gentle circles on my skin. The simple gesture sent a shiver down my spine.

"I know things have been a bit crazy lately," he said softly. "With my schedule, and Ellie, and everything else. But I want you to know how much I appreciate you,

Natalie. How much you've saved my ass these last couple of weeks. How much you mean to me."

I felt my cheeks flush, and not just from the champagne. "Dylan, I-"

"I've just been thinking about a lot of things lately," Dylan said. "Am I the right person to raise this baby? Can I still play football and take care of her? And I keep coming back to the fact that I'd be lost without you. So thank you."

I looked down. I didn't know what to say. I managed to bring my eyes back up with a nervous laugh. "Well, I guess you've brought me to a nice restaurant. That makes up for a lot of it."

"You deserve it, and more. You deserve-"

The waiter cleared his throat. He had brought the fourth course, which was apparently the main course, even though I felt like I had already eaten enough. A Beef Wellington with mashed potatoes and about a dozen other garnishes was set in front of me.

Dylan must have seen my eyes dilate, because he laughed. "Why don't we discuss the heavy stuff after you've eaten?"

I didn't even wait for him to finish talking before digging in.

30

FANCY HOTEL TIME

Yes, I am a nurse. No, I don't want to look at it.
-Nurses not at work

NATALIE

AFTER AN AFTER-DINNER SOUP and a cheese course, we finally had our dessert. I would have said that I couldn't eat one bite of the chocolate mousse in front of me, but we all know that dessert goes in a different compartment.

We remained undisturbed through dinner. After paying (over the insistence of the maître d'), there was one more guy who came up to ask for an autograph. Dylan handled it as graciously as the first one, but then ushered me to the door.

Someone tried to intercept us, but Dylan put his hand on the small of my back, guiding me toward the door.

With Dylan standing between myself and the fan, I felt protected, almost as if he was my bodyguard.

We got in the car without any more fans getting in the way. He seemed relieved when he finally settled into his seat.

"Are you okay?" I asked. "You've seemed distracted tonight, like you have a lot on your mind."

Dylan laughed and shook his head. "Actually, with you around, everything seems a lot clearer."

I smiled at him. "Is that right?"

"I've told you before how close I am to getting cut from the team at the end of the preseason, right?"

I just nodded.

"I was able to play at 100% on Sunday. Because of that, they're going to play me this Sunday, and that makes the actual season look realistic. I wouldn't have been able to concentrate on the game if not for the help you've given me."

"Dylan..." I didn't know what to say. "You're welcome. Thank you for bringing me into your world."

He flashed me a grin as he pulled into traffic. "You just like my world because the food is good," he teased

"Yes, and I get free beer at your football games," I teased back. I reached for his hand, giving it a gentle squeeze. "And thank you."

"Always," he replied, pulling up to a new valet parking space.

I looked outside. This wasn't our apartment building. I gave Dylan a confused look.

"I figured that, as long as we had Alex watching the baby, we might as well stay somewhere else tonight," Dylan said, a sheepish grin on his face.

"And what makes you think I would agree to that?" I asked with a wry grin on my face.

"Well, I kind of asked while I was kissing you earlier," he said. He looked me up and down, taking in my looks. I flushed again. "And you didn't say no."

I laughed. "Then take me home."

We left the car with the valet and headed in. He held my hand as we walked in. I expected him to go to the front desk, but he walked straight toward the elevators.

A guy was in the lobby, talking on the phone. His eyes went wide when he saw us. "Holy shit, it's-"

Dylan waved and kept walking, picking up the pace a little bit. At the elevators, he scanned his card and pressed the elevator button. One of the elevators opened immediately. The guy in the lobby was still staring at us as we got in the elevators and Dylan pressed the "Close Doors" button.

"Friend of yours?" I asked.

"Everyone in this town is a friend of mine since we won," he said as he scanned the card again and pressed the top floor button. "But don't worry about that. Where were we in the car?"

"Right about here," I said, getting on my tip toes and kissing him deeply. Immediately, his hands wrapped around my waist, gripping me tightly as he slipped his tongue into my mouth.

As the elevator doors opened, Dylan's lips were still on mine. He guided me backward, his strong hands at my waist. I barely registered we were moving until I felt the cool air of the penthouse on my skin.

"Welcome to-" Dylan began, and he waved his hand over the room as if he were going to give me the grand tour. Before he could start, I cut him off with another kiss. His words dissolved into a low chuckle against my mouth.

We stumbled further into the room, neither of us willing to break apart. I heard the soft thud of my purse hitting the floor, but I couldn't bring myself to care.

Dylan pulled back slightly, his eyes twinkling. He turned back to the room. "I thought you might like to see-"

I silenced him again, my fingers threading through his hair as I pulled him close. He responded eagerly, his hands roaming down my back.

After a moment, he tried again. "There's a stunning view of the-"

This time, I nipped at his lower lip, effectively derailing his train of thought. He groaned, his grip on me tightening.

"I am *trying* to show you the fancy hotel room," he whined, but I could hear the smile in his voice.

I grinned up at him. "Less talking, more kissing."

He obliged, capturing my lips in a searing kiss that made my toes curl. We moved further into the room, bumping into furniture neither of us could see.

"Careful," Dylan warned, steadying me. "There's a-"

I silenced him once more, my hands sliding under his jacket to feel the warmth of his body through his shirt. He shrugged off the jacket, letting it fall forgotten to the floor.

I pulled back slightly, meeting Dylan's eyes with a mischievous grin. "You know what? The only thing I want to see right now is the bedroom."

His eyebrows shot up, a slow smile spreading across his face. "Well, if you insist," he said, his voice low and husky.

Dylan took my hand, leading me through the penthouse. I caught glimpses of luxurious furnishings and floor-to-ceiling windows, but my attention was solely on the man in front of me. We reached a set of double doors, which Dylan pushed open with a flourish.

The bedroom was spacious and elegant, with a massive king-sized bed as the centerpiece. But I barely registered the details. My focus was entirely on Dylan as I stepped closer to him, my hands coming to rest on his chest.

"Now, where were we?"

I slid my hands up to his shoulders, pushing his suit jacket off. It fell to the floor with a soft swish. Dylan stood still, his eyes dark with desire as he watched me.

My fingers moved to his tie, slowly loosening the knot. I took my time, savoring the anticipation building between us. Once the tie was undone, I let it slip through my fingers, joining his jacket on the floor.

Next, I turned my attention to his shirt buttons. One by one, I unfastened them, revealing more of his tanned skin with each movement. Dylan's breath hitched as my fingers grazed his chest, but he remained motionless, letting me set the pace.

When I reached the last button, I pushed the shirt open, running my hands over his muscular chest and abs. Dylan shivered under my touch, his restraint clearly wavering.

"Natalie," he breathed, his voice rough with desire.

I silenced him with a kiss, pushing the shirt off his shoulders. It fell away, leaving his upper body bare. I broke the kiss to admire him, my hands tracing the contours of his muscles.

Dylan's hands twitched at his sides, clearly itching to touch me, but he held back. I appreciated his self-control, how he was letting me take charge.

My fingers trailed down to his belt, and I looked up at him through my lashes. "Is this okay?" I asked softly.

He nodded, his eyes never leaving mine. "More than okay," he replied, his voice barely above a whisper.

I unbuckled his belt slowly, then moved to the button of his trousers. As I lowered the zipper, Dylan's breath caught in his throat. I pushed his pants down, and he stepped out of them, kicking them aside.

Now clad only in his boxer briefs, Dylan stood before me, his desire evident. I took a moment to appreciate the sight of him, my eyes roaming over his athletic body.

"Your turn," Dylan said, his voice husky with lust.

I smiled, turning my back to him. "Unzip me?"

I felt his warm hands on my shoulders, then the slow drag of the zipper down my back. His fingers trailed down my spine, leaving goosebumps in their wake. The dress loosened, and I let it fall to the floor, stepping out of it carefully.

I turned back to face Dylan, now in just my underwear and heels. His eyes widened, taking in every inch of me. The heat in his gaze made me feel powerful and desirable.

"You're so beautiful," he said, his hands hovering just inches from my skin, waiting for permission.

I closed the distance between us, pressing my body against his. The feel of skin on skin sent a jolt of electricity through me. Dylan's arms wrapped around me, pulling me even closer.

I wrapped my arms around Dylan's neck, pulling him down for a deep, passionate kiss. His hands roamed my back, tracing patterns on my skin that sent shivers down my spine. The heat between us was palpable, electric.

Dylan walked us backward until my legs hit the edge

of the bed. I sat on the edge of the bed and scooted back, beckoning him with a crooked finger.

He followed, crawling onto the bed with a predatory grace that made my breath catch. Dylan hovered over me, his eyes roaming my face as if committing every detail to memory. Then, slowly, he lowered himself, pressing his body against mine.

The weight of him felt right, like he belonged there. I ran my hands down his back, feeling the play of muscles under his skin. Dylan kissed me again, deep and slow, as if we had all the time in the world.

His lips left mine, trailing kisses along my jaw and down my neck. I tilted my head back, giving him better access. When he reached the sensitive spot where my neck met my shoulder, I couldn't help the soft moan that escaped me.

Dylan chuckled against my skin, the vibration sending a new wave of sensation through me. "I like that sound," he murmured, nipping gently at my earlobe.

I gasped, my fingers digging into his back. "Dylan," I breathed, not sure if I was pleading or praising.

He pulled back slightly, his eyes meeting mine. The intensity of his gaze made my heart skip a beat. "I want you, Natalie," he said, his voice rough with desire. "More than I've ever wanted anyone."

His admission sent a thrill through me. I reached up, cupping his face in my hands. "I want you too," I whispered back.

Dylan smiled, a mix of relief and joy crossing his features. He leaned down, capturing my lips in another searing kiss. As our tongues danced, his hand trailed down my side, leaving goosebumps in its wake.

I arched into him, craving more contact. Dylan groaned, breaking the kiss to rest his forehead against mine. "You're killing me," he panted.

I grinned, feeling bold. "That's the idea," I teased, rolling my hips against his.

His hand slid lower, tracing the edge of my underwear. I held my breath, anticipation building as his fingers danced along the fabric. When he finally touched me through the thin material, I couldn't hold back the moan that escaped me.

Dylan's eyes never left mine as he continued his gentle exploration. I felt like I was on fire, every nerve ending alive and singing under his touch. My hands roamed his back, his arms, anywhere I could reach, wanting to touch every inch of him.

His fingers slowly and carefully pushed down the fabric of my underwear, and then they pressed against my entrance. I gasped at the feeling of him touching me, wanting more. His fingers moved up a little bit, touching my clit and rubbing softly.

He looked into my eyes, his own full of desire and love as he pleasured me. His other hand moved to my breast, teasing a nipple through my bra with his fingertips as he continued his slow, gentle exploration.

I arched into him, my body begging for more, but I didn't want him to stop. It felt too good. The combined sensations were almost too much to bear.

"Dylan," I murmured, my voice hoarse from need. He looked up at me, his eyes dark. I reached down to pull my panties the rest of the way down, working them off as he continued to rub my clit. When they were finally off, I could only whisper. "Please."

He understood. He pulled his fingers from my clit, leaving me aching with desire. In one swift motion, he stood up, pulling his boxers off as he moved.

Naked, he stood above me, his virile cock erect and glistening. I reached up, taking him into my hand, stroking him slowly, feeling the heat and the texture of his skin beneath my fingertips.

With that, he positioned himself at my entrance, wanting me to take him inside of me, but I wanted to start slow. Still, as he held himself there, I found my hips rocking back and forth, trying to take him in just like he and I both wanted.

Dylan slipped inside of me slowly, inch by inch, his eyes locked with mine. He slid his hand between us to massage my breast, his thumb brushing over my hardened nipple through the lacy fabric. I gasped at the dual sensation of fullness and pleasure.

He started to move, his hips rolling in a rhythm that echoed the wild beast within him. I met his movement with my own, my body moving in time with his, desire and lust the sole guiding force.

I looked up into his eyes, drowning in the depths of his love for me. And, for a moment, all else faded away. It was just him and me, two souls connected in a dance of passion and desire.

We found our rhythm together, lost in the moment, oblivious to the world around us. The sounds of our skin hitting skin echoed in the silence of the room as we explored each other's bodies, learning every curve, every peak.

Without pulling out of me, he rolled over onto his back, pulling me with him. I cried out a little as he went deep, but then I steadied myself as my hips straddled his body. His hands went to my ass, holding me as he began to thrust upwards.

I leaned back and felt him plunge deeper into me. I reached behind myself to undo my bra, removing the last piece of clothing between the two of us. When he saw my uncovered breasts, he quickly let go of my ass and grabbed them roughly. In a few moments, he leaned up and buried his face in my chest, licking my nipples hungrily.

We writhed against each other as he reached behind me and pulled me in closer with those muscular arms of his. He drove himself deep inside of me and then looked up into my eyes.

In that moment, I could tell that he was close. He realized it too, and slowed down, as if considering pulling out of me, and there was no way I could let that happen.

"Keep going," I moaned before leaning down and kissing him. I tried my best to rock my body against his, keeping the momentum up. I didn't have to work hard for long. As soon as he saw how badly I wanted him, he moved his hands lower, grabbing me around the waist, and sped up his pace.

I moaned loudly as I felt him swell within me. His eyes darted around my body. He bit his lip as he pounded into me. I felt him tremble as we danced, both of us desperate for release.

Suddenly, he held me even tighter around the waist, slamming into me. I reached down between us and touched my clit, rubbing it fiercely as he put me exactly where I needed to be.

"Yes," I cried out. "Do it!"

I felt the splash within me as he groaned in pleasure.

The dual confirmation of his release sent me over the edge. I felt my eyes roll as I gripped his cock tightly in my body, my muscles spasming against his rigid pole.

After a few more thrusts, he fell backwards onto the bed, and I felt him shoot one last time into me. I moaned as I fell down on top of him, exhausted from the Earth-moving orgasm I had just experienced.

When I finally recovered, I propped myself up on my elbows. He was squeezing his eyes shut. His hands roamed all over body as he thrust gently, still within me despite just coming.

I danced my fingers up his chest. "So, do I get that tour now?"

He kept his eyes squeezed shut. "No tour. Just bed."

"But you were so excited before," I said with a giggle. I looked around as much as I could without losing his dick inside me. "I'm sure I heard you say something about a stunning view."

"I have the only view I need right here," he said, patting my butt gently.

"How can you see the view if your eyes are shut?" I asked. I slowly got my knees under me and pushed myself up, gasping softly as his cock finally left me. "I'm going to go take a shower, and then maybe we can check in on Alex and Ellie."

"No baby. Only bed."

I laughed again as I got up out of the bed. I grabbed the robe that was hanging on the bathroom door, then looked inside.

"You didn't tell me this place had such a cool shower!" I called out as I saw the misting feature.

"I tried to!"

31

WHAT COULD BE

"You can't fix crazy, all you can do is document it."
—Anonymous

NATALIE

"HAVE FUN IN THE GARDEN, PENELOPE," I called out as the goat left to ride up on the elevator to her penthouse garden. My aunt waved for her. We'd made it back from the hotel just in time to see Penelope off to the garden.

Alex had bolted the moment we'd arrived home. I'd never seen anyone look so tired. I couldn't blame him. Being a single dad to a baby and a goat wasn't easy.

"We are going to have to find a new goat-sitting solution soon," Dylan commented, coming out of the bedroom, his hair damp from the shower. He looked at his ruined recliner that Penelope claimed during the times she wasn't up in the garden or sleeping in the bathtub and sighed before heading to the kitchen. To be honest, the goat situation we did have was only working because Dylan's housekeeper was an amazing woman.

And Dylan paid her a lot.

It wasn't going to last. We couldn't keep Penelope in an apartment forever, even if she did love being up in my aunt's garden. She deserved to have a real life out on a farm with grass and freedom.

This was just a pit stop. A holding pattern.

Just like everything else in our world at the moment. There was a lot of things that were up in the air.

They'd won the game on Sunday, but Dylan was still unsure of his place on the team. Dylan said that the meeting to go over the game on Monday was the best day at work he's had in months.

Dylan was off the medical roster and officially on the team, but he was still afraid of being traded. The uncertainty of his future with the team ate at him. I could see it in the way he read the playbooks every moment he had a chance, the way he practiced catching and holding a ball when he thought no one was looking.

Another unknown was Ellie. I knew the DNA results for his daughter hadn't come in yet. Dylan didn't want to talk about it, but the uncertainty of her future hung like a dark cloud around the edges of our happy sunshine mornings. If she wasn't his, that meant she belonged to someone else. It meant that someone could take her from us.

And us? As a couple? We hadn't had that official talk yet. Were we a couple? Seriously dating? I wasn't sure. I mean, I was sure that I was in love with him, but that didn't mean that we had any idea of what our future together could hold. What if he got traded? What about school? What if we didn't have Ellie keeping us together?

So many what-ifs floated up in the air, just waiting to rain down ruin upon us. It made the beautiful morning feel cloudy. We just had to wait to find out when and how bad the rain would be.

Dylan brought me a steaming cup of fresh coffee without being asked. He even added the fancy sugar-free syrup I liked in just the right amount. This guy was a keeper. The warm happy feeling that someone truly knew and cared about me was almost as good as the caffeine kick.

"So, what are our plans today?" I asked as he settled on the couch next to me. "It seems all three of us have the day off."

Ellie cooed from her playpen. She liked to lay in the pen and stare at the lamp next to the couch. Lamp was her favorite thing other than Dylan.

"Yeah, that baby girl works too hard for her own good," Dylan agreed, sipping at his own coffee. He looked me over and licked his lips. "I have some ideas of things we could do."

My cheeks heated. Even though I was spending the night every night, I didn't have work, and I still wasn't used to the way he looked at me. It was like he couldn't get enough of me and my body. Every chance, he had a hand on me, stroking my arm, playing with my hair or just resting on my thigh. I craved his touch, finding ways to sit just a little closer so he could wrap an arm around me or stroke my hand. I had never felt so beautiful or so wanted in my life as I just sat in my sweatpants and bedhead hair with a gorgeous man basically drooling over me. A man that brought me coffee.

"Again?" I teased. "Last night and this morning weren't enough?"

He leaned over and kissed me, tasting of coffee and desire.

"It's never enough," he whispered, his voice low and raspy, sending little shivers down my spine that made me warm instead of cold. He grinned at my blush and leaned back, pleased with his efforts and watching me like I was everything he could ever want.

I sipped on my coffee and tried to think, but it was distracting with him sitting there, in gray sweatpants, a t-shirt that wasn't tight but didn't hide his muscles, and lounging like I didn't know that all I had to do was nod my head and he'd have me naked and moaning in seconds.

"Um..."

He grinned, knowing that he'd sent all the blood in my body away from my brain. I made a face at him. "I just need more coffee."

He laughed, smiling at me as if he knew how much I enjoyed being flustered by him. I loved the way he made my body react and yet feel so safe and wanted at the same time.

"What if we tried out the fancy new stroller Alex insisted I buy?" he offered, pointing to the very fancy black and gray stroller sitting by the door.

"You mean the one McKenna convinced him to buy with your credit card?" I asked. "I think he was just trying to impress her."

Dylan nodded. "It isn't my thing, but I am always happy to help my friends get laid."

I smacked his arm.

"I can't help it if girls like the baby carriage," Dylan replied, keeping a straight face. "I also can't help it if Alex has strange taste in women."

"McKenna is awesome," I countered, smacking his arm again.

"And I think it's sweet you stand up for your very strange friends," he continued, getting out of my reach knowing that I was going to smack his arm again. Instead, I stuck my tongue out at him making him laugh.

"But, seriously?" I asked, looking at the stroller. "I thought you didn't want to go out in public with her yet."

Dylan sipped at his coffee, obviously buying time as he decided how he wanted his words to come out.

"If anyone asks, she's Alex's niece," he said after a moment. "Since Alex has had multiple babysitting adventures with her, that's not unbelievable. She could be his niece or even his cousin."

It looked like he wanted to add something, but changed his mind.

"I'd love to walk around the park with you," I said. I pulled up the weather app on my phone. "It's supposed to be cool until lunchtime. We could pick up sandwiches on our way back."

He grinned. "You always have the best ideas."

We didn't bother to change out of our comfy clothes as they were appropriate for a walk outside, even if his gray sweatpants looked way too good on him to be allowed in public. Dylan did pull a baseball cap with the Twister icon low over his head and put on a reflective pair of sunglasses. I teased him about being a secret agent and he hummed the theme songs to both *Mission Impossible* and *James Bond* in the elevator.

Ellie loved being in the stroller. She gurgled and cooed, waving her hands at the warm sunshine. There weren't many people out on this fine Tuesday morning, which suited us both. I didn't want to have to lie to anyone, but luckily, since I worked the night shift, no one knew who I was. The baseball cap and sunglasses seemed to be working as no one asked for his autograph or tried to take his photo.

We walked the sidewalk to the park, taking our time instead of chasing a goat this time. The trees rustled in the warm sunshine and the fountain gurgled.

"We need a picture," Dylan announced, taking a seat on the fountain's edge and pulling Ellie out. She blinked at the bright sun, but happily stared at the fountain. She seemed to like the noise and I filed that away. I could play it during nap times and...

Would I still be there for nap times in a few days? When the DNA test came back, Dylan could hire a professional nanny. He wouldn't need me or my strange work hours. My chest tightened. Since we were sleeping together, I hoped and assumed that I'd still see him, but I wouldn't be the main caretaker for Ellie anymore. I didn't know if that made me excited or terribly sad. It was a conversation I knew we needed to have, but I didn't want to have it.

"Natalie, you need to be in the picture," Dylan said and I realized I was just standing there, staring at the fountain. I shook myself, sitting next to him on the stone fountain's side. He pulled out his phone and put it on selfie mode, balancing Ellie on his lap. He took off his sunglasses, setting them on the side of the fountain.

He frowned slightly as he looked at the camera screen, then wrapped his arm around me and pulled me into him. Pulling me into the picture of his life. The smile I gave to the camera was real.

He lowered the phone and grinned at the image. "We look pretty good."

I had to agree. The lighting was decent, and all three of us had looked at the camera and smiled. Even Ellie. We looked like a little family.

"Excuse me," a woman said, making me look up. I had thought we were alone. "Can I take a picture for you?" She motioned to the phone and mimed taking the picture again.

Dylan froze. He still had on his ball cap, but he'd taken the sunglasses off for the photo. The woman was probably in her mid to late thirties. She didn't have on any football gear, but that didn't mean that someone in her life didn't have Dylan's picture on their wall.

"That's really nice of you, but--" I started to say, but the woman cut me off.

"Please? As a mom, I never have any good photos of me and my kids. I'm always the one snapping the photo, so all I have are terrible selfies with my kids. Let me take the picture so you have a good non-selfie one."

"Sure," Dylan said, handing over his phone. He pulled me into him again, smiling for the woman.

She grinned and started snapping photos, even kneeling so that the "light would be better." She made silly cat sounds to make Ellie look at the camera. I began to wonder if she was a professional photographer and this was all some kind of elaborate setup.

"Thank you," Dylan said when the woman handed him back his phone.

She beamed at him. "You have such a lovely family," she gushed. "And thank you for letting me do that." She turned to me. "Make sure you get some pictures of yourself and don't always hide behind the camera. It's easy to do as a mom."

We thanked her again and she jogged off down the path and away from us.

"Do you think she knew who you are?" I asked when she was out of earshot.

"Nope. She just thought we were a cute family," Dylan assured me. He showed me the screen of his phone. "These came out really good."

The screen showed the three of us, all smiling and laughing. The sky was blue, the fountain lovely, but it was the soft way that Dylan held me to him in the photo, the way that Ellie leaned against us both, that had my heart spinning.

We could have been on a commercial for the city. *"Bring your family for the perfect family adventure!"* My throat tightened.

"Make sure to send me a copy," I said, wanting to have a piece of this day forever. I wanted this feeling forever. The three of us. A family. A life. Even if it was all just a dream, even if this all ended in a fiery ball of pain in two weeks, I wanted a record. I would treasure that photo until the end of my days.

"I think she's getting hungry," Dylan remarked,

putting Ellie back in her stroller. We started the short walk back home.

"Ellie, or you?" I asked, noticing that Ellie was not sucking on her hands, or showing any other signs of hunger for that matter.

"Me," Dylan confessed. "I've been thinking of those sandwiches all morning."

I laughed, my heart feeling light and heavy at the same time. I was so damn happy to be in this moment, I could float. I was floating. But I knew that this was temporary. Things were going to change. They had to change.

And I was afraid they might change in a way I didn't want.

But I refused to think about that. I refused to consider any future right now that didn't have a happily ever after with all three of us growing old together. Well, Ellie could leave when she turned eighteen to go become a famous scientist. That was acceptable.

"So, I've been thinking," Dylan said in the elevator. I held my breath when the doors opened and we went into his home.

"Thinking about what?" I asked. The words *"So, I've been thinking"* were rarely good in a relationship as young as ours.

"The apartment next to me is going up for sale next month. What if I bought it and made Ellie a real bedroom?"

"I didn't know Mr. Chandler was moving," I replied, focusing on keeping my feet underneath me. Ellie fussed as I took her out of the stroller. She clung to me, her eyes heavy and ready for a nap. To be honest, I was ready for a nap too. I was used to sleeping at this time of day.

"You aren't the only one with contacts in the building," Dylan informed me with a teasing smile.

I raised an eyebrow.

"He offered to sell it to me early," Dylan admitted. "But I haven't said yes. When he asked, I didn't think I needed the extra room, but with Ellie..."

I yawned, my jaw cracking.

"It looks like I have two very tired girls," Dylan said, crossing his arms and looking at the two of us. "I think you both need a nap."

"It's fine..." I started to say, but he ushered us both into the bedroom.

"Come lay down and dream with me for a moment," he said, patting the big bed. He pointed to the wall before closing the curtains and making the room dark. "That's the other apartment. It only has two rooms, but I think it could work."

Dylan flopped onto the bed so I could hand him Ellie. He tucked her into the nook of his arm and then motioned to me. I snuggled into both of them, using his bicep as a pillow, my body curving around the already sleeping baby nestled between us like an egg in a nest.

I sighed with contentment, my body relaxing into the bed and into Dylan.

"We'll put her nursery in the room there," Dylan explained, pointing to a wall. "We can paint it pink."

"Pink?" I shook my head. "Teal. Teal is the new pink."

Dylan paused, thoughtful. "Okay. Teal. But I want to get her a tea set. A real one, not something plastic. I want real tea parties."

The idea of this big strong man drinking tea out of a teacup with his small daughter was ovary exploding, heart-achingly beautiful. I smiled, my eyes growing heavy.

"I like that. Keep telling me more. I want all the dreams."

He smiled over at me, rotating onto his hip so that we faced each other in the darkened room. We were in our own world. Our own magical little space where nothing bad ever happened. Where dreams and hopes were real and joy was always an everyday thing. This place, this moment was safe and wonderful.

"We can have so many plans," he whispered. "You can go to school. I could pay for it so you don't need the scholarship. We'll get a nanny. Maybe we'll get a house. A yard would be nice. Then we could keep Penelope."

My eyes were so heavy, but I giggled. "She needs a farm, not a yard."

"Okay, we don't have to keep Penelope, but she could at least come and visit," Dylan amended. I liked hearing these dreams. It was soothing to hear him ramble these lovely ideas in a soft voice. But they weren't real plans. These were sweet nothings. Dreams that would fall apart as soon as we opened the curtains and let in the light.

"You are so beautiful," he whispered, his voice so low I almost didn't hear him. I assumed he was talking about Ellie, but then he brushed the hair from my forehead.

A delicious, wonderful warmth filled my chest at the simple gesture. At his dreams of us together. I knew they were just dreams, but I loved the idea of them. I loved the way they filled my lungs with hope and my heart with a joy so bright I was sure I was shining in the dark. Sleep pulled heavy on me, leading me into real dreams of what we could become.

I felt Dylan carefully pull his arm out from under my head and make sure that the pillow that replaced it was soft and perfectly placed. I felt him carefully tuck a blanket around me, warm and soft. I was mostly asleep as he picked up Ellie, leaving me to sleep the day away in his bed. My body relaxed, my breathing slow and even as I slipped into a deep sleep.

"I love you," he whispered, leaning over to kiss my forehead. "I want those dreams. All of them. More of them. And always with you."

He left me sleeping in the dark, my heart pounding with love.

32

FORCED TO PARTY

*I can't guarantee that anybody in the world will be alive
Sunday, so I can't guarantee who will be on our roster on
Sunday*
-Kyle Shanahan

DYLAN

"DO I HAVE TO?"

Coach glared at me from under bushy eyebrows. "Yes. It's mandatory."

I would have rather run laps for hours. I would rather flip tires, run drills, sprints, anything... anything but this.

"Besides, it's a fundraiser for a good cause," Coach continued, ignoring my best attempt at puppy-dog eyes. "Delano is out sick with the flu. We have to send someone.

Your star is back on the rise and the team owners requested you specifically."

I shifted from one foot to the other and wished I could run out of Coach's office.

"I can't," I told him.

He raised an eyebrow and asked "Why?" in that tone that made me double check my uniform was on straight.

"I just... It's Friday and..." I didn't have a babysitter tonight. Natalie was working and I'd promised her I would never ask her to watch Ellie on workdays. Alex had a date with McKenna and had made me promise I wouldn't interrupt with anything short of a nuclear disaster.

I didn't have anyone else I could ask at this point.

But I couldn't tell Coach about my daughter. Not yet.

"This isn't a request. This is for your career," Coach reminded me, his voice low and dangerous. "You need all the good publicity you can get right now. You're not clear from being traded. This is the best way for you to get in good with the Clarences and stay with this team."

"And the Clarences requested me specifically?" I asked, more to buy time than as a real question.

Coach nodded. "I'm telling you that this is the only way to survive this season," he said. He sighed. "And I want you to stay here, Dylan. I really do."

If that wasn't enough to make me feel guilty for the rest of my life, I wasn't sure what was. Maybe I could kick a puppy. I didn't want to let Coach down.

"Then I'll be there," I said, deciding I could find a solution. There were always solutions, right?

"In a tux," Coach added. "I expect you to be on your

best behavior. Remember we have a game Sunday and I need you to be ready."

I left Coach's office with my shoulders deflated and without a plan.

I would just have to ask Natalie. I'd pay her extra. So much extra. I would make it up to her somehow, but I needed her to watch Ellie tonight. I didn't have time to find someone else. I couldn't trust anyone else.

I slumped into the empty locker room. Everyone was already gone for the day since I'd had to stay late to talk to Coach. I was glad. The last thing I wanted was for Marcus to ask me to come have burgers or Franklin to need advice. I thought about asking one of them to watch Ellie and shuddered. That wouldn't work. They couldn't know about her yet.

I sat down on the cement bench dreading the text message I needed to send. I wasn't even going to try calling first. I was too much of a coward.

My phone had three missed calls and a new very important email. I swallowed hard. I wasn't ready to read that email that said if my daughter was truly mine. I loved her. I knew that, but if she wasn't my blood, that meant someone else would want her.

My hands trembled. I didn't want to open that email, so I did the other horrible thing I needed to do.

"I need you to watch Ellie tonight. It's important. I'll pay you extra."

Shame washed over me as I hit send. She was going to be so furious and I couldn't blame her. I'd promised I wouldn't do this, but I didn't see much of an option.

I glanced around the empty locker room.

With a deep breath, telling myself that it didn't matter,

that I had to do this, that it would all be okay, I opened the email and read the results.

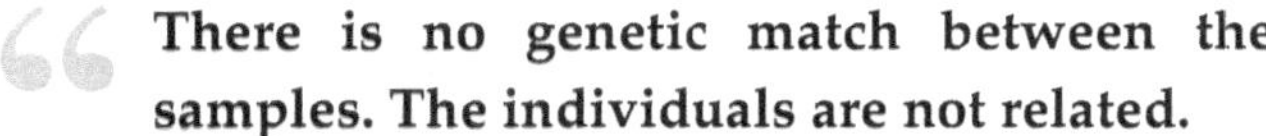

> **There is no genetic match between the samples. The individuals are not related.**

The words swam across the screen. I swear she had my eyes, but... they were someone else's eyes. That nose wasn't mine. Her amazing little grip had absolutely nothing to do with me.

Ellie wasn't my daughter.

The phone clattered to the floor as it fell from my hands.

She wasn't mine.

Heartache so deep I wanted to howl and scream raged through me, but at the same time, I couldn't move. I was frozen to the bench, my eyes not seeing the room around me. The world spun around me so hard that I thought I might throw up.

"Hey man, you okay?" Alex's soft voice echoed through the empty room. I looked at him, not really registering anything.

Ellie wasn't mine.

"You read the email." Alex sat down next to me on the bench. "I'm really sorry. You've been a really good dad to her."

I didn't have words. I didn't know how to talk anymore. A bone deep hurt, an ache I didn't even know I could feel reverberated through my being.

And Alex just sat with me. He didn't say anything else. He just sat with me, keeping me company as I worked through the horrible emotions rolling through me. There was no judgment. Just friendship. He knew how much this hurt, so he just gave me the silent support I needed. Without words, I knew that he was there for me. That he understood.

"She's not mine? Are you sure? The test isn't wrong?" My voice cracked with the wild hope that the testing company had screwed up and sent me the wrong results.

"I talked with your lawyer," Alex replied. "There is no doubt on the test."

The little flame of hope blinked out of existence. I sank into darkness.

"What do you want to do?"

Alex asked it with such softness in his voice, yet each word stabbed like a knife. What did I want to do? She wasn't mine. Another man could be looking for her. Another father might not know she was out there, but would he love her the second he saw her? Would he be a better father than I could ever be? He was her real father.

She wasn't mine. She wasn't supposed to be my responsibility.

Yet all I could think of was her little fingers. The fact she loved anything by the Beatles and Taylor Swift but would scream the minute we put on any 90s music. The way she milk drunk smiled at me.

"Do you know anything about her real parents?" Those words hurt coming out. Her real parents. Not Natalie and me.

"There isn't anything in the system for her mom," Alex replied. He sighed. "But there is a DNA hit on the father."

Hope, fear, disgust, and anger all rose up inside me at the same time. I thought I might throw up.

"He's not a great guy," Alex continued. "Your lawyer

says he won't be a problem with whatever you choose to do."

"What do you mean?"

Alex handed me his phone. A news article filled the screen. The man that shared DNA with my Ellie was wanted for several felonies and was last seen in Mexico running from the authorities. Anger sizzled down my veins. How could he do this to his daughter? How could he abandon her like that?

Because he didn't know. I knew that was the answer. The anger evaporated as quickly as it had come.

I looked at the picture of the man. He had similar coloring as me, but only in a generic sense.

"He's not going to contest any custody arrangements," Alex said, taking back his phone.

"He looks familiar," I said, leaning against the wall and staring up at the ceiling. "Do I know him?"

"He used to live in the building. He lived in the apartment directly below yours," Alex replied. "I spoke with the front desk. He was a real ladies' man. Apparently, he would tell all the women he brought home that he played for the Twisters." Alex scoffed. "He was an accountant. I doubt that man even knew what a touchdown was."

I thought about what the front desk lady had said.

The damn Twister player. We were not the same. Again, anger buzzed through my veins, but there wasn't enough steam in it to do anything.

The ceiling didn't hold any answers, so I looked down at my hands. I remembered the feel of my daughter.

"So, she's not mine. Her dad is scum. Her mom is a ghost." My fists clenched. "And I need a babysitter for tonight."

Alex winced. "Non-refundable tickets."

"Is your cousin available?"

Alex shook his head. "I mean, I can ask, but it's one of the boy's concert's tonight. He plays violin. I'm already in trouble for missing it to go on this date that I am about to be late for. My whole family is going, so they're all out."

"I asked Natalie." My heart continued to sink. Today sucked. "She hasn't responded yet."

"She'll be fine with it," Alex assured me, his voice full of false bravado. We both knew she wouldn't be. "Pay her extra. Maybe bring flowers or something."

"Penelope will just eat the flowers," I replied, feeling that plan going down the drain as well.

"So it's a win-win, everyone is happy," Alex tried to laugh, but it came out strangled.

"I don't know what to do, Alex." Despair filled my lungs.

"About a babysitter? I told you, flowers and extra money."

"No, I mean..." I sighed, running my hands through my hair and wishing I could punch something. "I'm not Ellie's dad."

Alex didn't say anything.

"Do I keep her? Do I do the single dad thing?" I asked him, not really expecting an answer. "She's not mine. I mean, I can adopt her, but what if she ends up hating me for it? I keep reading about all these terrible adoption stories online."

"You shouldn't believe everything you read..." Alex began.

"What about your cousins? They want her. Would they be better?" I didn't wait for him to answer. "What about

Natalie? This will break her heart. She loves the kid. She's practically Ellie's mom, but I've known her for all of a couple weeks. She's not really Ellie's mom and I can't ask her to make that life choice on two weeks. She has her own dreams. It always supposed to be a short term solution."

"You are going way above my pay grade," Alex said after a moment of silence.

"I pay you. I can afford you," I replied.

Alex sighed. "I don't know, man. I wish I had answers for you. Hell, I don't even know what I would do if our situations were reversed. It's a shit sandwich. There is no good way to eat it. Every option is hard and sucks." He sighed again. "*Mi abuela* would say, 'pick the option that sucks less,' but I don't know what that is."

We sat in silence for a moment.

"But I'll support you no matter what you choose," Alex promised. "I'm here for you, and not just because you pay me. Whatever you choose, I've got your back."

"They might trade me." The words hurt coming out.

"Well, can you try and get someplace warm?" Alex asked. "I don't want to deal with snow if I can help it, but I think I could get into hockey if absolutely necessary."

"You'd come with me?" An ache behind my chest grew to the point an alien should have exploded out of it.

"Someone's got to keep an eye on you," Alex replied with a shrug. "*Abuela* would be pissed if I didn't make sure you ate once in a while. She likes you."

"No, she doesn't," I said, thinking of the grumpy old woman that always glared at me when I visited.

"She bets on you every week," Alex replied softly. "She's up over ten grand because of it."

"No way." I shook my head and scoffed. "I lost every game but the last one. She can't be up."

"She started betting on you in college," Alex explained. "Overall, you're a winner. *Abuela's* never wrong."

I stared at him in surprise. I couldn't believe that his grandmother, a stern woman who didn't speak three words of English, had believed in a scrawny boy who was friends with her grandson enough to bet on him. And keep betting on him.

"You've got this," Alex said. "You'll figure out the best option. You always do. Not every play works every time, but you have the best record I know. You can do this."

A little of the darkness surrounding my heart lightened.

"Thank you."

"Now go take a shower. You reek." He made a gagging face. "I'll go find you some flowers and a tux. You should ask her to babysit wearing the tux. Girls love a guy in a suit."

I didn't feel much better, but at least now I had a plan.

33

FORCED NOT TO PARTY

If you take my good pen, I will cut you.
-Nursing Staff Everywhere

NATALIE

I COULDN'T BELIEVE he had the audacity to show up in a tux.

A freaking tux.

I was calling out of work at the last minute so that he could go to a damn party. I thought something big had happened when he'd asked, something that his team really needed him for, but no. He was going to a *party*.

"Are you serious?" I stared at him, absolutely dumbfounded. "We had an agreement. I am supposed to work tonight. You promised me that you would never do this."

"It's an emergency," he tried to tell me.

"Emergency? I didn't know tuxedos were the new emergency wear. What kind of emergency? Is there a ball-room that needs dancers? Perhaps some champagne that is about to go to waste?"

"It's not like that," he snapped at me. "I didn't have a say in this. Coach is making me."

"Right. I see him twisting your arm." I glared at him. I would have slammed the door in his face if I wasn't in his apartment and not my own. Also, it would scare Penelope and Ellie. "How would your coach react to you calling in two hours before a game?"

He didn't answer.

"I'm so sorry, Coach, but I don't feel good. I need to go to a party," I mimicked in an unflattering voice. I would have stomped my foot if I knew it wouldn't make me look like an angry child. "We are short staffed tonight. Do you know how unprofessional it is for me to call out with less than four hours notice?"

I inwardly cringed at the memory of telling Sherri I would be late tonight. The disappointment flecked with panic in her voice as she tried to figure out how to staff an ER on a Friday night.

I tried to take a breath. I tried to calm myself down. Ellie was already fussing, sensing the rising tension in the room, but I was furious.

"I didn't know about this until today. I got called in," he informed me. I hated that he looked really good in that tux. The fact that I liked the way he looked in it just made me madder.

"Call Alex."

"I did. He can't." He held out the flowers. I did not take them.

"Oh, that's right, he had a date. Glad to see what your priorities are." I walked away from him, leaving the flowers and pretending that Ellie needed her blanket from the coach.

"That's not fair," he growled at me, tossing the flowers onto the table.

I tried the deep breathing technique the labor and delivery nurses had taught us to calm laboring mothers in the ER. I could be calm. I could be a grownup. I didn't have to be a mean vindictive bitch. Even though he deserved it.

A *party*.

He didn't even have the decency to invite me to go with him. Not that I really had anyone to babysit, but that was beside the point. He didn't know that. He'd just assumed that I would watch Ellie.

"I can cover the first four hours," I said through gritted teeth. "You have until one am. Then I need to go to work. My boss is pissed, but that is the best I can do."

He looked like he might reject that proposal and I would have flipped out on him. Nothing good in the world happened after one in the morning at parties with alcohol. Nothing that he needed to be a part of, anyway.

I stomped to the kitchen and began making Ellie a bottle.

"I can say that I'm tired and need to rest so I'm ready for Sunday," he said. "No one will have an issue with that."

"And you can't use that now?" I asked, repositioning

Ellie in my arms. She was wiggling and fussing for the bottle even though it wasn't ready yet.

"No. This is a mandatory fundraiser. I am expected to be there. The owners of the team asked for me personally. I don't really have a choice," he replied, anger sharpening his voice into something that didn't sound quite like him.

"Sounds rough." Sarcasm echoed through every word. I saw his jaw clench.

"Here, I'll take her. You can finish the bottle," he offered, the words kind but the tone harsh.

"And have her ruin your tux? Nope." I put the nipple on the bottle a little harder than was necessary. "I won't be responsible for her ruining your suit."

"Doesn't matter anyway," he mumbled. "She won't be my problem for long."

"And what's that supposed to mean?" I asked, giving Ellie her bottle. She quieted once she was being fed.

"It's not important," he hedged.

"Oh no, now you get to explain." I moved next to him, staring up at him and daring him to defy me in this as well. "What do you mean your daughter doesn't matter anyway?"

"That's not what I said," he spat. He stared at me, anger and something I couldn't figure out in his eyes. It didn't suit him. "But she's not my daughter."

The world could have gone up in flames and I wouldn't have noticed. A brass band could have marched through that kitchen and Penelope could have started singing opera as a soprano and I wouldn't have blinked.

"What?"

He ran his hand through his hair, messing up the

careful hairstyle he had obviously spent time making look nice for his party.

"I don't have time for this right now, Natalie," he said, heading toward the door. I cut in front of him like one of the defenders on the opposite team.

"No, you will make time." I stood firm in front of him.

"The DNA results came in. She's not mine." His voice was flat. Emotionless. Like he didn't care that this beautiful little girl wasn't his.

"Were you ever going to tell me?" I asked softly, clutching her to me.

"Of course, I was going to tell you!" he yelled, anger and hurt clouding his face. "I just fucking found out!"

I took a step back, the force of his anger pushing me away.

"You said she won't be your problem for long." Righteous anger was flaring white hot inside of me, replacing the red hot anger of being told what to do. "You going to abandon her and go back to all your parties?"

Hurt flashed across his features for a second before he snarled, "I don't know what I'm going to do! I don't even know what the fuck I am doing! I was never supposed to be her father, don't you get it? She was never mine! I don't deserve her!"

I took another step back. I knew that he was hurting. I knew that he was in a terrible emotional upheaval and that I should be kind.

But I was still mad. I was seething angry that he'd kept this from me. That he was going to a party after dropping that bombshell.

"So, what? You're going to put her on her real dad's doorstep?"

"Alex has a cousin in the countryside that wants her. They will give her a better home than I ever could." His words were calm. All the fight went out of him. He refused to look at me, instead turning to the door and opening it up.

I didn't have words. I just stood there staring after him as he walked away and closed the door, leaving me and his daughter, no, the unwanted baby, behind.

I looked down at Ellie, happily sucking away on her bottle and oblivious that her entire world was about to be rocked. Everything she knew was about to change.

I slid to the floor, unable to keep myself standing. This wasn't how this was supposed to go. We'd been planning such a beautiful life. I felt the dream evaporate like smoke around me and I knew I'd been foolish to believe in the sweet plans we'd made.

They were just whispers of a future that could never be.

I didn't even want to think about what getting rid of Ellie meant for our relationship. I wanted to believe that he loved me and we'd figure this out. But he hadn't consulted me with any of this. Not the party, not the DNA test, not the fact that he'd apparently had Alex put in adoption papers for his cousin.

I wasn't a part of the plan. I wasn't a consideration. If I wasn't even being consulted about where Ellie would end up, why did I have any reason to believe that he'd want me in any other parts of his life? I'd just been a convenient babysitter that put out.

"Don't catastrophize," I told myself, but it was too late. I was already imagining and believing the worst possible scenarios. A sob welled up from somewhere deep inside of me, painful and shocking in its intensity.

"I don't want you to go," I whispered, feeling my throat go tight with tears. I kissed the top of Ellie's head, my heart aching and feeling the world about to crumble around the both of us. "I hope Alex's cousin needs a babysitter. You won't be getting rid of me that easy."

And then I sobbed.

34

PARTY TIME DECISIONS HAVE CONSEQUENCES

Football is, after all, a wonderful way to get rid of your
aggressions without going to jail for it.
-Woody Hayes

DYLAN

"LET ME TELL YOU, having four hundred pounds of man on top of you is not that pleasant." I laughed, but my heart wasn't in the story. Luckily, none of the guests seemed to notice. They all chuckled and smiled, giving the appropriate party etiquette laughs.

"I don't know, I think I could learn to live with it," one of the ladies in a low-cut red dress said with a laugh. I noticed her husband took the glass of wine away from her.

"There you are, Callahan," Coach said, coming up

behind me and putting a hand on my shoulder. "The owners wanted to have a word with you."

I swallowed hard, but smiled and nodded at the rich guests who were donating lots of money to a children's charity. They had moved onto another conversation before I had even taken a step.

"Thanks for coming tonight," Coach said, walking beside me. "I know you had other plans, but I do appreciate this. It's for a good cause."

I looked around at the banners proclaiming that all the money donated would go to fighting children's cancer. If I had known that, I would have volunteered. I didn't want to think about Ellie having anything worse than a stuffy nose. I could only imagine the pain that would cause both me and Natalie.

I winced.

I wouldn't have cared a month ago. Not really. I always cared about kids, but it wouldn't have been personal. Apparently having kids changed things.

The ballroom was packed with glittering gowns, perfectly tailored suits, and more champagne glasses than I could count. Coach and I weaved through the party guests, and I stayed away from the champagne. I straightened the lapels of my tux, feeling out of place, like a linebacker at a ballet recital.

"Hey, there's our star tight end!"

I turned at the sound of the voice and made myself find my calm. I really wished I had a glass of champagne now. It was the owners of the team. The ones who signed my checks, controlled my future, and could ship me off to some other team whenever they felt like it.

"Mr. and Mrs. Clarence," I said, shaking Mr. Clarence's

hand with just enough grip to seem manly but not enough to shatter his fingers. Mrs. Clarence, of course, went in for a hug, and I managed not to drop my nonalcoholic drink.

"Look at you all dressed up! I hardly recognize you without a helmet on," Mrs. Clarence laughed, her eyes crinkling with genuine warmth. "I keep telling my husband we need to host more events like this just so we can see our players looking civilized for once."

"Oh, you mean not in uniform?'" I joked. "Or just not covered in mud?"

"I like the mud," the woman in the red dress called out.

"We really liked seeing you play this week," Mrs. Clarence said, ignoring the other woman.

Mr. Clarence chuckled and clapped me on the back. "Exactly. You're doing well, son. Really well."

My throat went dry. I had no idea where this conversation was going, but I knew it was important. Owners don't make small talk with their players unless there's something big coming. They hadn't asked me here tonight because they wanted to hear my bad jokes. I braced myself for the worst.

"We wanted to talk to you, actually," Mr. Clarence continued, his tone suddenly serious. "There's been a lot of chatter, as you probably know, about trades. Especially with your contract situation coming up."

I nodded, trying to look casual. Inside, I was anything but. I'd heard the rumors. Hell, I'd lived the rumors, every time I walked into the locker room and caught guys whispering about who was going where. The NFL is a business, and loyalty is just a nice word they print on t-shirts. Beside me, Coach tensed.

"We've been watching you," Mrs. Clarence said, her

voice softer, like she was trying to put me at ease. "We see the work you've been putting in. Not just on the field, but off it. The leadership, the attitude... you're a big part of this team. Coach has been telling us all the extra you've been doing the past couple of weeks."

I swallowed hard. "Thank you. That means a lot."

"And it's obvious you *want* to be here," Mr. Clarence added. "That's important to us."

Okay, now they had my full attention. They weren't talking like people who were about to hand me a plane ticket to some other city. This was... different.

"We started this franchise with a vision," Mrs. Clarence continued. "A vision for the future. Our kids are going to inherit this team one day. They're too young to understand it now, but we're building something we want them to be proud of. A legacy."

"And you're a part of that," Mr. Clarence finished. "You belong here. You've earned your place. We're not trading you, son."

For a second, I forgot how to breathe. No trade. I wasn't getting shipped off to some random team, some random city where I'd have to start all over again. Relief washed over me so hard, I almost hugged them both, but I figured Mrs. Clarence might not appreciate my drink being spilled down her dress since my hands were shaking so hard.

"We want our children to grow up knowing they're part of something bigger," Mrs. Clarence said, glancing at her husband. "And that's what you're helping us do. We're proud of what we're building, and you're going to be a big part of it."

I smiled a real smile, not the half-hearted one I gave

reporters when they asked the same questions after every game. "I'm proud to be a part of it, too."

As they moved on to mingle with other guests, I stood there, letting it all sink in. I wasn't going anywhere. I had a place, a future.

"Good job," Coach said. "You've made it."

And then, like a blitz from nowhere, it hit me.

This was exactly the kind of conversation I'd been waiting for, wasn't it? The reassurance that I wasn't just a replaceable piece of machinery, that I was valued. And I hadn't even realized how much that mattered until now. But the truth was, I wanted that kind of certainty somewhere else in my life, too.

My girls. Natalie and Ellie.

They were the kind of certainty that I wanted. They were the only things I wanted.

I had been acting like there was always more time, like I'd eventually get around to telling her how I felt. But there was *never* time, not in this life. We only had this one chance. If I didn't take it, it would be gone forever.

If I could stand here in a room full of billionaires and tell them I was all in for their legacy, I could damn well tell the woman I loved how I felt about her. That I wanted to raise our daughter together. That I wanted to have more children with her. That I wanted to give her every dream she could ever want and make sure she always knew how much I loved her. That I wanted to grow old with her and never spend a day without seeing her smile.

How much I just wanted to be with her.

I downed the rest of my drink, set the glass on a tray, and came up with a plan. Time to stop being a coward.

I needed to make things right. I pulled out my phone, ready to make some calls.

Then, in true football fashion, I fumbled my phone, dropped it, and almost knocked over a waiter trying to pick it up.

Yeah. This was off to a great start.

35

COME TO THE GAME

*"Don't piss off nurses. They're like the mafia. Piss off one and
you piss off the rest."*
— Unknown

NATALIE

"WILL you be watching the game today?" Dylan asked.

I considered being a bitch and saying no.

But he had come home last night by eleven and given me a really nice packed lunch with my favorite energy drink, apologized for wasting my time, and handed me several crisp hundred dollar bills.

When I'd come home from work Saturday morning, there was a cooler full of Mexican food waiting by my door. The salsa told me it was from Alex and his family, but the note just said, *"For Natalie. Love Dylan."*

It was a bribe not to be mad at him, but one I was willing to take. Still, I'd spent all of Saturday crashed out after the crazy night working, and I cowardly didn't want to talk to him in the evening. I knew he had pregame rituals, so I pretended that I was really doing him a favor by not bothering him.

This morning, I'd come over and he handed me the baby and asked if I would be watching the game.

"Ellie likes watching it," I said. "And it's better than that weird bald-kid show."

"High praise," Dylan replied with a grin. "Then, if you're watching, know that I'm playing for my girls today."

He kissed my cheek faster than I had time to react, not that I would have stopped him. I liked those kisses on my cheek that felt so safe and normal. A man kissing his wife before he headed off to work.

And then he was out the door and off to the stadium.

It made me wonder if Friday night had just been a fever dream. If I had imagined our fight, or maybe I'd missed the part where we made up. I really hoped I hadn't missed that part, because make-up sex was usually pretty awesome.

It was Penelope's last few days in the garden with my aunt. I felt bad that I didn't really have a plan for her after this weekend. Dylan had been so busy this week that I doubted he'd had time to set up placement on a farm. Bitterly, I wondered if Alex's cousin also wanted a goat. They could just have everything then.

"Are your ready to watch Dylan on TV today?" I asked Ellie, enjoying the toothless smile she gave me. I almost said, "Are we going to watch Daddy on TV today?" but I managed to catch myself. I understood why he didn't want the single dad life for a child that wasn't his. I knew he loved Ellie, but I also knew that it was a big ask. Not to mention, I wasn't sure what all the legalities were since he wasn't her biological parent. I was just really glad that Dylan was rich enough to be able to afford all the lawyers who could figure this stuff out.

There were perks to being rich.

I tried not to be sad or angry. I tried not to cry as Ellie and I snuggled on the couch, but it was hard. I didn't want to lose this. I didn't want these wonderful Sunday mornings to go away. I turned on the pregame, but wasn't really paying attention.

I was starting to recognize names: Marcus, Franklin, Cameron; and positions: quarterback, center, and running back. I now understood, thanks to Annette, how the game was scored and I didn't feel like a complete idiot at least, but it was still a foreign language most of the time. Besides, we still had several hours before the game actually started.

I did my laundry and made Ellie and I a snack. We snuggled and napped like we usually did on our days together. It was simple and felt normal, yet my heart ached with the idea that this could be the last time. I hated that I might not have these baby snuggles. That I would watch her grow via Facebook photos and random birthday invites. I wouldn't be in her life like a parent anymore.

Even though I loved her like she was my own flesh and blood.

I would die for this kid. I would chop off my arm if it meant she would have a good life. I kept catching myself dreaming about parent-teacher conferences and school dances. Would she be sporty or bookish? Would she like princesses or Pokemon? What books would we read together?

So many future things that I wasn't going to experience with her.

I knew that those things were never guaranteed anyway. I wasn't married to her dad. I was a glorified nanny, but still... that didn't stop my imagination from wanting a life with her.

I was glad when the game started and I had something outside of this apartment to focus on. I almost didn't want to watch. I hated watching as Dylan got hit and tackled, but I loved watching him run. He made a great play and the camera zoomed in on him, and even through his helmet, I could see the joy of the game on his face. He'd faked out two guys and made a gain of thirty yards. Even the announcers were impressed.

"We have the old Callahan back!" they cheered.

It looked like we were going to win the game. I say we, because I did consider the team mine now, even if I hadn't done a darn thing to justify the win. No, that wasn't true. I'd worn the Twister's jersey Dylan had given me for my first in-person game. And my lucky underwear.

Just because I wasn't thrilled with Dylan's choices at the moment didn't mean that I wasn't going to support him with everything that I could.

I was a team player.

My phone rang. Alex's number popped up.

"What do you want?" I answered sounding mad but smiling so he could hear the teasing in my voice.

"I need your help," Alex replied, his voice not full of teasing or smiles. I sat up straight.

"What do you need?" The teasing vanished. I was already switching into nurse mode.

"I need you to come to the stadium," he replied. I could hear voices in the background shouting, but it sounded like he was in the VIP suite watching the game. "It's an emergency. I think I may need stitches."

"I can't give you stitches. And I have Ellie. If it's that bad, you need to go to the ER," I told him. "You can call McKenna. It's a good excuse to talk to her unless the date went badly last night."

"The date went amazing, thank you very much," he informed me. "But she can't help me. I need you for this. I can't explain it on the phone, but it has to be you."

I sighed and rolled my eyes. He probably just needed a band-aid or something. Besides, didn't they have EMTs at the games? I was sure he could get better help than what I could give.

"I have Ellie," I reminded him.

"Bring her." Alex sounded confident again. "Please. I need you to get to the stadium. Please."

There was something in his voice that made me want to hop in the car and drive. It wasn't fear. It wasn't pain. It was something earnest and sincere.

"The game is almost over. The traffic is going to be insane," I whined, glancing at the TV. It had been a close enough game that no one had left early. "And I really hate lugging that baby car seat everywhere."

"I promise I will make this easy," he coaxed.

"There is nothing easy about hauling a four-month-old baby into a crowded stadium, Alex," I informed him.

"Come on," he pleaded. "I never ask for anything. Just this."

"You ask for plenty!" I said with a laugh. "Remember who got you your girlfriend?"

"Please, Natalie." Something in his voice had me pausing again. *The sincerity.*

I sighed. "Fine. It'll take me a while to find parking, but I'll go get us in the car."

I heard more voices on the other end of the line. "I have a driver coming to get you. He's got a car seat base already installed. You don't have to deal with a thing. Thank you. I promise you, this is important."

I glanced down at the phone to make sure I was still talking with Alex. How had he fixed that up so quickly? I guess he probably had all sorts of contacts being Dylan's personal assistant, but getting a private driver with a car seat installed was pretty impressive.

When I got Ellie and her car seat down to the lobby and into the car, Alex's skills had me even more impressed. The base was the correct model for Ellie's car seat. There was also my favorite brand of energy drink, snacks, diapers in the correct size, and a bag of new wipes.

Alex was getting good at this.

I stared nervously out the window as the driver expertly worked his way through the traffic. The radio played softly overhead.

"Dylan Callahan had his best game this season," the first radio announcer enthusiastically yelled.

"Considering it's the first game of the season, it's not that impressive," commented his co-host.

"Given what we saw during preseason, it's his best. I would even say better than last season," the first continued. He then went on to list Dylan's accomplishments for the game. Even if I wasn't dating the guy, I would have been impressed.

I tried not to fidget, but my knee bounced in a quick tempo rhythm to drummers only I could hear. Ellie dozed in her car seat next to me and I tried to prepare myself for whatever this could be. What could possibly be so important for Alex to summon me like this? He couldn't need something medical, since there were better medical professionals available in the stadium. I was a nurse, and while that was pretty awesome, I was not a paramedic with a full ambulance at my disposal.

So, logically, Alex wasn't calling me to the stadium for him. He had to be calling me there for Dylan.

The announcers hadn't said that he'd been hit or had another injury, but I wasn't sure they would if he wanted to keep it quiet.

Anxiety ate at my soul, especially since I hadn't been able to set things right with him yet. I loved him. I hadn't told him that yet, but I wanted to. I needed to. I wanted him to stay in my life. I wanted him.

So I just hoped this whole emergency trip to the stadium was Alex being an idiot.

The driver pulled into a secret parking area that was probably reserved for the really important VIPs. This is where the superstar celebrities got to come into the stadium. They didn't have to wait in traffic or go through the security lines. Alex and several men in maroon jackets were waiting for me. Outside, I could still hear the thunderous applause and cheers of the fans celebrating the win.

"Leave the car seat here," Alex instructed, looking like

he did not need any kind of medical help. "They'll make sure it stays safe, but it's too bulky."

I frowned at him, but he didn't give me anymore information. I unhooked Ellie's straps and cradled her in my arms. The men in maroon coats ushered the three of us down a cement hallway, past what I assumed were the locker rooms, and into a conference room full of reporters and cameras. The head coach was speaking and answering questions with a huge smile on his face.

I would have backed out of the room, but Alex was right behind me.

"I'm going to take Ellie out to a quieter spot," Alex said, holding out his arms. "You need to stay here."

I opened my mouth to protest, or at least ask what was going on, but up front the Coach said, "And now the man you all want to hear from, Dylan Callahan!"

In that moment, Alex swiped the baby out of my arms. I glared at him, but didn't want to make a scene, not with all these reporters here. Instead, I turned and looked at Dylan.

He wore a team branded t-shirt and his hair was wet from a hasty shower. Everyone in the room was clapping.

"What changed for you this game?" shouted a reporter. "You played like a totally different player!"

Camera flashes sparkled as Dylan grinned at the question. "You mean, like a good one?"

The room filled with good-natured laughter. Dylan looked around the room, his eyes finally settling on me. His shoulders relaxed and he took a deep breath before answering.

"My daughter. The reason is my daughter."

The room stopped laughing. Reporters looked at one

another, unsure of what they had just heard. Dylan Callahan had a daughter?

Alex was on the stage beside him, handing Ellie to Dylan. The reporters buzzed, all of them looking around for where the baby had come from. And I realized that Dylan had asked Alex to hand him Ellie so that the reporters wouldn't suspect me as Ellie's birth mom. He was protecting me, because if I had handed him the baby, all those cameras would have been pointing at me as the baby mama.

"This is my daughter," Dylan announced, holding Ellie up high enough that the camera's had a good shot of her snuggling into him. Luckily, she didn't seem phased by the lights or the strange sounds once she was safely nestled in Dylan's arms. She gave the most adorable little yawn and snuggled into him with a happy little sigh that made everyone in the room let out an, "aww."

I, however, was very fazed.

I just stared at him, my heart pounding a mile a minute and hope flooding my system so hard I thought I might float away on it.

"I adopted her officially this morning," Dylan continued. "But that ball I caught today, I just started imagining it was her. I don't dare drop it now."

The reporters all laughed and the cameras flashed.

"Is there a mom in the picture?" A reporter called out.

"As I said, this was an adoption. This little girl came into my life and there is no way I can let something this good slip through my fingers. So, I am never letting her go. I know a good thing when I see it." Dylan's eyes met mine. "And I'm not letting a good thing go without a fight."

I knew he meant that for me too. He wasn't just talking about Ellie. He wasn't going to let me go without a fight either. I nodded, my chest and throat so tight I couldn't have said a word even if all those reporters hadn't been there.

Dylan gave me a huge smile that lit up my world. Tension left his shoulders and suddenly I could breathe again.

"Oh she's asleep," one reporter noticed. "Should we keep it down?"

"Oh no," Dylan said, shaking his head. "She needs to learn to sleep through noise, so just don't scream questions at me and we'll be fine."

He did the rest of the press conference with his daughter sleeping in his arms. I couldn't pay attention to a single question after that, and they were all football and game related so they didn't matter to me anyway. What mattered was that Dylan was keeping Ellie. That Dylan wanted me to know that he was playing for both of us now.

36

HAPPILY EVER AFTER

What do you call a lineman's kid?
A chip off the old blocker

DYLAN

One Week Later

I STOOD in the kitchen and observed my world falling apart.

I couldn't have been more pleased.

The contractor had marked up the walls and we were in the demolition phase, so my apartment was a disaster area. Luckily, Natalie was willing to let me come stay at her place while mine was covered in dust and work tools.

I grinned as I looked at the chaos. Natalie had no idea the surprise I had planned for her. She thought that I was adding a nursery and an office for myself, but the truth was that the office was for her. I'd already had Alex find all the books she would need for her first semester of school and the contractor already had plans made for a gorgeous bookshelf, complete with a rolling ladder.

In the meantime, I'd hired a professional nanny to help watch Ellie. Natalie had been less excited about that until she'd found out that Maria was willing to work nights and weekends. This meant we could now go on dates that hopefully didn't conclude with us running down the street chasing after goats. And hopefully, more sleep as well. It also meant that Natalie could come to more of my home games. I knew that I would play better knowing she was cheering me on in the stands.

I wandered around the apartment, picking up stray things that would just turn into a mess again by tomorrow with the contractors, but I was trying to find something to do to keep busy until Natalie got home.

Was I behaving like a love-sick teen boy waiting for his girl to call? Absolutely.

I closed the hall closet door, making sure that it fully latched shut. There was a shoe box on the top shelf that looked unimportant. At first glance, there were just a random assortment of household items- keys, letters, random coins, and even a pair of lucky socks. But wrapped up in those lucky socks was my mother's engagement ring. I'd picked it up from my safety deposit box after the game last Sunday.

My parents had a wonderful happy marriage, so I considered the ring to be good luck.

I wanted it close because I knew I'd be asking Natalie a very important question someday soon. I just needed to wait for the right moment. And probably the end of the season because trying to do anything while the season was active was just too much.

Still, I knew deep in my bones that Natalie was the one for me.

The one that made my heart sing.

I smiled at the closed closet door and felt a wonderful anticipation. It was like waiting for Christmas morning. Something good was definitely coming that would absolutely be worth the wait.

"Honey, I'm home!" Natalie called out as she walked into the apartment. Her nose wrinkled at the mess but she smiled as soon as she saw me.

That smile made my heart do fabulous things. The kiss she gave me made other parts of my body do fabulous things as well.

"Well, I did what you asked. I got rid of the kid," I told her once I'd thoroughly kissed her. "I gave her to Alex's cousin. They couldn't be happier to have her."

Her jaw fell and her eyes went wide.

"You what?" She looked frantically around the room. "But she's your daughter! I saw the paperwork!" Her voice rose to a screechy level typically reserved for bats.

Unfortunately, that supersonic level also had the tendency to wake the baby. Ellie began to cry from her crib in the bedroom.

Natalie's face turned to confusion as she followed me into the bedroom. I'd tucked Ellie in for a nap while the contractor and I had spoken. It was about the end of her nap time anyway, so she was just mad that we'd left her alone.

"But you said you got rid of her," Natalie said,

reaching out for the baby. Ellie happily snuggled into her arms, glad that her mother was home.

"I told you I got rid of the kid," I replied, grinning at my own cleverness. "I gave Penelope to Alex's cousin since they live out on a farm. And, I technically did offer them a kid at some point, so I owed them."

Natalie rolled her eyes. "I hate you."

"I know." I grinned at her.

"But the goat is happy?" she asked.

I pointed to my chest. "The GOAT is happy, thank you."

She groaned again but smiled at me like I made her happy too.

"I love you," she whispered, coming to kiss me.

And I knew that we'd live happily ever after.

IF YOU LIKED THIS BOOK...

Escape With Me: A Midlife Love Story

* * *

"I gave it all up to be happy. I'd give it all up again for you."

They say life begins after 40, but Cassie ain't feelin' it. Divorced and feeling trapped by her job, she wants to let loose for her friend's tropical beach wedding. She decides to let her hair down and get a little unpredictable. That's when she meets a handsome bartender, Wyatt.

Despite a few grey hairs, Wyatt's the liveliest man that Cassie has ever met. She knows that there's got to be more to his life story than just being a bartender, but this is just supposed to be a vacation fling. And after sunny days spent breaking all the rules on the beach together, Cassie realizes that nobody has ever listened to her the way that Wyatt does.

His carefree life is enviable, his kisses are intoxicating, and she can almost imagine a life with him. But all vacations come to an end. And when Cassie invites him to visit her hometown, Wyatt reveals that he can never go back. Not to her town. Not to America. Not to civilization.

Cassie leaves, confused and heartbroken, wondering just who she got herself involved with. Suddenly, her predictable life gets turned upside down when she sees her picture splashed across the Internet. And when the tabloids come looking for the mature woman who found the lost billionaire, she has no idea what to do...

...until he comes back.

Escape With Me: A Midlife Love Story

ABOUT THE AUTHOR

New York Times and USA Today Bestseller Krista Lakes is a thirtysomething who recently rediscovered her passion for writing. She is living happily ever after with her Prince Charming. Her first kid just started preschool and she is happy to welcome her second child into her life, continuing her "Happily Ever After"!

Thank you for supporting an indie author. Anything you can do, whether it be writing a review, or even simply telling a fellow reader that you enjoyed this, helps me out immensely. Thanks!

Krista would love to hear from you! Please contact her at Krista.Lakes@gmail.com or friend her on Facebook!

Further reading:

Bad Boys and Babies
    Family Doctor's Baby
    The Billionaire's Baby Arrangement
    Crime Boss Baby

Kinds of Love
    A Forever Kind of Love
    A Wonderful Kind of Love

An Endless Kind of Love

Billionaires and Brides
Yours Completely: A Cinderella Love Story
Yours Truly: A Cinderella Love Story
Yours Royally: A Cinderella Love Story

The "Kisses" series
Saltwater Kisses: A Billionaire Love Story
Kisses From Jack: The Other Side of Saltwater Kisses
Rainwater Kisses: A Billionaire Love Story
Champagne Kisses: A Timeless Love Story
Freshwater Kisses: A Billionaire Love Story
Sandcastle Kisses: A Billionaire Love Story
Hurricane Kisses: A Billionaire Love Story
Barefoot Kisses: A Billionaire Love Story
Sunrise Kisses: A Billionaire Love Story
Waterfall Kisses: A Billionaire Love Story
Island Kisses: A Billionaire Love Story

Other Novels
I Choose You: A Secret Billionaire Romance
His Every Desire: A Billionaire Seduction
Wolf Six's Salvation: A Shifter Love Story
Burned: A New Adult Love Story
Walking on Sunshine: A Sweet Summer Romance
An American Cinderella: A Royal Love Story
Mr. Darcy's Kiss: A Contemporary Pride and Prejudice